Life by the Red Oak

Steve Marchand

All rights reserved. This is a work of fiction. Names, characters, places, and incidents either are the product the author's imagination or are used fictitiously. Any resemblance to actual persons, living or dead, events or locales is almost entirely coincidental.

No part of this publication may be reproduced, distributed, or transmitted in any form or by any means, including photocopying, recording, or other electronic or mechanical methods, without the prior written permission of the author, except in the case of *brief quotations* embodied in critical reviews and certain other noncommercial uses permitted by copyright law.

Please see the last page for the author's website address.

Copyright © 2020 Steve Marchand

ISBN : 979-85-65385-77-9

Special thanks to my family and friends for asking *how's the book coming?* in a way that showed you really cared. Your support is, as always, high motivation.

Thank you to Louise Brown for an initial review and for your good words.

Thank you Anne Martin for taking the time to read this story despite your busy schedule. Your advice, your comments and your kindness meant the world to me.

CHAPTER 1

Jonathan Foster lowered the binoculars and squinted to bring the distant scenery into focus. His target, a woman as far as he could tell, had become a dot to his naked eye. A tiny dot that had now just derailed his plan to hit the sack right after dinner.

"No way in hell," he mumbled.

His round to secure the warehouse — the building he'd been calling home since the initial wave of the virus — was almost finished, albeit much earlier than usual. His end-of-day ritual had taken him to the roof last as always. This was where he listened for suspicious noises nearby and made the final determination on whether or not it was safe to call it a day. He was about to go back inside and lie down when movements at the top of the hill, east of the City, had tickled the corner of his right eye. No one had used that road in weeks; ignoring such a sighting was not an option.

"No way in this brand-new hell," he said again, raising the binoculars this time.

The woman's wheelchair appeared to disobey her commands to roll forward in a straight line. Her troubles grew as she gained speed after she pushed her wheels down the long steep hill that would take her to the south end of the City's outskirt, not too far from where Jonathan lived.

It was the truth of her predicament he was questioning. She couldn't have survived until then on her own, he thought. Not in a wheelchair, and certainly not one that appeared to be such a dud.

He theorized the woman was used as bait, part of a scheme to rip poor saps of their belongings. Tapping into people's good nature impulses had become an effective luring tactic as of late. Jonathan himself, though far from gullible, had walked head first into a similar trap three weeks earlier. In his case, the lead character in the setup had been a young boy feigning distress. And so a woman pretending to wrestle with a wheelchair wasn't that much of a stretch.

But when the chair came to a brutal stop and then flipped, sending its occupant flying from her seat and onto the pavement, her fall erased many of his doubts. That tumble was as real as it was violent. No accomplices jumped out of the bushes to rush to her aid either. The woman took a moment to gather her wits. She then crawled across the road to recover parts of her chair, reattached them, pulled herself back up and resumed her descent.

Jonathan's instincts defeated his common sense and he left the warehouse to go get a closer look.

Sleep would have to wait a little while longer.

Venturing out there was always a rough proposition. If

he had to, he preferred to do so wrapped in the safe blanket of darkness the night provided. There was still an hour of daylight left when he had first zoomed in on the woman. At that hour, he calculated, danger was multiplied by a factor of about ten.

After his encounter with the kid three weeks earlier, he had also promised to himself he would never again try to help someone in need. He knew better now; he had paid, and he continued to pay, a hefty price for his latest attempt at kindness. These short minutes would haunt him for the rest of his life, however long that was going to be. He was certain of it.

The scene that had now just played out in the distance had somehow lit a spark in his darkened sense of empathy.

Jonathan ran across the South Side Bridge. He zigzagged between the destroyed stores, the deserted office buildings and quite a few decaying bodies. He had combed the streets of this part of town often enough in the last eight weeks to know which ones would take him in a single piece to where he estimated the woman would arrive after her trip down the hill.

He paused every once in a while and listened. The silence in which the world had gone and plunged itself had become a great advantage to the mindful. The noises Jonathan heard could mean the difference between life and death. So did the ones he made.

He found a safe spot in a back alley and waited.

Coming from the adjacent main street, he soon heard the unmistakable sounds the defective wheelchair made as it moved on the pavement's rough surface. It was indeed a woman.

When she appeared in his line of sight, between two

buildings, he got his first close look at her. She was disheveled, dirty as can be and Jonathan could tell she had been wearing the same clothes for many days. The backpack she carried on her lap contained very little.

He took a step forward but stopped, making good on his own promise not to engage. He would play it safe and follow and observe her for the time being, nothing more. Easier said than done; Jonathan had never seen anything so compelling. The advanced state of decrepitude of the woman's chair, as well as the injuries she had sustained in her fall earlier, made each yard she covered look like an Olympian exploit.

She was also moving toward the hot zone, which gave Jonathan cause to worry. This main road on which she was traveling would eventually deliver her to the worst elements the City had to offer.

If she were to move too close to the downtown area, he thought, he would approach her and warn her of the dangers ahead. Much to his relief, she took a sharp right turn and opted instead to use the same alley from which he was spying on her.

Every once in a while the woman paused to gaze at her hands and blow some cool air on them in an apparent attempt to ease the pain from her injuries.

She tore open garbage bags and rummaged through all the bins she came across. At times, she would bring a find near her face and inspect it. After some hesitation she would either throw away the piece or shove it in her mouth. More often than not, she spat it back out and coughed in disgust.

It wasn't a scheme. Jonathan was overwhelmed by her situation, the worst he had seen since the beginning of this mess back in April.

It always came down to food. Every survivor's life had been reduced to a never-ending quest for something to eat. Water wasn't a problem for anyone with some sort of a container and a functioning brain. Even this woman, obviously deprived of luck and all other necessities, took a bottle with some of the precious liquid out of her bag to sip on it at some point.

Food was the constant worry. Going out to look for it was a gamble whether armed to the teeth and dressed in fatigues, like Jonathan was, or not. Finding it was equally perilous. Decency flew out the window at the sight or smell of food. A kind and sweet old nun could kill the leader of a biker gang in his sleep for a bite of a dried out Pop-Tart if she ever saw it in his hand.

So the more Jonathan observed the woman in the wheelchair, the more he softened his position. Inside an hour, he had switched from keeping an eye *on her* to keeping an eye out *for her*. He would stay within earshot until sunrise.

Then, he would try and make contact with her.

Night descended before she could go very far. The deserted alley was now lit by nothing but the half moon shining above the woman and her stalker. Plenty of darkness for some much-needed protection from a distance, but enough of a glow for Jonathan to still distinguish the tones of the woman's clothes.

After her *meal* she found room behind a dumpster, pulled the remains of a blanket from her bag and settled down for a nap.

Jonathan sat on the ground just shy of a hundred feet from her, his back against the brick wall of a structure that had perhaps once been a factory of some sort.

Difficult to tell since most of the buildings had been ravaged — first by rioters, then by scavengers — after the virus had struck. He retrieved an army ration from his backpack, but thought better of it; such a feast would be inappropriate after what he had just witnessed. Even the energy bar he ate felt over the top.

Though his eyes were locked on his target, he allowed his mind to slowly drift toward his own situation. Less to what it had become and more to what it had once been. Getting lost inside a thick haze of memories was easy, especially at that hour. This stillness, mixed with the kind of obscurity the night now imposed, was a powerful agent of reflection. The virus, and the violence that had raged in its wake, had killed almost everyone in the City. More than six hundred thousand souls had gone silent there; the remaining few could finally hear themselves think.

He had Facetimed his mom and dad before all communications were cut off, so he knew they had made it through the first wave of infections. That was it. That was all he knew. If the virus hadn't taken them in the second wave, the lawlessness that had ensued had surely claimed many of his loved ones. The woman he'd been following this evening, however, had revived some of his hopes for them. If she had managed to survive this entire time, on her own and without the use of her legs, perhaps a few members of his family were still alive back home. Had he lived closer to them, he could have helped save a few more.

Or were they all gone already?

He was exhausted. At the time he had left his building earlier, he had been up for more than twenty-four hours. Wondering about those he once knew, and worrying about their fate, was far from reinvigorating. His inability to get to them was a heavy burden. The weight of these daunting *perhaps* and *maybes* found its way to his eyelids.

The moment he closed his eyes he thought of Kat, of course. No matter how hard he fought them, he couldn't stop the images of her from flickering in his mind and hammering at his heart.

There she was, in bed, facing him and smiling, her soft, warm hand on his cheek. There she was again, leading the way as the two hiked along the punishing Skyway Trail. And there she was, standing in the kitchen, holding a grocery bag over the counter as though she was just about to set it down. Motionless, her eyes wide opened, stiff as a rock and disfigured beyond recognition.

"Kat, gimme the bag, babe."

"Kat, gimme the bag..."

"Gimme that bag, bitch."

"Oh crap," Jonathan muttered as he jumped to his feet. He had fallen asleep. Two thugs were now attacking the woman in the wheelchair, trying to rip her backpack from her hands. She was giving it her all to fight them back.

By the time Jonathan had risen to his feet, one of the thieves had hit her across the face with such force she had flown out of her seat and landed on the ground. His friend grabbed the chair, spun around and tossed it high in the air. When it crashed back to the earth, one of the rear wheels came off and rolled to the opposite side of the alley.

"All you had to do was let go of the damned bag, lady. Come on Bud, let's get going," one of the men said.

"We can't leave her like that. That's just mean. We should put her out of her misery," the other answered.

The woman looked down and appeared to whisper a few words. One of the two attackers walked up to her. The order came just as he was about to put his hand on her head.

"Don't touch her."

The bullies turned around at the sound of Jonathan's voice. Though the light from the rising sun was quite dim, he could see the *Oh Shit* looks on both their faces.

There was nothing impressive about his physique. He was thirty-four years old and of average built and height. It was the clothes he wore and the tool he held that signaled bad news to the two men. The chances of finding themselves at the wrong end of a silenced M4 pointed by a soldier in full army gear had been slim to none. Until that moment, that is.

Right then and there, they knew. They knew were toast and that there was little they could do about it. If stealing from a woman in a wheelchair and killing her afterwards were offenses that now went unpunished, so was ending the pathetic lives of those willing to do these terrible things.

"Drop the bag," a calm Jonathan said to the one holding it.

After the backpack hit the ground, he directed the men to walk toward the corner of the street from which he had just rushed.

"Now move this way."

Cooperation was the culprits' last hope of escaping this alive. The fact that the soldier hadn't killed them on the spot had also given them a hint of comfort.

But when the three men turned the corner, and Jonathan was certain they had disappeared from the woman's view, he did the deed.

He couldn't have allowed them to live.

Letting them walk away was the equivalent of sentencing to death other people like that poor woman.

Their kind never gave up, anyway; they would have come back for him. They always did.

That lesson too, Jonathan had learned the hard way.

These guys now outnumbered the weak and the good by a depressing margin. Lack of decency, combined with the absence of law enforcement, had guaranteed the survival of so many of them. Laziness played its part too, of course. Doing the right thing meant a lot of work and was often synonymous with danger. They couldn't be bothered. The bad elements had become the strongest, not because they were big or they could lift massive weights. They were the strongest because they were just too lazy to give a damn.

Jonathan thought of them as nothing more than cowards who viewed the most vulnerable as low-hanging fruits. They showed no mercy and seemed to enjoy going out of their ways to act like assholes in the process.

The woman was lucky; it was just a couple of losers this time. They usually traveled in well-armed groups of five to ten and attacked on sight.

This drive they had to refuse to walk away no matter how outgunned or outwitted they were made them unforgiving. It also made them unforgivable.

Jonathan returned to the woman.

The left side of her face had started to swell from the beating she had received moments earlier. Her hands and forearms were bleeding after her two spectacular falls on the pavement within a few hours from each other. She was sitting up, holding against her chest the wheel that had come off her chair.

He had never seen that expression on a person's face before. Her eyes were fixated on the remains of her chair as though her entire world had just crumbled. Sure, her world looked even messier than Jonathan's, but it was hers. And now she couldn't go anywhere in it.

"Bastards broke my, hum, my chair," she said in a voice shattered by despair.

"Are they gone?" she asked.

"Yeah, they're gone. They won't bother you anymore. My name is Jonathan and I mean you no harm."

"You understand we can't stay here, right? All this commotion is bound to have alerted others. We have to go now," he added while looking in all directions.

The urgency in his tone was justified. The curiosity that had plagued civilization prior to its recent demise had not been eradicated. When something out of the ordinary occurred, survivors would flock to the scene to see what had caused the ruckus. *"Maybe there's food there"* was everybody's first thought.

Still, a minute ago she had been assaulted by two jerks that had threatened to put her to death. And now, this man who had confronted them without blinking, was offering his help. Was she supposed to just trust him?

"I'll get you a new chair. I promise."

His words had escaped his control.

He didn't have a clue if or how he could ever live up to that pledge.

"Can you climb on my back? I'll take you somewhere safe."

The woman raised her head to try and get a better look at Jonathan. Everything was happening too fast and the blow to her face had rendered her vision blurry.

All she could really see were his army fatigues.

She did notice a deep gash above his left temple. It appeared fairly recent.

She put a hand on his shoulder, a gesture of resignation so much more than one of assent. Jonathan saw in her eyes she had accepted there was a distinct possibility he might end up being the one to kill her later. Her situation was that dire; this faint chance to keep on living, if only for a few more minutes plagued by uncertainty, was all she had left and she was willing to go for it.

The sun was peeking above the horizon and they had a walk long of at least an hour ahead of them. The woman, who had obviously been deprived of food for some time, was light as a feather but Jonathan had to use both hands to secure her legs. Being unable to hold his weapon added to his anxiety.

At the halfway mark, he announced he needed a break. There was a familiar building nearby, he told the woman, one he knew would make a good place to lay low. What he really had in mind was to better assess the health of his cargo.

"Is this where you, hum, you live?" the woman inquired.

"No. But I've been here before. We should be safe while we rest a bit and regroup."

It then dawned on him he hadn't asked for her name yet.

"Anna," she answered.

"Are you hungry, Anna?"

She averted her eyes, as if in shame, and nodded. Jonathan retrieved an energy bar from his backpack. Before he handed it to her, he made Anna promise to eat it one small bite at a time. She agreed, but before he could stop her she had shoved the entire bar in her mouth and could barely breathe.

He took a bottle of water out of his bag, poured some of its contents on a piece of cloth and brought it near her face so he could wash off some of the dirt. Her initial reaction was one of retreat, but after she looked at him in silence for a moment, she accepted his help and leaned forward.

Anna was scared and in excruciating pain, but it was the feeling of fresh water revealing clean patches of her skin added to the sweet taste of proper food that turned out to be too much to bear.

As Jonathan saw his first real look at her face, he also saw her first tears.

The longer they stayed stationary, the greater danger grew. Jonathan cleared the space of all traces of their interlude and took Anna on his back again. This time, they would walk straight to his building.

"It doesn't look like much on the outside, but I assure you it's quite comfy inside. Ready?"

Anna no longer had the strength, nor the will, to answer. She was now just going with the flow. Jonathan, understanding her state of mind, didn't repeat his question. It couldn't have been later than six in the morning but the exact hour was irrelevant. He hated being out there during the day, period. In his opinion, only the bad or the stupid went out in daylight. He had time to waste with neither of them.

About a block away from the bridge they had to cross to reach his hideout, Jonathan got on one knee and instructed Anna to hold her breath, to keep silent. He wanted to listen for signs of activity in the vicinity of his quarters. When he felt confident enough, he ran across the bridge and proceeded toward a red brick warehouse that had been severely damaged by fire.

He walked along the building and stopped in front of a dumpster on wheels near the back corner. He pushed the dumpster to the side and a wide entrance door attached to it followed the motion.

"Didn't see that coming," Anna whispered.

Her reaction drew a laugh from Jonathan, though he asked Anna to remain quiet. Once inside, he sat her on the ground, slid the door back into position and locked it. The place was now dark as night. Jonathan fired up his flashlight, which blinded Anna.

From the little she managed to see, it looked smaller than it did on the outside. And it was in complete shambles. She began to fear she had been deceived. Panic was about to grab a hold of her when Jonathan walked to a second dumpster filled with junk like rusted metal and burnt wood. He pushed this one to the side also, this time to reveal a set of stairs.

He took a nervous Anna in his arms and went up to the top floor. Upon reaching the last step, he opened an iron gate and flipped a switch, a surprising move since power had gone out everywhere a week after the first wave of the virus. Anna surveyed the room. It wasn't a mansion, far from it, but it was a home and she agreed; it did seem comfortable.

Jonathan sat her on a gigantic vintage leather couch and went down again to camouflage the stairwell. After he came back up, he tried to get Anna to relax by offering her some filtered water.

"Maybe I'll just stay, hum, stay until I get a new chair. Then I'll be out of, hum, of your way."

"You're my guest, Anna. Not my prisoner. How about we just take it one day at a time?" Jonathan replied.

Her second sip of water was interrupted by cries only a very small animal could voice.

Jonathan looked at a cardboard box in the left corner of the room.

"Right. The Fur Ball," he said.

CHAPTER 2

Seven and a half weeks earlier.
April 20, 2021. East coast, the United States.

Early in the afternoon, reports from Australia, South America and Africa began flooding social media platforms, and some time thereafter the airwaves, concerning bizarre instances of people struck by what was described as deadly freezing spells.

India and Japan announced their first cases within the hour. Then Europe was hit. Given the late local times, and the massive chaos the fast-moving outbreak was leaving in its wake, the accounts relayed from the first impacted regions were sketchy at best.

It seemed those infected had suddenly become immovable, every muscle in their bodies having contracted with a force so overwhelming it had killed them. Witnesses referred to it as rigor mortis on steroids. Although death was swift —

within seconds of an infection — the expression on the victims' faces showed signs the process had caused excruciating pain.

While the virus, or whatever it was, had already killed a great many in multiple and vast areas, the way it selected its preys was unclear. Some described having survived the infection while standing inches away from people who hadn't. Theories about the randomness of infections, some more plausible than others, circulated amid the reports. Among those was the rumor that anyone suffering from one form or another of allergy was a primary target. The spread was so rapid, so systematic and wide, that none of the presumptions put forth would ever be validated.

As for the origin of it all, except for those who had been living under a rock prior to the outbreak, it was easy to ascertain. Everything pointed to what had happened in Antarctica nine days earlier.

A mere six hours after the first cases had surfaced in Australia, in the evening of April 20th, North America was introduced to the virus's brutal and arbitrary reach in spectacular fashion.

Jonathan Foster's beloved Bruins were about to face off against the Canadiens at the Bell Centre in Montréal. His passion for the Bruins had been handed from fathers and mothers to sons and daughters in his family for generations. The iconic B was tattooed on many Foster hearts, no matter where they lived in the world.

Jonathan was especially grateful for Boston's postseason success this year, which had given his mind an escape from the political and social madness spawned by the fracture in Antarctica.

Against all odds, his team was one win away from sweeping its eternal rival and moving on to the next round of the playoffs.

There had been talks earlier in the day of all public gatherings, such as sports events and concerts, being canceled because of the devastation overseas. North America, however, was still recovering from a punishing second wave of COVID-19, which had begun in the fall. At long last, the newly discovered vaccine was helping rebuild an economy the yearlong pandemic had seriously crippled. The population, depressed by a long period of isolation, was longing for entertainment and flocked to the arenas by the thousands to cheer on their favorite bands or professional athletes.

So, with much money at stake, the National Hockey League had opted to play on as scheduled. They had nevertheless planned to honor those lost earlier in the day with a moment of silence prior to the game.

And silence they got.

Before the puck was dropped, during the singing of O Canada, the virus invaded the arena. Members of the two teams, the fans, the journalists and TV crews: most people were infected. The shocked few hundreds that had been spared ran in all directions, stumbling and tripping over the thousands of dead bodies in the stands. The feed was eventually cut off.

Word quickly spread that Canada had been hit. What for now remained of the five hundred and eighty million North Americans tuned in to CNN, Fox News and MSNBC to get the latest reports. They were treated instead to the most frightening images ever shown on live television. Cable news anchors, most of them working from studios in the New York, Washington and Atlanta areas, began freezing on the air. Since the majority of the employees in those buildings were also infected, no one could pull the plug this time.

Jonathan had just landed on CNN when it happened. Their poor anchor got the worst of it and by far. In a cruel and ironic twist, he was in the midst of describing the apparent effects of the virus on the human body unaware he was about to experience them himself.

He stopped talking mid-sentence and continued gazing through the camera lens for a few seconds, though his expression had changed to reveal he suspected something horrific was about to happen. He was right.

The man looked down at his right arm while it rose in front of him, obviously against his will. He was about to scream his pain when viewers clearly saw the left side of his neck contract and wrinkle as the muscles underneath his skin reacted to the virus. His head then tilted in unnatural fashion toward his left shoulder. He still wanted to scream, but the virus had gotten a hold of his throat. Someone did scream on his behalf after a commotion was heard out of the camera's view. Everyone in the studio was now getting infected, some not as silently as the anchor, though the live shot's focus remained on him.

His ordeal ended when the virus crawled up his face and ordered the muscles in his right cheek to pull on his lower jaw until the microphone captured the disturbing dry sound the bones made when they snapped and dislocated. Twenty-eight seconds had elapsed between the moment the man had stopped talking and the moment he had stopped breathing.

At the conclusion of this scene, when Jonathan heard

the anchor's bones fracture, he let out a loud "Oh crap" of disgust while he pointed at the TV. His brain was about to surrender to fear when he averted his eyes from the screen and looked at his apartment door instead. He brought a shaking thumb to his mouth and chewed on the nail while he gathered his thoughts. A moment later, he jumped off the couch and ran to the small plaza a stone's throw away from his complex.

The proximity of that mini mall was why he had moved there in the first place. Everything he'd ever need — bus stop, convenience and grocery stores and a friendly burger joint — was within walking distance.

He entered the grocery store, grabbed a cart and rushed down the aisles to secure as many nonperishables as he could. None of the shoppers present seemed to be aware yet of the events that had just occurred in the country's other major cities. They looked at a frantic Jonathan push patrons out of the way, sweep items off the shelves one full arm's length at a time, and presumed he was either off his meds or in the midst of an anxiety attack.

As he threw batteries, bottled water, canned and dried foods in his cart, the store's evening manager went and followed him.

"Sir? Sir? We're going to ask you to calm down a bit."

"Really? You're gonna ask me, huh?" Jonathan said in a sarcastic tone.

"Well, you're scaring our customers, sir."

Jonathan had an epiphany. He paused and stood up straight.

"Would they feel better if I left?" he inquired.

"Quite honestly, sir, I think it would be best," the young man answered.

"I'll make a deal with you," Jonathan said. "Go to the front, clear one of the lanes so I can pay for all of this real quick and I'll be out of here in no time. I swear."

He couldn't believe his luck when the manager complied. The cashier gave Jonathan an exasperated look and asked him if he needed bags. After she scanned the last of his items and he paid the four hundred seventy-four dollars and twenty-one cents he owed, Jonathan approached the manager and whispered a few sentences in his ear.

The young man spun around to look at the people in his store. They all stared at him, waiting to see what he would do next. He walked slow and easy to an empty cart. He grabbed it and he too hustled down the aisles to fill it with canned goods. Other customers, despite having no clue why, did the same.

Jonathan had made it near his building when he saw those who didn't have as fast a reflex as he did flock to the streets and storm the stores. Panic, and all that was to be expected to come with it, had been set in motion.

The service elevator was Jonathan's safest way to reach his apartment without his fellow tenants seeing him with all these fresh supplies.

In his absence, Kat had returned early from her shift at the hospital located midtown. She looked shaken to her very core. And she was, in part by what she had been watching on TV, but also because of the way her employer had chosen to handle the crisis.

Since those infected in other parts of the world weren't sick per se, and since nothing could be done to save them, the hospital director had instructed most of the support staff, along with a few nurses, to stand outside the main entrance and evaluate all incoming patients for triage. As per his orders, no infected bodies were to be carried inside if the virus ever struck the area. He panicked at the sight of the news anchors freezing on the air and scratched his original plan; the nurses were told via texts on their phones to return inside, but in as discreet a manner as possible. The building was then put on lockdown. Non-essential personnel such as Kat, wasn't allowed back in.

She had caught a ride home with a coworker and she was now watching a local channel. Reporters were doing what they could to describe the events. In most cases, however, all they had to work with were feeds from cameras aimed at whatever they were capturing at the time their operators were infected.

Kat rose from the couch, went to Jonathan and hugged him while she sobbed.

"I was texting you. Why didn't you respond?" she asked.

"I was stocking up on food, babe," he answered.

They remained by the door for some time and held each other while they stared at the television. These images looked more like a low-budget apocalypse movie preview with a cast of B-list actors than actual news.

"This isn't real. This isn't happening," Jonathan kept thinking to himself.

It was real. Hundreds of thousands, if not millions, had perished in the Big Apple alone. Canada, the West Coast and the southern states had also been devastated. Reporters were at a loss and couldn't decide where to focus their coverage: the terrible implications of the illness itself or the complete chaos it was leaving behind.

As far as Jonathan and Kat knew, their part of the City

seemed to have been spared. He rolled the grocery cart to the kitchen with its content still in it and returned to the living room to comfort Kat who was scared to death. He put on a brave face to try and hide it, but so was he.

The Facetime request he sent to his parents from his iPad to theirs went through. They were both fine, although they had heard of many infections in their town, a rural area more than nine hundred miles southwest of the City, where Jonathan lived.

At the very start of their chat, fearing they could lose the connection at any moment, he gave them strict instructions to barricade themselves inside their house. He stressed there was no way to tell how people would behave after such shocking events, not even in a small community like theirs. His dad, Mark, a veteran known by all to keep his cool no matter the crisis, didn't really need his son's advice but he appreciated it, though he too showed signs of great worry.

"I love you guys," Jonathan told his parents before touching the screen to end their conversation.

Kat wasn't having the same luck with her parents. She called them every thirty seconds, but no one answered and she became more agitated after each failed attempt. Jonathan had to take the phone from her hands and try on her behalf.

The chaos shown on TV had reached epic proportions when, seconds to midnight, all channels switched to color bars.

Jonathan speculated that the government had deemed the situation to be beyond their control. Their last hope to contain the madness, as he saw it, was to stop the flow of information.

Kat joined him in the kitchen to help put the food away. She handed the bags to Jonathan who took the items out one at a time and laid them on the counter while he recited reassuring words; at least they would have a bit of food and water until the authorities regrouped and then worked to beat this thing. At least, for now, they were safe.

And at least, they were together.

"Everything's going to be fine, I'm here now. Wink, wink!" he said to brighten the mood as he grabbed the next bag from Kat's hands without looking at her.

She wouldn't let go of it.

"Kat, gimme the bag, babe. Kat, gimme the bag…"

CHAPTER 3

Jonathan spun around and saw Kat. He tried to take a deep breath. He needed it so desperately. But he couldn't. Shock had flipped the air in the room upside down and it could no longer find its way into his lungs.

Kat's face, which he had often described as that of an angel, was frozen with the same expression it would've had if a thousand volts had passed through her body.

Jonathan, having seen on television what the virus could do, moved to stand in front of her and braced for the infection and for the pain to come and overpower him. It didn't.

From the day he had met Kat, all he had ever needed to do to guess her state of mind was to look into her eyes. Worry, joy, sadness, anger; she couldn't keep anything from him if he stared long and deep enough.

When life left Kat's body, it was her eyes that delivered the shattering news to him. He saw it being extinguished like the flame of a candle slowly dying.

His mind went blank.

The trauma took a while to let go of its grip on him, at which point he became aware of his surroundings again. He now remembered that, at the same time Kat had been infected, there had been screams coming from other units in the building as well as heavy and hasty footsteps in the hallway just outside his door, so he knew he wasn't the only survivor.

He took Kat in his arms and then to their bedroom where he laid her on her side of the bed. He used her phone to send an email to her parents in case they were still alive. His message, although succinct, included an apology to them for having failed to protect their precious daughter. His calls and Facetime requests were no longer getting through to his parents. He also sent them an email to inform them he had lost Kat and repeated his advice to barricade themselves inside their home.

He signed off with a promise he would somehow try to get to them.

Both messages appeared to have been sent, but there was no way to tell whether or not they had been received. As a matter of principle, he dialed 911 a few times to report Kat's death. As he had expected, no one answered his calls.

The late hour and the speed at which the illness had struck the west outskirt of the City where Jonathan's complex was located meant there were no riots yet. He knew this calm wouldn't last; the streets would soon be crowded with looters and distraught people as had happened everywhere else. He killed all the lights in the apartment but lit two candles, one in the living room and one by Kat on the bedside table.

Each move he made was mechanical, almost against his will, as though an external force was pulling the strings to guide his thoughts and his actions.

Kat had bought him an oversized and sturdy backpack in the fall after her sustained efforts to convince him to take up hiking with her had paid off. He filled it with changes of clothes topped with some of the food he had bought at the store earlier. He made sure to include his laptop and his iPad to the lot.

At four o'clock in the morning, Jonathan was resting the now heavy backpack against the wall in the living room, when someone knocked on his door. It was a timid knock, not the kind that would startle anyone. Since there were no cries for help, he chose not to answer. Whoever it was didn't insist and moved on to the next unit. No one else on his floor responded to the visitor either. This didn't mean anything, really. If Jonathan had refused to open the door, other survivors could have decided to play it just as safe.

The radio on his iPod found mostly dead air. Some of the stations still had music playing, but in all likelihood it came from automated playlists. He surveyed the streets through the different windows to monitor movements outside. Except for a man walking at a fast pace, he saw nothing remarkable.

With each passing minute, the intuition he was only postponing the inevitable grew in him. The uncertainty the outbreak had brought to the entire planet was likely to last awhile. And no doubt the person who had shown up at his door moments ago had been the first of many more to come. The knocks would only grow heavier and more impatient. He had to go.

The idea of leaving Kat behind was tearing him apart. He sat on their bed and looked at her, as if to confirm beyond any doubt there really wasn't anything he could do. Her face, just like the rest of her body, was as hard as a rock. She was no longer there.

Not only had Jonathan known for a few hours already that he needed to flee, he knew exactly where he was supposed to go. His mind kept showing him the one building where he was convinced he would be safe. He could also hear Kat whisper to his ear that he had to run to that shelter, and run now.

He sobbed again, apologized for leaving her and kissed her forehead.

"I'll come back for you," he said before blowing out the candle.

A few weeks earlier, Mr. Dean, Jonathan's boss who had taken quite a liking to him over the years, had finalized the purchase of a small warehouse with the plan of transforming it into a machine shop. It was located at the south edge of the City, about twenty miles away from Jonathan's apartment complex.

Both he and Mr. Dean had inspected the building prior to the deal and they had agreed on its great potential for an expansion. Its size, but also its location just across from the South Side Bridge on the outskirt of the City, were a perfect match for what they needed. Their assessment, based on a business decision at the time, still held for the situation at hand. For now, getting farther away from the core of the City was a safer bet than remaining idle so close to it.

Jonathan put on his winter gear and tightened the straps of his backpack around his waist and shoulders.

He got out of the apartment and locked the door behind him, making sure to limit the noise. He tiptoed to the stairwell and then listened to confirm he was alone before he headed down.

The building's rear exit was next to the lockers where the tenants kept their bicycles. He got on his mountain bike and pedaled as fast as he could. Though downtown was a couple of miles behind him the magnitude of the chaos echoing from there made him stop, turn and look toward the City. Horns, alarms, screams and gunshots; he heard them all.

Adams River bordered the City's west side all the way down to the south. When Jonathan reached the road along the water, he estimated he would be at the warehouse before sunrise. He crossed paths with only a handful of people, but he took good note of their demeanors. Some were in obvious despair. Others were going about their business, oblivious to the tragic events unfolding around the world. A City worker behind the wheel of a street sweeper, for one, smiled and waved at him.

Jonathan made it to the one hundred yards South Side Bridge at around six o'clock. His destination was the very first building to his right on the other side of the river.

The warehouse was old and unassuming, meaning it was built to last: two floors of red bricks, four large windows on the lower level but only one on the top floor.

The structure wasn't very big; forty feet wide by eighty feet long with a fifteen-foot ceiling on the main floor. It stood far enough away from the road and was hidden behind plenty of mature trees. A heavy delivery sliding door on the left side, near the back, was the sole entrance. That corner of the warehouse, no more than ten yards away from the river, was also it closest point to the water.

The feature that appealed the most to Jonathan, and the main reason behind his fleeing there, was the second floor. The large room covered a bit less than the rear half of the building and could easily be transformed into livable quarters. A metal door gave direct access to the roof for a view of the City's tallest skyscrapers in the distance, just above the tree line by the river. The roof was the perfect belvedere from which to keep an eye out on the bridge or wannabe intruders.

He broke the sliding door's lock and figured that, whenever this whole thing would blow over, Mr. Dean would understand and forgive his trespassing. He was a great and accommodating man, although Jonathan expected the cost of these damages would be deducted from a future paycheck.

Mr. Dean had already had a number of items delivered in the preceding weeks like pallets of bricks and bags of cement for small repairs. Some of the expensive production tools and machinery had also arrived, as did piles of metal sheets and tubes of various sizes and thicknesses.

The second floor was just as Jonathan had remembered it.

The previous tenants had divested themselves of an enormous brown leather couch and an equally impressive matching chair. There was also a table, benches and a patio set for the roof in the summer months. To his left was a separate room with wide windows, most likely used as the manager's office, complete with a full bathroom and a shower.

Jonathan removed his backpack, crashed on the couch

and disappeared inside a cloud of white dust. His cell phone was showing a strong signal yet he still couldn't get through to anybody, including Mr. Dean. While he had been able to send emails to his and Kat's parents earlier, nothing was coming in or going out anymore. He used a bunch of rags he found in the office to dust off the couch. He then lay down to try and rest. This was just for the form; he knew there was no way he would fall asleep, just as he knew it would be impossible for him to ever make sense of the last twelve hours.

Why did Kat have to die, but not him? He was inches away from her, and yet he had been spared. He thought of himself as weak, a coward even, first for having survived and then for abandoning his girlfriend in the middle of the night. And this reflex he had to flee now felt wrong. Hiding in an isolated warehouse? How on earth would he keep informed on the state of the world if he couldn't see it?

He rose, grabbed a patio chair and went out on the roof for some fresh air.

As he ate a cup of cold oatmeal, he heard vehicles drive by the building at high speed. At around ten o'clock, one of them took a turn in the driveway. Jonathan nervously ventured by the ledge to get a look.

The red pickup truck moved at a slow pace and then stopped by the entrance. He knew that truck quite well, having driven it himself many times. He ran back inside, flew down the stairs and opened the door to reveal his presence.

Mr. Dean took a few steps in Jonathan's direction and looked behind him as if he hoped with all of his heart to see Kat also emerge from the warehouse.

"Are you alone?" the old man asked, quite aware of the terrible implications in his question.

Jonathan's knees buckled and he fell to the ground, his face buried in his hands. Mr. Dean covered the rest of the distance and helped him up so he could give him refuge in his arms.

"You did the right thing by coming here, kiddo," Mr. Dean reassured him.

"I broke the lock. I'm so sorry," Jonathan confessed.

"Well, that's quite alright. I'll just adjust your pay accordingly," his boss said as he smiled and winked.

He asked his employee for a hand in getting some supplies out of the bed of his truck. Before he obliged, Jonathan also had a question.

"Mrs. Dean?"

It was the old man's turn to bow down from the pain. He looked away and grabbed a firm hold of his truck's tailgate.

Jonathan didn't need to hear the words.

The two took a few minutes to regain their composure before they began unloading the truck.

CHAPTER 4

Two months before the world changed, Anna Cobb had been a vibrant and rising artist enjoying the generous fallouts of her fairly recent and unexpected status as an online celebrity.

She had paid her dues, years worth of them, by working early hours at the trendy *Pierre et Daniel Bakery* in the north end of the City while looking forward to the afternoon so she could trade butter and pans for brushes and canvases.

Her gift was undeniable, but as is often the case for those afflicted with creative propensities, feeding both herself and her passion had been an ongoing challenge. She had once pointed out that for someone who spent most of her days in dough up to her elbows, very little of it ever landed in her pocket. Her salary and the money she raised by selling a few of her pieces here and there had kept a roof over her head, albeit barely.

Anna approached painting the same way she did everything else in her life: with pride, poise and a mind wide open. She was *one of those people*. Those blessed with talent, sound reasoning and jaw dropping looks, though her appearance ranked dead last on her list of priorities. And since she was *one of those people*, the less she cared about it, the more beautiful she was.

Her younger brother Matthew had enrolled in a night course with hopes of pursuing a career as a Social Media Strategist. At twenty-six, he had finally decided to heed Anna's advice to put his own artistic impulses to good use. He too would paint, but with a keyboard instead of brushes and on a computer monitor, rather than a canvas.

He featured his sister, as well as some of her paintings, in a series of clever Twitter advertisement spots for an assignment. When the short clips went viral, both his and Anna's lives were turned upside down.

Their story found its way into a slew of articles in popular online publications. Orders for Anna's pieces came in steady, some by well-connected people who then promoted her work. The snowball effect allowed her to quit her job at the bakery, rent a live-in atelier and focus on her craft.

Matthew was rewarded with a position in one of the City's major media firms at the end of his course.

Not a single day went by Anna didn't reflect on how she had attained this level of comfort and on the luck she had to be able to earn a living doing what she loved the most. She reimbursed Matthew's tuition fees and took him to happenings and gallery openings as her date as often as he would let her.

It was after such a chic soirée that her fate was once again given a shove in a different direction. Matthew was taking Anna home when a drunk driver t-boned his car on the passenger side a block away from her studio. He was mostly unharmed, but Anna sustained a brain trauma that left her in a coma for nine days. When she awoke from it, the doctors informed her that she would never regain the use of her legs. She also had fractures to her ribs, right arm and right shoulder.

Her brain injury, mild all things considered, had resulted in some hesitation when she spoke. This struggle to say what was on her mind was as great a source of frustration as her inability to stand up and walk out of that hospital to go grab a decent meal. Anna had been a master of the retort, a loveable but first class smart ass, so she responded with rage when her mouth refused to translate her thoughts at the speed it did before the accident. She often interrupted herself with "hum" mid-sentence and repeated words.

Despite her disappointment with it, this minor change in her speech pattern made her sound endearing beyond measure; it was impossible not to come to a standstill and listen to her whenever she attempted a conversation.

A devastated Matthew was at his sister's bedside when she regained consciousness. After the doctor had spoken to her and left the two alone, Matthew had told Anna that giving her the life she had always wanted with his publicity campaign had been his greatest accomplishment. And now he felt responsible for taking it all away from her.

His tearful apology sat near the top of a long list of heartbreaking moments that had marked both their lives. Anna reacted to his words with sadness, but also with a dash of anger, in part because of her difficulties in expressing her thoughts on his apology. She did manage to make him promise never to say something like that again. She knew he wasn't at fault and took all the time she needed to tell him so.

And while her condition was serious, it wasn't half as bad as what they had been through two decades earlier.

"Remember Dad?" she asked her brother.

Their father Paul had also been involved in a car crash, though he hadn't been nearly as lucky as Anna. Every single detail of that cold September week was etched in Anna's memory: from the rain, to the fear when the police had shown up at their house, to the smell of that damn hospital.

On her first visit to Paul's room, Anna had searched in vain for familiar traits in the face of the man lying in that bed. She was all but eleven years old, yet no one had to tell her he wasn't going to make it. Matthew was seven at the time.

Three days after the accident, both Anna and Matthew had stood in a corner of the room and held hands while they watched their mother Julia sign the papers authorizing the medical staff to turn off the ventilator. Anna had long tried and wished, but she could never erase from her memory the sound of her mother's cries mixing with the flat, continuous tone of Paul's heart monitor before a nurse clued in and killed the switch.

After the funeral, Julia had entered a state of deep depression and spent the greater part of the nine following years sitting in a chair in the family home's living room, chain smoking.

Before she was even a teenager, Anna was in charge of the house, cooking the meals, making sure Matthew did his homework and wore clean clothes to school.

When Julia died of a heart attack at the age of forty-four, Anna began her life on her own. Uncle Lou and Aunt June, who lived nearby, took Matthew in. Lou had made Anna promise she'd come and have dinner with them twice a week. This way, she would maintain a close relationship with her brother and remember she still had a family that loved her.

"Family is the True North of your life. Know where it is and you'll never lose your way," Lou told Anna more than once.

She made and kept the promise.

A month after she had regained consciousness, following what felt like an endless succession of surgeries, Anna was transferred to a physical rehabilitation facility seventy miles east of the City.

There were many aspects to tackle; she had to learn to go about her life without the use of her legs, recover strength in her right arm. She also sat with a speech therapist five afternoons per week.

Each day seemed to bring about something that highlighted the harshness of her new reality. And each one of those changes, no matter how minor, was a steep hill to climb. Being taught to use a catheter to relieve herself, among other things, had been a pride crushing part of her rehabilitation.

Matthew came by every day to assist her as best he could, though spent the greater part of his visits recording his sister's progress with his phone. Anna put on a smile and a brave face for the camera. At times it was genuine, but the tight schedule imposed by the Center was exhausting and she was demoralized at even the smallest of setbacks. Many nights she had cried alone in her room, dispirited by what she secretly called *the unfairness of her destiny.*

Through it all, however, Anna was thankful for Matthew's constant presence and for the great new friend she had found in Josie, a kind older woman who was also at the Center as a result of a car crash. The two had bonded over their common fate and their love for the arts. Josie, much more at peace with her situation, was a rock on which Anna could lean on tougher days.

On the night of the outbreak, Matthew was with his sister as usual. Anna's rehabilitation had improved at a rapid pace in the preceding two weeks. She was able to get in and out of her wheelchair without help and go unassisted anywhere inside the Center, which included the arts room. She stopped by there every day after speech therapy to practice holding canvases, brushes, paint tubes and palettes. She didn't paint, though. She wasn't ready for that just yet.

Intrigued by the commotion in the hallways, Matthew and Anna followed the crowd to the rec room where everyone had gathered in front of the television to watch the reports. Anna stopped her chair next to Josie's who then offered a full recap of the events.

The sixty people present in the room — the Center's entire population — stared at the TV and saw what the rest of the country saw. Given what was happening, and at Matthew's urging, the nurses extended visiting hours.

Everybody was still glued to the TV screen when, at around ten thirty, a scream detonated at the back of the room.

A nurse had just noticed that a doctor, standing next to

her, had been infected. Seconds later, it was her turn to succumb. The virus then took multiple people at once, causing panic and incomprehension among the others. Anna, fearing they were all about to die, grabbed a hold of her brother's arm and pulled him closer so she could hug him.

The next two minutes felt like an eternity. People screamed and sobbed as the virus circled the room and selected its victims at random.

Calm eventually returned. Anna let go of her grip on Matthew, believing the attack was over. She turned to Josie and saw she was crying. Anna motioned to reach for her friend's hand to give her comfort, but stopped when Josie's feet began tapping on her chair's footrests. Her legs, which she hadn't been able to move since her accident, then extended in front her.

The virus had decided it needed one more life.

"God no, please," Josie shouted while she looked at Anna and tried to reach for her hand. Matthew pulled his sister's chair away before the two could make contact.

The virus seemed to take longer to finish its dirty deed on Josie than it had on the others. It moved from her legs, which she couldn't feel, to her arms, which she could. The muscles response to the infection outlined the path the virus followed: from her arms, to her shoulders and then to her chest where it split to travel up her face and down to her belly.

The screams Josie let out during her agony were so long, loud and horrific that Anna fainted before she could see her friend take her last breath.

In the end, Matthew and Anna were both spared. Forty-two others around them didn't share in their luck. The Center's staff, now reduced to just a few, calculated they would need all the support they could get to maintain care and order. The visitors were invited to stay and help with the patients who hadn't been infected.

Matthew took Anna to her quarters, but returned to assist in carrying the dead to the exercise room where they were covered with bed sheets.

Added to the terror of what had just happened was the sadness of watching guests saying goodbye to those they had come to visit and who were now lost. The reaction of survivor patients left alone and more vulnerable than ever as their deceased loved ones were taken away was difficult to absorb.

Five of the visitors who had just lost someone decided to leave the Center to try and reach their families, bringing the total number of people alive in the building down to thirteen; six patients, four visitors, two nurses and one big custodian named Benny.

In the days that immediately followed the infection, the survivors experienced a kind of anguish they hadn't known before.

The Center was in a fairly secluded area, away from the City and no one from any levels of government or law enforcement showed up to rescue them.

Their only contact with the outside world came from a couple of radio stations that still had sporadic broadcasts. It was difficult to follow, let alone believe, their grim accounts of the events. At first, it was just a bunch of kids goofing off behind the microphones after they had broken into the studios. Adults soon took over and did what they could to report the news. Their efforts were incoherent at best.

There were nonetheless recurring themes in the little

information they all relayed: madness, chaos, violence.
   And death.
   Death everywhere.

CHAPTER 5

Mr. Dean sure hadn't shown up at the warehouse empty-handed: sleeping bags, foam mattresses, propane tanks, a camping stove and a sizable amount of food.
Once the goods were unloaded, Jonathan suggested they rolled the truck behind the building to maintain its unoccupied look.

The second floor required a lot of attention. Mr. Dean had the utilities turned on the week before; water and electricity were running just fine, which helped them transform an archaic and dusty room into livable quarters. Toward the end of the afternoon, on the day after the wave of infections, both men were exhausted.

They sat down, Jonathan on the couch and Mr. Dean in the big chair. A long and heavy silence filled the room. Jonathan broke it with a question.

"You think this will blow over soon?"

His boss lowered his gaze and shook his head while he searched for the right words.

"With what I saw earlier today? Not any time soon, no."

This, coming from someone admired by all for his common sense, was a terrible pronouncement.

"Why? What did you see?" Jonathan asked.

The old man hesitated again.

"Death ... despair ... chaos. Absolute chaos," he answered.

Mr. Dean's drive to the warehouse from the north end of the City hadn't been as uneventful as Jonathan's ride from his apartment complex in the west. He had left his house much later and had found the highway blocked by cars that had piled up after their occupants had been infected. Other major roads were obstructed by either more pileups or by debris from planes that had crashed on their approach to the airport, also located North of the City.

He had been forced to go across town where madness was raging in broad daylight. There were countless bodies in the streets. High-rise buildings were on fire and looters were fighting over useless things like large screen TV's and booze. People had also thrown themselves on the hood of his truck, begging him for his help. Stopping anywhere before making it to the warehouse would have been a dangerous move, if not a fatal one. He knew that. And for a man of such compassionate nature, ignoring pleas this desperate had been heart wrenching.

Whatever "this" was, its consequences were devastating, widespread and he warned Jonathan to get ready to work hard to set up their den for a long stay.

"A lot of people died yesterday. If things ever return to normal, and that's a huge if, it'll be quite a while."

They had dinner and spent the greater part of the evening describing their losses from the previous night. Before Mr. Dean could give the gruesome account of what had taken place at his house, he reached inside one of the boxes he had brought and retrieved a bottle of Whisky.

"I'll only have one glass. But I'm gonna need it," he declared.

◆ ◆ ◆

Mr. Dean's sleeping bag was empty. The door leading to the roof was ajar. Jonathan, not fully awake yet, joined his boss outside. The old man was scanning the part of the City that peeked above the trees with his binoculars.

Jonathan was taken aback by the amount of smoke coming from what he estimated to be the downtown core.

"What you said yesterday, kid? About giving this place an unoccupied look? I don't know if that'll be enough."

Mr. Dean had gotten up early and spent the first minutes of daylight circling the yard, pondering on ways to deter people from even thinking of entering their hideout.

"I may have figured it out," he announced.

The smoke rising from the City had given him an idea.

While they had breakfast, oatmeal again but warm this time, he explained his plan to give the illusion the warehouse had been destroyed by fire. They would have to break the windows on the ground floor, burn the bricks above them to turn them black and then block the gaping holes from the inside with the thickest metal sheets they had.

Hiding the only way inside the warehouse was critical. There were dumpsters on wheels by the building next door, so they could use those as camouflage. He also wanted to conceal the tools and other work supplies on the main level behind a wall of trash and scrap metal; if anyone ever got a look inside he hoped they'd move on, put off by the sight of worthless junk. The upstairs quarters would need to be better insulated, locked and reinforced.

As for his truck, it should only be used if an emergency ever arose. It was too noisy, too visible and gas would soon be as rare a commodity as food. They couldn't take the risk of being tracked back to their home or finding themselves stranded somewhere after a breakdown.

He asked Jonathan what he thought of his plan.

Jonathan shrugged. "When have I ever argued with you?"

It would never have crossed his mind to question the man's reasoning. He had, after all, followed his lead for the last fifteen years. And it had paid off too. Under his guidance, Jonathan had become a skilled machinist, a trade for which he had neither training nor interest before he met his boss.

Mr. Dean was nearing retirement age when a young Jonathan had shown up in his office, fresh out of college and disillusioned by his employment prospects. Dean Mach Inc. wasn't a big enterprise, but it had just landed a contract with a much larger distributor and there was a need for new, strong hands.

The man was proud of his shop and though he cared

deeply for each of his employees, Jonathan stood out from the pack. He was green, yes, but his maturity, his wit and his energy had led Mr. Dean to like him immediately. He hired him on the spot and took him under his wing. In time, but very little of it, Jonathan had risen through the ranks and become the son he and Mrs. Dean never had. Everyone expected that one day, sooner rather than later, the business was going to be turned over to him. So the idea of his boss leading the way in this new life of theirs brought immense comfort to Jonathan.

By the end of their first full day together at the warehouse, the two men had already completed many of the tasks Mr. Dean had listed in the morning.

"You should take a shower while you can," he told Jonathan.

"What do you mean?"

He warned his employee; if things continued to deteriorate, and he was certain they would, electricity and water were bound to shut down at any time. When Jonathan came out of the bathroom, Mr. Dean had piled up wood pallets and covered them with the foam mattresses to make two beds.

"Never thought of us as hip, and yet here we are" he joked.

After a week's worth of effort, the lower level of the building looked like it had been struck by multiple tragedies while the top floor was transformed into a home.

Their food supplies, however, were already depleted.

Jonathan told Mr. Dean he wanted go out to see what he could find. He planned to leave at sun down and walk toward the City. Since he couldn't predict what would arise along the way, and because he needed to be fast and light, his boss would have to stay behind and guard their home. This excursion would also serve as an opportunity to assess the situation in the area. He expected to be back in the morning with a full report and if all went well, breakfast.

While Jonathan was getting dressed, Mr. Dean repeated the same set of advice to him over and over again.

"Don't approach people; not loners, not groups, nobody. Don't rush into anything either. Take your time. Observe, listen to what's around you."

Once he was wrapped in warm and dark clothes, and his backpack was secured around his shoulders and waist, Jonathan looked Mr. Dean in the eye and reassured him he had a clear understanding of what he was about to do. With the same confident tone, he promised he'd return in one piece. Still, after he exited the building he stopped, leaned his back against the sliding door and took a moment to focus.

Mr. Dean stood on the roof and faced the road, hoping to get a glimpse of Jonathan. Although the power was on, their area wasn't well lit; he appeared, but only for a few seconds as he crossed the bridge and he headed toward the City.

The old man retreated inside, sat in the large chair and stared straight ahead. There would be no way he'd get any sleep until Jonathan came back.

Ten minutes later, the main entrance door slid open. Someone began climbing the stairs. Mr. Dean's heart rate increased with each footstep he heard. The gate to the second floor swung open. Jonathan rushed in, walked to the light switch and flipped it downward.

"We can see the light in here through the window," Jonathan said.

For all the precautions they had taken to secure the warehouse and make it look abandoned, this whopper of a detail had escaped them. Every night since they had moved in, they had signaled their presence to potential survivors across the bridge. It was pure luck no one had noticed or cared.

"I'll keep it off for tonight," Mr. Dean said. "We'll make shutters tomorrow."

Jonathan left again. When he looked back at the building from the other side of the bridge, there was now nothing but darkness.

It must have been nine-thirty, ten o'clock at the latest, when he reached the fringes of the City and saw the flickering sign of a grocery store on the horizon. This more populated area, although at a good distance from the downtown core, should have been buzzing with traffic and noise at that hour. It was eerily quiet. The wind sweeping through the City carried the scent of the recent desolation in Jonathan's direction.

It was a blend of smoke, fumes and bodies in early stages of decay. The bodies of those who had fallen victims to the virus, but also those lost to the violence in the aftermath.

The supermarket didn't look promising.

Its doors were wide open. Carts, trash and a few corpses were scattered in the parking lot. Jonathan took position in a small patch of trees on the other side of the street to observe it anyway. When he felt confident enough, he ran and entered the store.

Every shelf of every aisle was empty. Maybe he'd have more luck at the back, where on normal business days the staff would have disappeared and then re-emerged with fresh supplies to replenish the displays.

He pushed the swing doors with caution, walked in and turned the corner. His heart stopped as he came face to face with two employees standing by a stack of boxes. He took a few quick steps backward, tripped over something and fell on his butt. His breath was cut even shorter when he realized he had landed among three bodies laid on the floor.

All of them had been infected. By the looks of it the two employees standing had died right where they were, but the other three had been carried to the back later.

Jonathan jumped back on his feet and regrouped. He hoped the presence of these corpses had been enough to discourage other scavengers. He did find some canned goods, pouches of dried soup, crackers, pancake mix and many bags of navy beans. He also got his hands on three jugs of spring water, which he emptied. The water was still running fine at the warehouse, but these containers could come in handy.

This wouldn't do it. He needed to make this trip count and concluded his best chance of finding food wouldn't lie in places like this one. It would be in houses that had either been abandoned or were occupied by infected people.

He pushed the swing doors to return to the front, but stopped and retreated upon hearing voices in the store. Through a small dirty window, he saw the silhouettes of four men inspecting the aisles.

Jonathan located the rear exit, which was locked, but next to it was a gray breaker box. The rear half of the building turned pitch black when he pulled the lever down. He erupted from the back and aimed for the front doors.

The lights in the parking lot put him in plain view of the others as he got near the entrance. One of the men screamed at him to stop. Jonathan ignored the order and kept going in the direction of the wooded area across the street. He dove in the high grass, crawled behind a tree and made sure no one had followed him.

Aside from Mr. Dean, these were the only people he had seen since the night of the virus. Instead of fleeing farther away, he stayed to observe the men and their demeanor. What happened next was a great disappointment.

The four men went back inside and came out later carrying items Jonathan had missed. A stranger on foot approached them and appeared to ask for their help. When his begging turned too insistent, the group attacked him and beat him to the ground. They almost ran him over with their truck as they left.

The scene shook Jonathan, but from a pure observational standpoint this was valuable information.

"Mr. Dean was right," he thought. "Don't go anywhere near people."

The man rose to his knees, sobbed for a while, then stood and limped his way inside the store.

Jonathan headed in the direction of houses nearby, choosing not to waste time with homes that had no lights on; those were too risky. He focused instead on the ones where he could peek inside. At the first signs of movement, or in most cases mere bad vibes, he kept on walking.

At about two o'clock, he came upon a house with the lights on at the end of a cul-de-sac. In the backyard, he stood by the patio doors and spied on the occupants.

An old man and woman were seated at the kitchen table holding hands, as though they were praying. Jonathan looked closer; both had been infected and had spent the last week frozen in that position. The door was unlocked. A quick tour of the rooms confirmed no one else was in the house. He grabbed all the food he could find.

The idea of taking what wasn't rightfully his repulsed him. It was, above all, quite creepy; there were people, sitting just a few feet away, ignoring him as he stole their goods. They were the ones who were dead and yet, it was he who felt like a ghost.

Half of his backpack was empty at the time he had fled the grocery store. There was still some room in it after he took the content of the old couple's pantry. Before he walked out, he looked at them and thanked them out loud for the supplies he had found in their home. It was a bizarre thing to do, but some expression of gratitude was in order he thought.

An hour passed before he deemed another house safe to enter. This time, there were enough provisions to fill his entire backpack. It was quite heavy, and Jonathan was more than capable of carrying it, but he feared this weight would slow him down.

Mr. Dean and the warehouse were well over two hours away by his own estimate. The last thing he wanted was to cross the South Side Bridge in broad daylight and perhaps be spotted by other survivors in the area.

He found a pace at which he could walk without the need to take breaks.

The horizon was beginning to turn orange when he made it to the river by his new home. Mr. Dean's best effort to remain awake hadn't paid off. He had fallen asleep in the big leather chair.

Jonathan couldn't blame him.

Only once had he sat in this massive monstrosity; the

moment his feet had hit the ottoman, he had slipped into a deep coma.

He tried not to wake his boss while he laid the contents of his backpack on the table in the middle of the room.

When Jonathan got out of the bathroom, after a well-deserved shower, Mr. Dean, all smiles and standing by the table, greeted him with an energetic "good morning" as he browsed through the food.

They had breakfast while Jonathan gave a detailed account of his night, after which he retreated in silence.

He too was satisfied with these fresh supplies.

What he had seen, however, was unsettling and plenty to reflect upon. He now agreed with Mr. Dean's assessment that it would be all but impossible to reconnect with anything that resembled the life they had before all of this. The virus had killed too many, left too much havoc in its trail, to allow for it.

He thought of the written promise he had sent to his parents about somehow getting to them.

It had taken him an entire night to travel but a few miles on foot. At no point had he felt safe or confident. Walking out there without being detected was slow and arduous.

His folks were more than nine hundred miles away. Reaching them could take months. That's if he survived the trip at all.

Then there was Mr. Dean.

Jonathan couldn't just leave him behind or expect him to undertake such a dangerous journey at his age.

There was a fair chance he would never see his family again.

Or know of their fate.

CHAPTER 6

The challenges he had faced in securing what could perhaps feed two adults for a week had been weighing heavily on Jonathan's mind. The canned goods would go fast. As for the rest, soup didn't qualify as a meal. Neither did pancakes for that matter. There were numerous bags of navy beans, but Mr. Dean had suggested they saved those for fall and winter.

The morning Jonathan had returned from his trip near the City, both men were working on shutters to cover the window on the second floor when the power went out. They looked at each other in silence as they let it sink in that their lives had just gotten much more complicated. They finished barehanded what they had started with the different machines and mounted the perfectly fitted folding panels into place.

Jonathan announced he would go out again that night. He wanted to try his luck in the opposite direction, farther south from the City.

He remembered that on the day Mr. Dean and him

had inspected the warehouse prior to its purchase they had also gone for a drive in the neighborhood. If his memory served him well, there was some sort of a home renovation depot, about five miles down the road. Perhaps there were things in there they could use.

"Maybe you should take it easy tonight and do this tomorrow," Mr. Dean said.

"Time isn't on our side, sir. Look at how fast all the food disappeared from the stores," Jonathan replied. "It'll be the same for everything else. Heck, if I weren't so tired, I'd be heading out now."

His boss agreed, but he insisted Jonathan slept for the rest of the day.

"No point in you going out there if you can't think straight, kid."

After sunset, while Jonathan was putting his gear back on in the glow of a propane lantern, he laid out his plan. It included using his bike to cut his travel time, even if only to get to the depot. He was prepared to leave it behind if he had to, though he loved that bike.

Mr. Dean had one more piece of advice for Jonathan before he left.

"Whatever you find, you don't have to bring it all back here tonight. If you see supplies you like, hide them outside nearby. We'll go get it later."

The depth of the darkness stunned Jonathan the moment he stepped outside the warehouse. His vision took a while to adapt. Strangely, when it did, this obscurity gave him a greater sense of safety than the lights had the night before. If no one could see him, he thought, then no one could hurt him.

The road's layout, flat and mostly straight, also played

in his favor. There were few buildings and lots of trees and empty fields along the way. So should a car come from either direction, he'd have plenty of time to ditch somewhere.

What he guessed was the depot emerged in the distance. His memory had failed him. There was indeed a Building and Renovation Center, but it stood among other outlets such as a flower wholesale warehouse, an arts and crafts store and a Take Paws Pet Distribution Center. Fields and patches of woods surrounded the plaza. The sight of a familiar company logo brought a smile to Jonathan's face.

"Jackpot," he said as he stopped his bike in front of the Great Mountain Coop, a renowned chain of outdoors sports and camping supplies stores.

He parked his wheels at the back of the building then tested the front and back doors. Both were locked, all the windows were intact; the place had been untouched by looters. He didn't want to shatter the glass at the front entrance, but he wasn't a seasoned burglar either. He circled around and spotted an office window, which he broke with his hands wrapped in his jacket. The glass fell inside with minimal noise and the hole it left was barely big enough for him, but he got in.

Winter sleeping bags, portable and reusable water filters, solar power equipment; Jonathan was a kid in a toy factory. He came upon a high pile of stacked tubs of cold weather meals, which he hugged. There were also boxes of energy bars, pouches of coffee, powdered milk and eggs, sealed jerky in all flavors and many more bags of beans to add to those he had found at the grocery store.

Mr. Dean's suggestion, the one about hiding the

supplies, echoed in his head. He found his way to the back door and carried all he could in high grass at the edge of a patch of trees, no more than twenty yards from the exit.

An hour later, sweating profusely, he filled his backpack with some freeze-dried meals and dozens of energy bars.

Before he left, he looked for the travel section out of curiosity. The sight of a bicycle trailer triggered another smile. This would make his life much easier by lowering the number of trips required to take his bounty home. The tools to attach the heavy-duty apparatus to his bike were right there on the shelves and he hit the road again.

His backpack and the trailer, both loaded at their capacity, slowed him down but he was quite anxious to share the news of his findings with Mr. Dean. He had to remind himself a few times to stay focused on his immediate safety. He made it to the warehouse as thirsty and as out of breath as he had ever been, but he couldn't help it; he ran up the stairs, opened the door leading to the men's living quarters and rushed in the dark room.

"Hold it right there," Mr. Dean yelled as he pointed his flashlight inches from Jonathan's face.

"Good God, sir. You almost gave me a heart attack," he said, grabbing at his chest.

"You? What about me? I'm the old fart here!"

They needed a minute, but they did find the humor in what had just happened and both burst out laughing. Mr. Dean told Jonathan he suspected his search hadn't gone too well since he was back so soon.

Jonathan's only answer was to flip his backpack over the couch to empty it.

The old man was speechless.

"There's a trailer full downstairs. I have to head back now. There's enough stuff for four or five more trips."

"Really?" his boss inquired with an eagerness that quickly turned to worries for Jonathan's safety.

He was adamant; what he had found had to be picked up now. Plus, he hadn't crossed paths with anyone on his way there or back.

He unloaded the trailer and he was about to sit on his bike when the door behind him slid open. Mr. Dean, though he hesitated a moment, stepped out.

Earlier in the week he had confessed he wasn't too keen on venturing back out there anytime soon. What he had seen on his drive to the warehouse the morning after the outbreak was seared in his mind. The pain in the man's voice had made it obvious to Jonathan the he would have to be the one to go out and scavenge for the both of them.

"Goddam it. Get in the truck," Mr. Dean blurted out.

"It's safer with the bike, sir."

"Five trips? No way. With me it's just one and we'll be back here before you know it."

Jonathan relented, but he suggested they break the old truck's lights to be as discreet as possible. He also described the layout of the parking lot, the locations of each of the buildings and where the supplies were hidden. Once out of the truck, they would have to remain silent.

And all of this had to happen fast; there wouldn't be time to neatly stack or inventory anything.

That last part wasn't a real rule. It was a wise crack aimed at his boss's legendary obsession with keeping a clean and well-organized shop, a fixation that had driven many of his employees to the brink of madness over the years.

Mr. Dean needed a few seconds to figure out Jonathan was pulling his leg. When he did, he gave him a heartfelt slap on the shoulder.

"Get in there, you smarty pants."

They drove in the dark at a safe speed and pulled in the parking lot shared by the different stores in a matter of minutes. Jonathan pointed to the corner of the Great Mountain Coop where he wanted the truck to back up and they began loading the supplies.

He noticed Mr. Dean's sustained looks toward the Building and Renovation depot in the distance.

They were on the move again after securing the last of the items, but Mr. Dean missed the exit turn and aimed instead for the depot. Jonathan was about to ask him what he was doing when the truck came to an abrupt halt and he was thrown against the dashboard.

"Go get these barrels, quick," Mr. Dean ordered while he pointed at them.

Confused, Jonathan jumped out of the vehicle, ran to a stack of three blue plastic barrels and swung them in the bed. He got back in his seat and felt relieved when Mr. Dean stepped on the gas pedal. He was thrown forward again a few seconds later.

This time, his head hit the windshield.

"Damn it sir, will you stop that," he said while rubbing his forehead to kill the pain.

"Come with me, kiddo."

Jonathan had no choice but to obey: his boss was out of the truck already and running toward the depot's main entrance with quite a purpose.

"There has got to be a small wood burning stove somewhere in there. We need one," he said.

There was no time to argue. Jonathan looked for the biggest rock by his feet and fired it at the glass door with all of his strength. The sound it made as it shattered echoed in the night.

The men split and rushed through the aisles to find the department where the stoves might be. It was Mr. Dean who located them. They picked the one they thought would be the easiest to carry, although it was still quite heavy.

"Now can we leave?" Jonathan asked.

The stove had taken a while to load and he was now on the verge of panic. Spending all of this time in the open was reckless, if not plain stupid, he thought, especially after the fracas the glass door had made when it had pulverized.

"One last thing," his boss answered. "See that pile of sheets of plywood. We need four of 'em."

They threw the sheets on top of the other items. At long last, they left the parking lot.

An angry Jonathan turned to Mr. Dean and gave him a long stare.

"What the hell do we need those for?" he asked, rubbing the bump on his forehead.

"Water, my young friend. Those are for water," Mr. Dean said as he smiled.

With the truck parked at the back of the warehouse, both men toured the building in silence until they knew it was safe to open the door and unload the supplies.

They looked at what they had amassed, what they had put their lives on the line to collect. Mr. Dean was happy and showed his appreciation with a tap on Jonathan's shoulder.

"That, kiddo, is quite amazing."

They celebrated with each a ration of cereal and a glass of orange juice.

"Let's get some rest," Mr. Dean suggested at the last bite.

CHAPTER 7

Eleven days had passed since the virus had killed three quarters of the staff and residents at Anna's Rehabilitation Center. Power had been out for four days. Thirteen mouths to feed meant the pantry was now critically under stocked. The survivors were worried and depressed.

The group held a frank discussion, at the end of which they concluded that someone had to drive to the City not only for food, but also a first-hand account of what was happening there.

Matthew eagerly stepped forward. Anna showed no reaction in front of the others, but after the meeting she took her brother aside and scolded him. She begged him not to go and raised every argument against it she could think of to try and convince him to stay put.

His mind was made up; he was strong, resourceful and knew the downtown area like the palm of his hand.

A young visitor who had lost his mother to the virus volunteered to tag along and the two made their plan to leave early the following morning. Matthew thought they'd first head to the Metro Police Headquarters located at the core of the City, a logical starting point to gather information. They would then search for food and, if possible, return that night.

And so at sunrise, through her quarters' window, Anna watched the two young men get inside the old beat up Honda Matthew had inherited from Uncle Lou. The car moved down the long driveway and soon disappeared behind a line of tall pine trees after it crossed the main road.

Anna wanted to be proud of her kid brother for showing this much nerve. In truth, she was sick with worry and a little mad at him for leaving her. With both hands pressed against the window, she took a moment to fight back the tears. She then came out of her room, approached the nurses and offered to help with those who were in worse shape than she was.

Until that morning, everyone at the Center had remained suspended in a waiting mode, convinced a rescue was imminent. That hope was still very much alive, but they had now accepted it could be a while before it materialized.

The time had come to organize and plan for a longer haul.

The Center's personnel took an inventory of the food and medical supplies while Anna visited the five patients. She brought water to one, helped another move in a better position in her bed and comforted for those grieving the loss of someone with just the right words. Within a few hours after Matthew's departure, she had become the most appreciated of the survivors.

A week after the infections, power had gone out as a

nurse was getting a patient ready for dialysis. Benny, the impressive custodian, had warned this would happen. The two nurses had discussed how they would use the limited power from the generator and shared their decision with the group; there would be electricity in the building for about four hours, three times a week, to allow for the treatment of this patient and to recharge one cell phone.

Since the days and the nights remained cool, Benny had taken the food out of the walk-in fridge and stored it outside in his toolshed with the hopes of preserving it a little while longer. He was also keeping all the jugs, bottles and canisters he had at his disposal filled with water and urged everybody to do the same. This, he thought, would be the next vital utility to shut down.

At dinner, on the day Matthew had left for the City, Anna had become silent. Night was now descending and her brother and the young man — Martin she believed his name was — had been gone for more than twelve hours. She knew it was too soon to worry, but she just couldn't help it.

Benny had climbed on the roof again to try and find a radio station still broadcasting. As it had been for the last four days, he heard nothing but dead air. When he walked back in the cafeteria and confirmed the continued radio silence, Anna's heart jumped into her throat. She finished her pasta and asked Benny to guide her to her room with his flashlight. She settled by the window to keep watch in case Matthew's car appeared on the road.

Multiple scenarios danced in her mind. There were the happy ones, those with Matthew driving up to the

Center in a car overflowing with supplies or better yet with law enforcement in tow, coming to save everyone. Though she tried, she couldn't brush aside the very plausible worst of outcomes, the one where she never saw her brother again.

Anna fell asleep, seated in her chair by the window, well after midnight. When she awoke and looked outside, the sun was rising already.

Matthew hadn't returned.

◆ ◆ ◆

Breakfast at the Center consisted of a bowl of cereal, and lunch, of a bowl of soup with crackers. A small portion of pasta and tomato sauce was served at dinner. The kitchen's giant stove worked on natural gas. It was pure luck that the tank by the side of the building had been filled the same morning the virus had struck and Benny made sure to use this resource wisely.

Anna's bright dispositions from the day before had made way to more somber ones. She still tended to her fellow patients by either helping them to the cafeteria or by bringing food, water and medicine to their room, but her upbeat attitude had all but vanished. In her limited spare time, she sat by the window in her quarters, staring at the road with a restless mind. She knew Matthew well enough to suspect that if he wasn't back yet something of importance was holding him.

Something else was bothering her.

Early in the morning she had rolled by the nurses' station and interrupted what could only be described as a heated discussion between the two. She didn't think anything of it at first, but when she caught them doing the same in the afternoon, she assumed some kind of hard decision was behind their argument.

She had considered approaching them to find out what it was all about or going to Benny with this information. In the end, however, she had opted to leave it alone. Things were already so difficult. There was no point in adding to anybody's anxiety. Or worse, cause divisions among the group.

Matthew had now been gone forty-two hours. Anna sat in her room, staring in the void of darkness outside her window. She was about to lose her fight against exhaustion when headlights, coming from the direction of the City, appeared in the distance. For a moment there, she wondered if she was dreaming and rubbed her eyes to confirm it was real.

The two brilliant orbs came to a full stop across the road from the Center then proceeded up its driveway. Anna pushed her chair out of her room to alert the others.

"They're here!" she screamed with excitement.

Benny rushed out of his office and ordered everyone to stay put while he went to meet with the two young heroes. His large silhouette, made even bigger by the beam of his flashlight bouncing off the walls, moved down the hallway.

When he made it to the foyer and pivoted to shine his light on the doors, he was greeted not by Matthew and his friend, but by a hail of bullets. Projectiles were still raining on him when he took half a step backwards and collapsed. The way he hit ground left no doubt as to his fate.

Despite the shock, Anna had the reflex to whisper to

the others to hide wherever they could. As the group scattered, men in the entrance could be heard praising themselves on the accuracy of their shots. Some argued about who should get credit for the kill.

Anna knew where she wanted to escape. Followed by the two nurses, she headed to the exercise room where those killed by the virus had been taken. Though Benny had opened some of the windows, the stench in there was suffocating. Anna almost threw up upon passing the door, but it wasn't enough to change her mind. This was her best chance at survival for now, she was certain of it. The three women lay down among the corpses, covered their bodies with spare bed sheets and remained still.

The attackers searched the building.

Anna's heart skipped a few beats each time they found someone hiding and dragged them, screaming or sobbing, to the entrance. One of the men stepped inside the exercise room. The foul smell and the sight of so many covered bodies stopped him from inspecting it any further. He warned his friends to stay away from this particular room before shutting the door.

The few hours that followed were quiet. Anna figured the thugs had come for the food and guessed they had taken the survivors they had found to a more remote part of the Center. At sunrise, she lifted her head from under the bed sheet and whispered to the two nurses she believed it would be safe to look outside or listen in the hallway. One went to the window while the other tiptoed to the door.

There was nobody in the parking lot, but the nurse at the door could hear muffled voices coming from what she thought was the cafeteria.

Anna remembered she had cookies in her backpack, which she kept hooked to her chair. Matthew, knowing these were her favorite, had surprised her with the box on the morning before the infections. She asked for her bag and shared some of the treats with the nurses.

The previous night's violent intrusion confirmed the grim radio reports from early on. Anna thought of Matthew again and wondered if the reason he still hadn't returned from the City was because he had a brush with these men along the way. Or maybe other men just like these.

The women spent the entire day either sitting or lying on the floor. They also whispered to each other because the attackers would sometimes step outside, to the front parking lot, which was right by the gym's windows. Anna listened to their conversations and tried to memorize their names as they called out to one another. She had identified four of them so far, but she believed there were more.

At sundown, after a round of cookies, the two nurses went to the adjacent change room and shut the door behind them. They let a bit of water drip from one of the faucets and drank some of it. A few minutes later, they returned to the main room with a paper cup full for Anna. The three women then hid under their bed sheets to try and get some rest.

Despite the fear, the hunger and the tensed atmosphere, Anna, who had slept all but a handful of hours in the last two days, quickly slipped into a deep sleep.

She awoke, as the day was about to break, and sat up to look in the direction of the two nurses. Their bed sheets were empty. She waited for them to come out of the change room, but when she reached inside her backpack and realized her cookies were gone, she put two and two together.

The nurses had used the cover of night to escape through one of the windows.

In all likelihood, leaving the Center had been the subject of the arguments Anna had witnessed between the two. The arrival of this band of murderous criminals had finally tipped the balance. Not only had they abandoned her, they had added insult to injury by robbing her of her food.

She crawled across the floor and went to the change room to get some water. One sip was all she could manage. She began trembling and crying, but covered her mouth to stay quiet. She had never felt so alone, so diminished.

And she had no clue as to what she was supposed to do next.

She could surrender to the attackers. She could also climb out a window like the nurses had done. There were wheelchairs outside near the entrance after all, so she could try her luck and flee.

No. No, her money was on Matthew. She knew he would return. She had to be strong and stay put for when he did.

Later that afternoon the men came out to the parking lot. They talked to each other the only way thugs could and killed time by staging wheelchair races. One of them cheated and tripped another contestant who fell on the pavement, prompting him to call his friend an asshole. Anna, eavesdropping from below the gym windows, nodded in agreement.

◆ ◆ ◆

This was Anna's third night among the corpses.

The stench around her, which at first had stained her nostrils and her throat, had now moved down to her stomach. She had taken breaks from it in the change room throughout the day, but she could only stay there a few minutes at a time. If the men ever decided to inspect the gym further, she had to be ready to hide.

She was rocking between sleep and awake under her bed sheet when bright lights in the parking lot interrupted her attempt to rest. She sat in her chair and pushed herself up so she could have a look out the window.

Matthew had just stepped out of his car. The back seat was stacked up with supplies. The success in his search for food was the reason he hadn't returned sooner, Anna thought. He, and the young man with him, gave a long suspicious gaze at the vehicle near the front entrance as they walked toward the building.

"Matthew, Matthew," Anna whispered through an open window.

Even in darkness, he recognized his sister's shadow. Intrigued to see her awake at such a late hour, and at that window, he was about to respond when the flashes and the sounds from the gunshots seized Anna. Her arms buckled and she fell back in her chair at the sight of the first bullets hitting Matthew and the young man. She tried to push herself up to look outside again, but couldn't find the strength.

There was no need anyway; she knew her brother had just been murdered before her very eyes.

She buried her face in her hands not only to cover her cries, but also as a normal reaction to the horrific scene she had just witnessed. Matthew's assailants drowned the already muffled sound of her sobs with their cheers and laughter as they emptied his car of the supplies he had brought.

This was the last straw.

She was starving. The nurses had deserted her. She was living among corpses.

And now, Matthew was dead.

In the morning, she would surrender.

Best-case scenario, they kill me too, she thought.

CHAPTER 8

It seemed the one and only hour of sleep Anna had managed to get had done her more damage than good. She felt weak and groggy. Her head was pounding.

The sun was now rising. She crawled to the change room to throw water on her face. Back in the gym, she sat in her chair and went by one of the windows.

She needed to see.

She needed to confirm that what she remembered from the previous night wasn't just the foggy remnants of a bad dream. The sight of Matthew's body, lying on his back near the thugs' car, triggered her tears again. Sadness became despair, which quickly turned to resignation.

She made her way to the door, opened it enough to peer in the hallway and listened. There was no noise, but it wasn't unexpected at that hour. Not all silences are the same, however. This one didn't feel quite right.

Anna exited her safe space and inhaled the fresh air for the first time in more than three days.

Her stomach was screaming from a hunger she had

never felt before. A type of hunger that made people do or think odd things; some joined a group, committed murder and laughed about it. Others chose to surrender to these murderers.

At the end of the hallway, as she entered the foyer, Anna passed by a pool of blood. No doubt it was Benny's, but his body was no longer there. The doors to the cafeteria were open; one of the thugs was in there, standing by a window and leaning against it, seemingly staring outside.

"Hello," Anna called out in a soft voice.

The man didn't respond or react to her presence. She moved in closer. Halfway between the door and the man, she tried once more to get his attention. He continued to ignore her. She reached the window and got a look at him from the side. The muscles in his face were tightly contracted, his mouth wide open.

Anna didn't understand right away what this meant. She went to the pantry and came upon another gang member in there, just as frozen. Only then did it dawn on her; there had been a second wave of infections during the night.

This second man had died sitting on a metal stool, a box of Frosted Flakes tightly held in his hand, which Anna did not hesitate to pry from it. She shoved handfuls of cereal in her mouth while keeping her eye on the door in case someone walked in on her.

This changed things. Surrendering was no longer the only option. Perhaps this was her way out, but she needed to find out how many people, good and bad, had survived this wave.

Anna finished the cereal then went to the kitchen to

grab a butcher's knife. She slowly and quietly entered each of the patients' rooms to inspect them. The first three were empty, but someone was asleep on the bed in the fourth one. She backed off and shut the door to think and visualize her next moves before going back inside.

Her wheelchair gave her the advantage of absolute silence as she moved forward on the floor's hard and polished surface. The man, lying on his side and facing away from her, was tucked in under the sheets all the way up to his eyes.

Anna pushed her chair past the foot of the bed then pivoted toward the man's upper body. His head was now within her reach. With the knife held high in the air, she pulled the sheets from his face in one swift gesture. She stopped the blade a mere inch above the thug's temple. There was no need; he was already dead. The virus had taken him too.

A thorough inspection of the building turned up six infected strangers in total, but there were no traces of the original survivors. When she screamed to call out to anyone who might still be alive, the echo of her own plea was all she heard. There was no one else in the Center.

Anna rushed to the parking lot, threw herself out of her chair and took Matthew in her arms. Her brother's lifeless body followed her rocking motion as she sobbed. She slid her fingers across his forehead to clear his hair from his eyes and closed them for him.

Their mother's depression had deprived Anna of her teenage years. Raising Matthew had occupied most of her time so there had been little of it left for friends, makeup sessions, parties or escapades to the mall. Not once had she ever complained about it or reminded

Matthew of all she had sacrificed for him. Acting as the only sound adult of the house had simply become a part of who she was.

Julia's death had separated the two siblings earlier than Anna would have wanted, but the two had never grown apart. Aside from having dinner with him twice a week, she had been there for each of Matthew's birthdays, his graduation and an extensive list of other milestones. She had also scraped him off the floor after his first break-up and she was there, beaming with pride, when he got his driver's license.

Aunt June, who had died on Matthew's eighteenth birthday, was the spitting image of her sister Julia. It was as though he had lost his mother for a second time in just over a decade. He was angry and withdrawn at the funeral. Anna, alarmed by his reaction, had a talk with him afterwards. Her words had been a soothing balm on his badly bruised heart.

Their conversation had ended in a pact; letting the sadness of their childhood steer their lives on the wrong path, or using their losses as permission to fail, would be the coward's way. They needed to toughen up and show up. The two had shaken on it in the form of a long hug.

She had been in awe of his strength and character after that day. In these difficult recent months, especially, he had been a rock.

"Not everyone has what it takes to, hum, to show up. But you did. You did, Matthew," she told him out loud before she went back inside.

On her way to the pantry, she stopped by the kitchen to shove a can opener and utensils in her backpack. She then set out to fill it with some of the food that was crowding the shelves thanks to her brother and the young man who had accompanied him to the City. If she was ever trapped again like she had been in the last three days, she wanted to be better prepared for it.

She was leaving the room when the door to the walk-in fridge Benny had emptied caught her attention.

A chain was rolled around its handle.

Anna stared at it for a minute, guessing at what was in there. She knocked and rested her ear against the cold metal to listen. There was no noise. She removed the chain and opened the door.

The bodies of the seven remaining survivors were scattered on the floor. None of them showed signs of violence. None of them had been infected.

Anna played out the scenario in her head. On the night they had taken over the Center, the attackers had gathered everyone they had found, walked them to the kitchen and locked them up inside the fridge. It was sealed tight, and so the group had slowly run out of air. Their death had probably occurred within a few hours of being trapped, before this new wave of infection.

The thought of what must have been a terrible agony made her stomach ache. These monsters didn't have to do this; it was a choice they had made out of pure malice.

Since there was nothing she could do, she shut the door closed. Leaving them there, in privacy and resting undisturbed, was the last bit of dignity she could let them keep.

With her bag filled with dried and canned food, along with two bottles of water, she went to the cafeteria to try and collect her thoughts. The man standing there frozen by the window, however, put out a lurid vibe. Her quarters and the entrance were no better; there wasn't a part of the building in which she could feel safe as long as the bodies of these men were dispersed all over the place.

They had to go.

Taking them to the exercise room was out of the question. She couldn't in good conscience put them anywhere near the decent people resting there.

Surely Benny kept some kind of rope in his shed.

The now familiar smell of death hit Anna once again when she opened the small shelter's door. The janitor's body was on the cement floor near the back. She went in anyway and found what she was looking for.

Back in the cafeteria, she laid a bed sheet on the floor behind the man who had been infected by the window and shoved him so he would fall on it. She then wrapped the sheet around his feet, hooked them to one end of the rope and tied the other to the backrest of her chair.

Dragging him on the polished floors proved easy, but it became a much more difficult task on the pavement in the parking lot. She pushed forward as far as her strength would allow and dumped the body on the left side of the long driveway.

Late in the afternoon, Anna dropped off the last of the six corpses. She backed off a few feet to take a good look at them. She had always been opposed to firearms, yet her fingers were tightly wrapped around the butt of the gun she had taken from the last man she had dragged outside. The other weapons she had gathered throughout the day were hidden under a high pile of dirty bed sheets in the laundry room. The one she now held would be hers.

"I hope you're all, hum, all rotting in hell," Anna screamed while using the gun to point at the group.

There wasn't an ounce of vindictiveness in her and

she had never said anything like this to anyone before. Then again, she had never met men like these either.

With the little energy she had left, Anna returned inside so she could work on what she believed was now her most pressing task: figuring out what came next.

CHAPTER 9

Jonathan and Mr. Dean had spent the greater part of their days improving their new home using the supplies they had found at the renovation depot.

The warehouse had a chimney, but the pipes to drag the smoke outside had been removed and the holes in the walls sealed off many years ago. The tools and the sheets of metal on the main floor, as well as the two men's expertise, had come in handy to remedy this situation.

The stove now sat in the right corner of the room, ready to be put to good use.

Installing the solar power equipment found at the camping store hadn't been easy. They also had no idea how much power they would get out of it. For now even with a kettle, an induction plate and a lamp plugged in at night, the system's batteries seemed to remain full. Perhaps they'd be able to use a heater in the winter to complement the stove.

The team's crowning achievement, however, was the water-collecting contraption Mr. Dean had imagined in a flash the night he and Jonathan had gone to the plaza.

They covered the four sheets of plywood with three coats of paint and three more of varnish to protect them from the elements. The sheets were then paired end-to-end to make two long panels. They mounted those on supports and joined them at the bottom with a custom-made gutter to form a wide V. Raindrops would fall on the panels, then glide down the gutter that ended above one of the blue barrels.

Mr. Dean looked at the result and seemed proud of what they had accomplished.

"First time in my life I'll say this kiddo, but I'm kind of hoping for rain."

They worked on their projects on the roof. It was the beginning of May; each day was warmer than the previous one, although the nights remained cool. They also felt safe up there. Unless they stood at the very edge of the roof and faced the road, no one driving by could ever see them up there.

At dusk the men retreated inside where they sat for long hours in silence and in reflection. The trauma they had experienced was obviously still quite fresh. So were their losses.

It had been a week since they had brought the supplies from the plaza. Jonathan told Mr. Dean he wanted to go back and spend more time exploring the Building and Renovations Center and see if there was anything left.

His boss was already less hesitant. No doubt Jonathan would be careful. Both had also become addicted to making the second floor of the warehouse more comfortable so the thought of new materials to take on additional projects was appealing.

Jonathan left at ten o'clock and reached his destination without a glitch. After a tour outside the depot to make sure he was alone, he went in. Others had come since he had raided the place with Mr. Dean, but there was still plenty to choose from.

Most of the tools at the warehouse were designed for metal, so he grabbed some more fitted for woodwork and shoved them in his trailer. He also found quality pots, cast iron pans and kitchen utensils.

The men would eventually want to expand their menu beyond freeze-dried food, so Jonathan went back to the camping store. He got his hands on equipment that could help him catch dinner in the fishing and hunting department.

He hit the road and pedaled in his building's direction with the trailer filled at capacity.

Despite the pain, the hard work and the stress of the last two weeks, he was able to acknowledge how beautiful a night it was. The sky was clear and the stars shining in a mesmerizing way. He seized on this calm and gave his mind permission to imagine what life with Kat would resemble in a world like this. The road on which he was traveling had become familiar enough to allow for it.

Kat loved the outdoors and thrived in settings that forced her out of her comfort zone. Had she been the one to survive the virus instead of him, she would have been just fine, he thought.

Mr. and Mrs. Dean were so very fond of her. Jonathan had taken Kat to the couple's fortieth wedding anniversary party for their first real date. She had often teased him by saying she had fallen for the Deans before she had for him, although not by much.

That night, Jonathan had presented his boss with a gift to mark the occasion; a stunning photo album with the front and back covers made of polished metal from the shop. Kat had been quite moved by Mr. Dean's reaction. The thoughtfulness of the present had also been her first glimpse into the heart of the man she had just begun seeing.

Had they both survived, perhaps Kat would be by his side, on this road, at this very moment, Jonathan thought. Or would she have opted to stay at the warehouse with Mr. Dean? After his horrific night from two weeks earlier, he would have enjoyed her company more than anything else in the world.

Mr. Dean was watching the events unfold on television while Mrs. Dean was on the phone with her sister. They still used a landline, which kept functioning flawlessly despite the growing chaos. Mrs. Dean passed the handset to her husband so he could reassure his sister-in-law and give her some advice.

Minutes into their conversation she stopped talking mid-sentence. Mr. Dean then heard a faint moan at the other end of the line. He called out her name a few times, but received no response. He hung up and told Mrs. Dean he feared her sister was gone.

He took his wife in his arms to console her, a moment of compassion which turned into a nightmare when the virus invaded Mrs. Dean's body.

She was a strong and heavy woman. Her grip on her husband was so tight he couldn't even scream his pain. He fought to breathe, trapped in her embrace, for nearly half an hour before he could free himself.

He had taken tiny steps all the way to the basement

descent where he had held on to a metal bar and dangled over the top stairs. Mrs. Dean had slowly slipped down to his waist, then along his legs, before falling down in the basement. The old man, ashamed of what he had been forced to do, had sat on a step and cried while he looked at his wife.

On their first day at the warehouse, he had shown his back to Jonathan. The two dark bruises formed the perfect outlines of Mrs. Dean's hands and forearms.

Jonathan was convinced Kat would have found the right words to ease some of the man's grief. At the very least, she would have found something better than the loud "Jesus" of disbelief he had let out at the sight of the injuries.

His thoughts were interrupted by two sets of headlights coming in his direction. He dismounted his bike and carried it deep into the gutter to hide. Three hundred yards from where he was kneeling, the lights came to an abrupt halt when one of the vehicles veered off the road to its right, in high bushes, and appeared to fall on its side. The other flipped more violently in a field to its left.

Jonathan approached the scene with great care, getting close enough to recognize the features of army vehicles. The only sounds he heard were from the engines still running.

He first went to the front of the truck that had crashed on the left of the road and pointed his flashlight at the cabin. The driver's face, and that of his two passengers, left no doubt as to what had happened; they had all just been infected. The three occupants in the second cabin showed the same condition.

Jonathan leaned against the hood, raised his head to

the sky and tried to measure the ramifications of this event. There had been another wave of the virus. There were now fewer people alive. The hope of ever returning to a normal way of life, however faint it was, had just been obliterated.

And he had been spared again.

He walked to the back of the truck to see what the crew had been carrying. There were crates upon crates of weapons, ammunition and explosives. Taking some of the lot would be wise, he thought, but he worried about leaving the rest. What if bad people got their hands on this type of arsenal?

The second truck's tailgate was bright orange, which was odd because it defeated the camouflage effort of the dark green color that covered the rest of the vehicle.

Its cargo was Jonathan's best find since he had left his home and moved in at the warehouse. Even the camping store was no match for what was in there: army rations, hundreds upon hundreds of them, with military gear and fatigues. It was a gold mine.

He took a few of the rations and turned both truck's engines off. He then erased their tracks and hid their presence with branches. On his way home, he kept an eye out for more vehicles that might also have veered off the road but saw nothing.

He wondered where these soldiers had come from and where they could have been headed. He didn't know of an army base in the area and there had been no signs of such personnel when he had ventured near the City. He would have to seek Mr. Dean's opinion to determine if it was appropriate to take the supplies. If it were the case, they would have to go now and use his truck again.

Jonathan climbed the stairs leading to the top floor of the warehouse. Mr. Dean had fallen asleep in the large chair again.

"Mr. Dean? Mr. Dean? You won't believe what just happened," he said as he went around the chair to stand in front of his boss.

"I was on my way ba…"

Jonathan raised his arms in the air and then grabbed his head with both hands. The muscles in Mr. Dean's face had reacted to the virus with such force that he could no longer recognize him.

The possibility that he might have been infected in this new wave hadn't even crossed his mind.

It was a resounding defeat.

This pain they had worked so hard to overcome in the last two weeks, this rough labor to turn the warehouse into a home so they could maintain some level of dignity through their ordeal, it had all been for nothing. At least, it had been for Mr. Dean. What had this man done to earn such a fate?

And what made Jonathan so special that he deserved to be spared once more?

The sole answer he received had nothing to do with his questions. There had been a first and a second wave, so there could be a third. And if his days were to be numbered, by God he would make them as safe and as comfortable as his luck would allow.

Jonathan stood and looked at Mr. Dean's watch. It read twenty past one. He pulled the keys to the truck out the old man's plaid shirt pocket, drove to the army vehicles and grabbed everything.

The food and gear required five trips. Four more were

necessary for the weapons and explosives. The sun was up by the time he unloaded the last crate from Mr. Dean's truck.

He didn't have the courage to go back upstairs. Not yet anyway. He came out of the warehouse's main floor, shovel in hand, and walked about twenty feet toward the river, stopping at the foot of a mature oak.

Mr. Dean had been quite a fan of that tree. He had marveled at it when they had first visited the building, and again after they had moved in, referring to it as a *Red Oak*. Jonathan had remarked there was nothing red about it.

"No? Wait until October, then we'll talk," had been the man's response.

Jonathan cleared a space of twigs and dead leaves and planted the shovel in the ground. The deeper he dug, it seemed, the sharper his pain became. It was the right thing to do, he knew it; he just couldn't accept the gesture itself. He paused several times to wipe the sweat and the tears off his face.

He later sat on the edge of the hole to cool down and meditate. The sun was high in the sky when he finally carried Mr. Dean's body outside. Jonathan tried in vain to break him from his seated position. The most comfortable and dignified rest he could offer the man was to lay him on his side and cover him with a thick and dark gray army blanket.

He then stood at the foot of the grave, his right hand on his chest, and attempted to say a few words. All he could manage was a weak whisper.

"Thank you, sir,"

Mr. Dean would have been fine with that speech.

Jonathan stared inside the grave in silence until he

found the will to finish what he had started, after which he dragged the shovel behind him all the way back to the warehouse with an empty heart. The phenomenal amount of food and weapons he had stockpiled during the night formed a maze that ended at the foot of the stairs leading to the second floor. He ignored it all and went up.

The oversized chair by the couch looked bigger now. It had become "the boss's chair" in the last two weeks. Jonathan had deemed it so, soon after they had moved in. Aside from that one time he had fallen asleep in it, he had made a point of always leaving it available for Mr. Dean.

Exhaustion had caught up to him, but sleep would be impossible. Not so soon after he had buried his mentor, anyway. He stood on the side of the roof that gave him a clear view of the grave below him while he ate an army ration of scrambled eggs.

The void he had felt since Kat's loss was now deeper, and so much darker, with Mr. Dean's death.

And there was this silence.

Silence had never been something Jonathan had sought or noticed, though Kat had often brought it to his attention while they hiked on remote trails. She reveled in it and often dedicated time solely to soak it in. He had thought little of it back then. Silence was an absence of noise to him, nothing more.

Now, as he stared at Mr. Dean's grave, silence was impossible to miss. It was everywhere. It was permanent.

It was an absence of noise because of the absence of people.

This is what they mean by heavy silence, Jonathan

thought. Its full weight was crushing him. After his meal, he used some of the water in the blue barrels to wash up and went downstairs to try on the army fatigues. He found a size that was a perfect fit.

The touch of new and clean clothes on his aching body induced much-needed comfort. There was also an unexpected burst of confidence that came with wearing a soldier's attire.

He went back up, sat on the couch and stared at the big chair.

He fell asleep an hour later.

CHAPTER 10

Anna had concluded that her best shot at survival would be to remain at the Center for now. Her plan was to lock herself in and stretch her resources for as long as she could.

Perhaps the authorities would regroup in the meantime then come and rescue her.

The shelves in the pantry were stacked with food again thanks to her brother. His murderers were an evil bunch, but they weren't stupid; they hadn't consumed too much of the fresh supplies in the few hours they had access to them. A single meal a day would suffice, she thought. If hunger ever became unbearable, she could always treat herself to small snacks here and there.

The water was still running, but she'd make sure to keep Benny's bottles and jugs filled in case his prediction of a shutdown ever materialized.

Before she locked herself in she got a pen, paper and a clipboard from the administrative office. She also grabbed two clean bed sheets and then headed for the parking lot.

Anna dragged Matthew's body under the porch by the

entrance, where at the very least he would be protected from the elements. She climbed back in her chair and wrote him a letter.

The two had spent so much time together in recent years, there was little left unsaid between them. Yet words still appeared in the trail of her pen as though they were leaking from a wet brush guided by her expert hand streaking across a blank canvas. She slipped the letter in the inner pocket of Matthew's leather jacket, took a moment to reflect and wrapped his body in a blanket. Before she covered his head, she pressed her lips against his cheek one last time.

This was the closest thing to a funeral she could arrange and apologized for not being able to give him the fuss he so would have deserved.

She approached the body of the young man who had gone to the City with Matthew and reached for his wallet to see any ID card he might have been carrying.

"Martin Fisher, twenty-one years old," she said out loud.

She thanked him for being by Matthew's side in the final days of his life, returned the wallet and covered him in a blanket as she had done for her brother.

Anna then sat up and looked on the horizon. The sunset was breathtaking. She was exhausted and dispirited, but some of the peacefulness managed to find its way into her heart.

Once inside, she secured the front and back doors with Benny's rope and the chain that had been used to trap the survivors in the fridge.

Since the bodies in the gym had kept the thugs out, she moved half the food from the pantry to the change room.

It would be safe in there with her if someone else ever came. She then rolled her bed from her quarters to the foyer for a clear view of the long driveway, the only paved path to the Center.

"No more surprises," she whispered.

Her first days of solitude were difficult. On the third night, a violent storm battered the area. The deafening bang from a bolt of lightning that had just struck a tree across the road from the Center shocked her out of her sleep in time to see the landscape and the inside of the foyer lit in a freakish way.

The glow of nearby cities no longer polluted the night sky. The perpetual humming of the world had been extinguished. Engines, sirens and honks from cars, vans, trains and planes had gone silent, as had the noisy heating and cooling systems of skyscrapers and manufactures. So when lightning and thunder struck in the dark, their effects were hair-raising.

Anna's heart pounded in her chest the entire hour the storm lasted.

Her schedule extended from sunrise to well after sundown. Such long hours made it impossible to ignore hunger. To get through tougher times, she occupied her mind by alternating from the front and back windows of the building to keep watch for signs of movement.

Her battle against the urge to eat was constant, but thus far successful.

Upon waking up on her sixth morning in isolation, Anna used the guest's restroom in the foyer to clean up as usual.

The water, coming out of the faucet in a steady stream at first, weakened to a narrow leak and then, to nothing.

The water works system had shut down just as Benny had warned it could.

It wasn't supposed to happen so soon. With such a strict rationing of her food and with the water flowing, she could have lasted up to a month with little worries. Now her plan, like the very last drop out of that faucet, had just gone down the drain.

If help hadn't arrived in a couple of weeks, she would need to be prepared to leave and seek it.

Anna remembered Benny's other thoughts on the matter; water was the one vital service the authorities would fight to preserve at all cost. If it were to ever stop running, it could only mean there had been a complete breakdown between the different branches of power. In short, it meant the government no longer existed.

She had continued to nourish the expectation that some sort of order would be restored. The way the six attackers had stormed the Center, murdered everyone and stayed there with no apparent fear of law enforcement ever showing up, had put a dent in her hopes but this couldn't possibly be the end of the civilized world.

Surely the army or the police would get their act together soon and save the day. They just needed time.

Benny had a wooden barrel collecting rainwater at the back of his shed, which he used to tend to plants and flowers around the building. It could work as an emergency supply.

Yes, life would be more difficult from that moment on, she thought. The key was to remain focused, vigilant, and she would be fine.

◆ ◆ ◆

It always began with a focus on the expression on Matthew's face: he was relieved to see his sister after a few days away from her. He then seemed puzzled; why was she awake at such a late hour? And why was she sitting there, by one of the gym's windows?

The flashes that accompanied the sounds of gunshots shed enough light for her to see his reaction to the pain as the bullets pierced his skin.

Not a night went by Anna wasn't afflicted by that nightmare. Like clockwork, she would awake at the part where Matthew had collapsed to the ground and she had fallen back into her chair. Tears inevitably followed her visions.

She loved her brother with all of her heart, but she wondered how much longer she would be haunted by these images. How many times would she have to ask herself if there had been something she could have done to alert him of the looming danger?

Added to the burden of reliving these events, was the fear of waking up alone in absolute darkness. She had no idea a terror so intense even existed. There were corpses everywhere, inside and outside the building. She had slept among them in the gym, but the two nurses were with her for the first night. They had also been there at the start of the second one. As for the third night, her mind was too preoccupied by the loss of Matthew to be aware of her surroundings.

Anna was now the sole member of her family left. For all she knew there was nobody but her alive on the planet. At times, to calm her nerves, she played along and tried to decide whether or not being the last person on earth would be such a bad thing after all.

Sure, she was afraid of the dark now, but she would get used to it eventually. She would also have to fend for herself, but if everyone were indeed gone there would be plenty of food to be found wherever she went. Keeping a healthy weight would even be a challenge. Painting all day, after settling down in a nice house by the ocean, sounded like a great plan. A one-story house, that is. *Pesky stairs*, she thought.

Flexing this creative mind of hers was a relaxing exercise. But a gust of wind outside the building or an odd noise inside, and there were many of those, was all it took to draw her back to reality.

No.

She knew there were others.

After what the thugs who had stormed the Center had done, after seeing how they could kill innocent people and then brag about it as if it were some kind of a feat, if some of those still alive out there were just half as bad, Anna wasn't in a hurry to cross paths with any of them.

This would be her true fear to conquer; she dreaded the moment she would have to leave the Center because she didn't think she would ever find the courage to approach other survivors.

If two certified nurses who knew her well could betray her by sneaking out a window in the middle of the night and abandon her at the mercy of a group of murderers, whom could she trust? And if they had stolen the last of her cookies, who else wouldn't hesitate to rob her of a backpack full of supplies?

These two had not only deserted her and taken her food; they had stolen her confidence.

The staff at the Center kept telling the patients they were

still part of society, that all they had to do was work hard and believe in their potential.

"Sky's the limit," they repeated.

What a load of bull, Anna thought. *They didn't even trust me to climb out a stupid window.*

◆ ◆ ◆

On her fifteenth night alone at the Center, Anna followed her usual routine before calling it a day.

She parked her chair by her bed so she'd be able to jump back in it fast if need be. She then checked the contents of her backpack: food, utensils, water, a change of warm clothes, one thick bed cover, a map, a pen, a flashlight and her gun.

The lot also included her very last catheter, which was causing her great anxiety. There were plenty of others locked behind the infirmary's heavy door. She had combed the entire building to find the keys and tried to pry the door open. None of efforts had been rewarded. Even the set of keys she had gone and retrieved from Benny's belt had been of no use.

Anna hooked the bag on her chair's backrest and settled for the night.

The images of her brother's death began playing in her head as always. Something was off, however. The course of the events was different than what she had been made to watch until then. The flashes from the gunshots lasted longer, as if in slow motion, and became brighter with each detonation.

Anna awoke and looked out the foyer's wide windows; headlights were coming down the driveway and getting closer to the Center.

She had rehearsed her escape to the exercise room so often she could now get there with her eyes closed. Darkness gave her great cover and in that room, at that hour, a bed sheet was the ultimate camouflage. Anna assumed position.

Though the gym's windows were shut, she heard the sounds of muffled voices and two car doors being slammed. Whoever was out there sure took their time checking the outside of the building. They then broke the glass doors at the main entrance, got in the foyer and surveyed all of the rooms with method.

Their last stop was the gym. Anna held her breath when the beam of a flashlight leaked through the sheet under which she was hiding. The strangers whispered to one another. There were three of them: two men and a woman. They returned near the entrance, where one of the men yelled, "Hello," then there was silence again.

Anna would have to spend at least one more night among the bodies. Being in the room with them wasn't as frightening to her as when she slept in the foyer. She thought of the corpses around her as brave soldiers keeping her safe.

After a full night awake, she cracked open the door to the hallway just enough to listen. Nothing. The sun had only begun to rise and she guessed the trespassers were asleep. Could she trust them? Were they the same type as the first group that had invaded the Center? She went to the window to take a look at their car. Any information about these people could help her gage their intentions. It was a car, just like any other.

Anna shook her head. Approaching them or being discovered were not options. They wouldn't dare enter the gym, but what if they decided on an extended stay at the Center? What would she do trapped in that gym? She had already accepted a while back that she would have to leave the building and get on the road at some point.

The time had come sooner than she had hoped, but it was here.

In the change room, she crammed more food in her backpack. Next was getting to the wheelchairs she had lined up under the porch by the entrance. With great caution, Anna pushed open one of the windows overlooking the parking lot and let her bag slide along the four-foot slab of concrete that separated the opening from the ground. Her best bet was to go head first with her arms stretched forward.

Once out of the room, she grabbed her bag and crawled behind a row of bushes all the way to the foyer's entrance, where it turned out the three trespassers had elected to spend the night. One of them was in her bed. The two others were asleep on leather love seats.

Anna was hesitant. The wheelchairs were parked to the left of the doors, which meant she'd have to pass in front of them and put herself in plain sight of those inside.

She could play it safe by hiding in the bushes the whole day and leave later that night. Or she could risk it all now. After a short deliberation, she opted for the latter and assessed that, if she played her hand to perfection, she wouldn't alert anyone to her presence.

Her eyes were locked on the prize as she crawled on her belly, pausing once to look inside. Matthew's body was the only obstacle blocking her way. She went around him, and then aimed for the chair that was the farthest from the doors.

Anna was hooking her backpack to the wheelchair's backrest when one of the men came out through the front doors, still half-asleep.

He stretched his arms while he let out a loud yawn a mere twenty feet away from her. He walked in the opposite direction, dragging his feet along the same bushes Anna had just used as cover. He stopped near the gym's windows, turned his back on her and unzipped his pants to relieve himself.

"Ugh, so creepy," he said while shaking his head after he took a quick peek at the bodies through a window.

Anna, hidden at the very end of the line of chairs, pulled her legs toward her. The man went back inside without noticing her.

"Let's go! Breakfast," he said to the others to wake them up.

Their voices grew faint as they made their way to the cafeteria. When she could no longer hear them, Anna sat in the chair but stayed put. Their words and tone were less threatening than that of those who had killed all of her friends. Maybe they were good people and wouldn't harm her.

She thought of all she had been through in recent weeks. Approaching these strangers appeared too great a risk, too complicated. Heading into the unknown, alone and in a wheelchair, seemed much simpler. She took one last look at the sheet that covered Matthew.

Leaving him behind like that, outside, by the Center's entrance, was tearing her apart.

"Come with me," she begged of him.

She reached the end of the long driveway and crossed the road.

She then pushed in the direction of the City.

CHAPTER 11

Anna had anticipated life on the road wouldn't be easy, but it was shaping up to be much tougher than she had imagined.

The contrast between the floor's smooth surface at the Center and the rough pavement on which she was now traveling was day and night. In the hour or so after she had left the Center, the ache in her hands alone had forced her to take two breaks already.

She didn't feel safe out in the open either. It was still quite early, but the area was devoid of buildings with empty fields and scarce patches of trees on both sides of the road. There would be nowhere for her to hide if she ever needed to.

What looked like a barn became visible in the distance and she set it as her target, a place where she could lay low until sundown. After tremendous efforts, and with excruciating pain in her hands and shoulders, she reached the path leading to the structure.

Her heart sank when she realized it was sand and mud. There would be no way for her to get to the shelter as she had so hoped.

She looked in the direction from which she had come. Maybe it would be best for her to go back to the Center. If the strangers were gone, she could reclaim her home.

"Don't be such a wimp," she finally lashed out. "One small problem and you're, hum, you're already giving up?"

She made it to a downhill portion of the road ninety minutes later. It wasn't very steep, but it was a long stretch and she had no clue how much pull gravity would have on her chair. She took the two sweaters she owned out of her backpack and used the sleeves as gloves in case she needed to reduce her speed.

The descent was quite smooth. The draft cooled the sweat on her face and even triggered the beginning of a smile. Three hundred feet into it, she heard music playing behind her. And it was growing louder by the second.

A car was coming.

Without slowing down, Anna steered her chair into the gutter to hide. The tumble was violent, but she was unharmed. She crawled up high enough to get a peek at the car. If these were the strangers at the Center, she could go back there. Today's excursion could easily qualify as mere rehearsal.

It wasn't them. Although she was disappointed, this close call still turned out to be valuable information. On a road that connected two fairly large cities, this was the first car to drive by her since she had left the Center three hours earlier. There were very few survivors in the area. While she didn't know how busy the highways or secondary routes were, this was good news to Anna. For now, she thought, the fewer people she met on her way to the City, the better her chances she would actually make it there.

She was about to drag her chair onto the pavement when she looked around her. The patch of high grass on which she had landed was adequate camouflage. The sky was clear and this end of May weather comfortable. She hadn't slept in almost a full day because her previous night's rest had been cut short. This was as good a place as any to have breakfast and take a nap.

She drifted in and out of sleep for much of the remainder of the morning and the afternoon. Aside from the motorcycle she heard in the distance, there were no other noises to break the silence.

In the moments she was awake, Anna lay on her back and tracked the thick white clouds across the sky above her. She didn't know the hour, or what day it was for that matter. Isolation at the Center had wrapped her in a cocoon so tight it had shielded her not just from the events in the outside world, but also from time itself.

She wondered about the City, about what Matthew had seen there. After he had left with the young man, her most pressing concern had been for his safe return, of course. But like everybody else at the Center she too had been anxious to hear the tale of his trip.

Now she had no way of knowing what the City was going to resemble. Her future rested on guessing at how many people were alive, which buildings were secure enough to enter and where she would find food.

That afternoon, Anna made the conscious decision to keep the good days and put them in the bank. What would feed or break her will to reach her goal, however, would be her ability to discard the bad ones on the spot.

Early in the evening, she finished the bottom half of the can of beans she had started for breakfast and waited for darkness to resume her trip. The moon barely lit the path ahead of her or the buildings bearing company logos that had begun appearing on each side of the road. All of them had paved driveways leading to their parking lots, but her inspection around the structures was time consuming and drained much energy out of her.

She wanted to find a building where she could get real rest and better assess her situation. The first two looked unoccupied but didn't provide for wheelchair access. The third one, a transportation outfit, did. She circled it, stopping every few feet to listen for potential occupants. Other than the normal sounds of nature, there were no hints of life either in the area or in the offices, though the windows were too high for her to see inside.

Anna parked her chair near the rear entrance, behind a van, to rest until daylight. She wanted to wait longer, observe some more to make sure she was indeed alone before she tried to get in.

All the rehab in the world couldn't have prepared her for the last twenty-four hours. Her body would need some time to adapt to this new regimen. Her hands, shoulders and now her back, were throbbing from the pain. She nibbled on a few crackers and fell asleep seated, wrapped in the blanket she had pulled from her bag.

Anna opened her eyes after what she thought were a few minutes, only the sun was already high in the sky. It wasn't noon yet, but it was late in the morning. She emerged from behind the truck and took the time to go around the building again. She didn't hear anything so she used the ramp to head toward the entrance.

"Get the hell away from here, this is my place," the deep voice screamed.

She had made it a third of the way up when a large bearded man came crashing through the door, yelling and hitting the handrail with a crowbar.

Anna sped away from the parking lot with no memories of how on earth she had managed to roll down the ramp in reverse without getting stuck. She made sure the man hadn't followed her, then stopped to catch her breath and collect her wits.

It could have been much worse, she thought. He hadn't attacked her or stolen her bag. This strategy of waiting, observing and listening was the wrong one.

Since someone lived in the first building she had tried to enter, she figured there could be more people in the other ones nearby as well. This area didn't inspire her confidence anymore, so she decided to keep going further down the road.

Early in the afternoon another car, coming from the City this time, appeared in the distance. Anna rolled her eyes and let out a heavy sigh.

"Not again," she said out loud.

It was unpleasant, but she didn't have a choice. She steered her chair off the road, hit the ground in a deep part of the gutter and laid low in the grass.

The car drove at reduced speed near where she had landed. Anna thought the driver might have seen her before she ditched and was now looking for her.

The vehicle soon took off. She played it safe again and spent the rest of the day where she was. In the future, she would have to stick to her plan of traveling at night.

That same evening, darkness came early because the sun hid behind thick and gray clouds. Anna got back to it and tried to remain focused on moving forward. It didn't help that she knew nothing of this area. The one time she had been on this road was in the medical transfer minivan that had taken her to the Center. Back then, her mind was more preoccupied by what lied ahead of her than what was around her.

She was surrounded by woods and went for a good part of the night without seeing a single building. A heavy downpour slowed her journey. The rain was cold and she hated herself because there wasn't a thing in her bag appropriate for this kind of weather. She pushed through a thick wall of water for two hours before an industrial garage, partially hidden behind trees, caught the corner of her eye. Anna observed it from a distance.

There were no lights inside and no cars in the parking lot, though something else on the ground there did grab her attention. A pile of branches or scrap metal, maybe? It was too dark and it rained too hard to tell.

For her peace of mind, she wanted to know before she went on to inspect the garage. She reached the stack and leaned above it. Only then was she able to identify what it was.

Or who it was, rather.

The two nurses, swept in the second wave of the virus, had collapsed on top of one another right there in front of the garage. Anna looked at the bodies and forgot about the rain and the cold for a moment. She had never wished bad omen on anyone, but this was irony in its purest of forms.

By abandoning her at the mercy of mass murderers, these women had stained their souls. They had then sold it for half a pack of cookies. The devil had come to collect the following night.

She had nothing to say to them.

While touring the property, she filled her two bottles with the water falling in a wide stream from the roof near the back. The door there wasn't locked.

"Hello? I'm just seeking shelter from, hum, from the rain."

Anna scanned the interior with her flashlight. There were a few drums, some red tool chests and a desk, but she was alone. She got out of her chair, dragged it inside and locked the door behind her. The two doors at the front of the garage, a large one for passage of heavy vehicles as well as a normal one with a window, were already secured.

She laid her wet clothes on the desk, put on dry ones and took out her map. The Rehabilitation Center was marked with a red dot. She tried to estimate her current location while she ate a granola bar.

Her best guess was that she had covered eight miles, nine at the most, in the two days she had been out on the road.

This was a harsh realization; she would have to be much bolder and braver if she wanted to reach the City before her provisions ran out.

The garage was a good place to rest. Anna felt safe in there. It was too close to the road and too isolated for a long stay, though.

With her blanket as a mattress and her backpack as a pillow, she lay down on the cement floor.

"One night," she whispered. "Two maybe, if it, hum, it hasn't stopped raining tomorrow."

The change in scenery did nothing to improve her sleep pattern. Whenever she dozed off, she continued to be awakened by the visions recreating Matthew's murdered. The images were now followed by the intense guilt of having left him behind near the entrance at the Center.

The role of big sister was one Anna had taken seriously her entire life. It was her job to protect him. In her mind, she bore some of the responsibility for his fate. She could have at least warned him as sooner after he got out of his car. She could have at least buried him. She could have at least…

Anna was able to fall asleep again, but it felt more like passing out and waking up, akin to how she had felt the day she had come out of her coma.

The rain hadn't let up in the morning. She decided to stay put until the weather changed. Taking this day off would help her recover and plan her schedule better. Anna parked her chair by the smaller door to read her map and keep an eye out for unwanted visitors.

The slow pace of time and the absence of movements in her line of sight afforded her the luxury of daydreams.

She thought of her brother, of course. And she thought of painting. God, she missed it so much. To her, there was nothing like the rush she got from the creation process. While she painted, Anna had the ability to split her mind in two entities independent from one another. The first controlled the brush she held. The second stood behind her shoulder, looked at the whole canvas, and whispered directions.

The more Anna reflected on her passion, however, the

more despair she felt. She was, now more than ever, an easy prey for negativity. This world didn't need artists, she thought, even less so an artist in a wheelchair.

This much free time and such deep silence also seemed to underscore her solitude, which was weighing on her quite heavily. She had spent the last two weeks at the Center completely cut off from whatever made up the rest of the world. Her latest human interaction had been with the man who had erupted from the building and scared the living daylights out of her.

She had to shake off the poisonous vibes of loneliness. Since she was longing for company, and since she missed her brother so much, her creative brain went to work.

Matthew was now there, with her.

She could see him walk inside the garage, looking for things he and his sister could use during their upcoming journey.

Anna followed him around and searched the tool chests and the desk asking, "Maybe this could be, hum, be useful? How about this, here?"

She found batteries, a rusty Swiss Army knife and a hammer, which she shoved in her backpack.

Rain was still falling at the mid-day mark. The inside of the garage grew stuffy. Anna opened the back door to let some fresh air in.

For a moment there, as she gazed outside and heard the soothing sound of rain drops hitting the leaves on the trees nearby, the bad feelings from earlier regarding her future and her place in the world moved aside to make way for a certain ease of mind.

She went back to the front door to mount guard while she dipped crackers in a can of cold tomato soup.

"You know you're going to be fine, right?" Matthew said, standing behind Anna.

"No, I don't know that," she answered.

"When did you become so negative, Sis?"

"When my, hum, my world ended."

"The world didn't end! Look out the window, it's still there."

"I didn't say *the* world, Matthew. I, hum, I said *my* world."

He was now sitting on the floor by Anna's feet, his back against the larger of the two front doors.

"Ever since our, hum, our accident, my world has been you. I was always looking forward to, hum, to seeing you arrive at the Center. The other patients thought I was the, hum, the luckiest girl alive to have such a, hum, a handsome visitor every day."

"Well, almost every day," she added after a pause.

Matthew raised his head to show Anna his *"Are you kidding me?"* face.

She grinned and said, "You did miss two days."

She became serious again and stared deeply into his eyes.

"When life return to, hum, to normal, I'll go get you back and, hum, and make things right."

Her brother's presence, albeit imagined, lifted her spirits. The rain stopped near the end of the afternoon. She went outside with her chair to look at the sky in all directions. The weather was clearing and she would depart at dusk, just a few hours away. She went back inside and took a nap.

This last day had served as a reboot. She tricked her brain into believing her trip hadn't begun when she had left the Center. It was going to start the moment she would leave this garage.

That night she was more driven, feeling less pain, and she even challenged Matthew from one given point to the next.

"First one to the, hum, the electric pole."

Anna had filled up on courage and positive energy during this breather.

She was going to need it.

CHAPTER 12

Jonathan accomplished little in the week that followed Mr. Dean's death.

He did kill some time by taking an inventory of the supplies from the army vehicles. It was quite an arsenal: twenty-six crates hosting four M4 carbines each and eighteen crates worth of clips of ammunition, suppressors, scopes and grenades.

While he wasn't a firearm enthusiast, he didn't mind them. He had gone hunting as a teenager, so he was familiar with the basics. These, however, were combat weapons and accessories; they would require training. The grenades were more of a concern to him. He carried those crates upstairs, to his living quarters, in the hopes of keeping them dry and safe.

The boxes with the rations finally raised his spirits. Considering the state of the world, the amount of food he now had under his roof was phenomenal. With restraint and a little common sense, he'd be able to survive up to two years just on these. This conservative estimate didn't even include the already impressive stash from the camping store. Rabbits sometimes hopped around the warehouse and ducks floated on the river. He was confident he could teach himself to hunt again.

Not having to worry about food was a clear advantage and Jonathan knew his good fortune. It could also make him a target. Starving and desperate people would stop at nothing to put their hands on just a fraction of what he had. With that on his mind, the rifles had found their purpose. He shot a few rounds in the early hours of each morning and rehearsed locking, reloading and cleaning his weapons.

While this firepower gave a solid boost to his sense of safety, he felt the need for variety. The rifles were great for long distance defense, but what about closer combat? What if he was caught without a weapon? The man was a machinist with many tools under his roof and plenty of free time to let his creativity run loose.

A crazy idea involving throwing stars germinated in his head, though the name itself was a turn off. It sounded pretentious and nerdy at the same time. After years of working with Mr. Dean's, coming up with solutions was second nature. He took less than an hour to draft what he thought would be a practical and effective design. He gathered a pile of metal sheets, each half an inch thick, and began cutting and buffing away.

What he held in his hand after a full day's work was far from nerdy.

His prototype was a real weapon: five inches in diameter, three distinct blades stretched in a swirl and edges sharper than anything he had ever done. It felt light enough and yet it had sufficient mass to fly a great and steady distance.

He threw it at a wood beam as a test. It was so well crafted that the way it had flown, and then sliced through the beam, had scared the hell out of him. As he struggled to dislodge the blade, Jonathan had prayed to God he would never need to use it against someone.

Given his aversion for its technical name, he decided to just call it a disc.

The next day he produced three dozen more, all based on his original design. He used plastic containers to make pouches, which allowed him to carry three discs in each of his pants' side pockets.

With practice he became quite skilled at throwing them, although he learned the hard way they were safer when handled with half finger gloves.

A week had now passed since he had buried Mr. Dean. Enough time for renewed energy and also curiosity as to how the second wave of infections had impacted the City. The only way to know if his protection was adequate was to get a better feel for the mood there and gage how many people were still alive. He was prepared to leave for more than a day if need be; he had the equipment, the weapons and the food to do so. And ever since he had moved at the warehouse, no one had tried to break in; the manner in which he and Mr. Dean had masqueraded the property was the ultimate cold shoulder for even the most inquisitive of eyes.

On the other side of the bridge, Jonathan turned around to look at his home, visible only thanks to glow of a near full moon. While he was confident it would remain untouched in his absence, he couldn't help but think how much more at ease he would be if Mr. Dean were there to guard it.

The stench from decaying bodies grew stronger as he neared the City. It was much more pungent than when he had walked these same streets a few weeks earlier. He didn't cross anyone's path, but he did see dimmed lights through the windows of a few houses and office buildings. He stayed away from those.

The silence in the alleys he walked near downtown was at times interrupted by commotions coming from inside some of the buildings. He couldn't tell if these noises were the work of people or stray animals. Whenever something fell or broke he paused, waited for his heart to restart and moved on.

Jonathan made it to the core of the City and spotted a small electronics shop with a clear view of what had once been a busy intersection. The windows were shattered on all sides, the merchandise gone. It was the perfect hangout to rest and spy on the comings and goings of potential survivors. All he wanted was to observe them and take note of their numbers and their behavior.

As the sun rose, he got to do just that.

In the week that had passed since the second strike of the virus, the City had become a hunting zone where the weakest were preyed upon like wounded animals.

Soon after sunrise, a man holding a plastic bag walked by the electronics shop at a quick pace. Seconds later, as Jonathan was getting his binoculars out of his backpack, two attackers snuck up on the man from behind, beat him until he stopped moving, then pried the bag from his hand.

The two ran in the direction opposite from Jonathan's hideout. The sounds of gunshots startled him. Another thief had just taken the men down, barely ten yards into their escape. The shooter then grabbed the bag, tore it open and let its contents fall to the ground, which he spread with his foot to get a definitive look. Disinterested, he went on his merry way.

Despite complete disbelief, and the pain from the knot in his stomach, Jonathan remembered he had come to the City to observe. He raised the binoculars to see what the coveted bag had contained: socks, track pants, a few t-shirts and a pair of running shoes. One man critically injured, two dead thugs and a murderer on the loose, all for dirty laundry.

And he hadn't even had breakfast yet.

He wasn't naïve. He had expected a dire situation, but seeing such raw violence play out in front of him was another thing altogether.

It seemed like an unfair determination, but until he had a better understanding of what his new life entailed, and a lot more weapons training, he couldn't risk his safety to save strangers. For now his rifles would serve for his own protection, nothing else.

More gunfire erupted, in the area and in the distance, throughout the day. Some of the shots were accompanied by screams so horrific they sent Jonathan's entire body into shivers. As the evening loomed, he had seen and heard just about enough and decided he would leave as soon as darkness would allow it.

He came out of the shop at around nine o'clock and followed the same path he had the night before. Only now, every once in a while, he had to look for safe spots along the way where he could crouch, take deep breaths and calm down. His observations of earlier in the day had awakened near debilitating fear and paranoia in him. He somewhat relaxed upon reaching the smaller backstreets, because it meant he was about to exit what he referred to as the hot zone.

The fragile balance he had regained tilted again when a woman burst out of a building, screaming at the top of her lungs, about twenty feet ahead of him. Three men rushed through the door a second later. They soon caught up to her, grabbed her and silenced her cries for help by covering her mouth.

Jonathan's body overpowered his brain, pushing aside the rules he had listed for himself that morning. He approached the three men from behind, his weapon aimed at them.

"Hey. Let her go."

They turned around to see who was addressing them. At least one of the thugs didn't seem all that impressed.

"Well, well, well, look who's here, guys. It's G.I. freakin' Joe in the flesh! What's you gonna do now, soldier?"

Jonathan had forgotten he was wearing the fatigues he had found in the army transports. To him, these were just clothes that allowed him to blend in the scenery. His goal wasn't to lure anyone into thinking he was the real deal.

But if these thugs believed it, he wasn't about to set the record straight.

"Let her go, now," Jonathan repeated.

"No way soldier boy, ain't never gonna happen."

The tallest of the three men, who seemed to be doing all of the talking, took a step forward. Jonathan had no intention of entering into a long argument with him. He was out in the open and he needed to wrap this up quickly.

"Do we have a learning disability here? You heard what I said?"

"Yeah, I heard. And I said, ain't never gonna happen," the man insisted, taking one more step toward Jonathan who in turn, fired a warning shot inches from his head. Realizing the situation had just escalated, the man raised his hands and reversed course, although not by much and with a defying grin on his face.

Behind him, his friends holding the woman released their grip on her. She fell to the ground.

"Miss, can you stand?" Jonathan asked.

Her lower lip was bloodied, both her knees scraped to the bones, but she slowly rose to her feet and nodded yes.

"Get behind me," he said to her.

He then told her to open his backpack and take the food inside, along with one bottle of water. The three men watched, with great interest, as she retrieved five army rations.

Jonathan instructed the woman to leave the area and to never come back. When the sound of her footsteps grew faint, his focus returned to her attackers.

They weren't charging or threatening him, but he had noticed the quizzical expression on their faces at the sight of the victuals that had poured out of his backpack.

"I'm gonna give you a chance," Jonathan said before he pointed to a bus shelter about fifty yards away from where they all stood.

"I want you to walk over there. Don't run, don't talk and no matter what, don't look behind you. If you do this, I'll let you live. Don't screw this up, guys."

While the two less combative ones marched toward the bus stop as they were told, their leader slowly walked backwards and stared at Jonathan, still with the same grin on his face.

"Are you stupid?" Jonathan asked as he feigned taking a step forward.

The thug spun around, but not before raising his middle finger at Jonathan. He then grabbed his two friends by their neck to bring them closer to him.

Jonathan hurried in the opposite direction. At the next intersection, he sprinted away. A few minutes later, he spotted a dumpster, leaned over it and threw up. He had never been this scared and could not believe what he had just done. This was a real weapon, which he had pointed at men and then pulled the trigger. He tried to shake it off by telling himself that these guys would have deserved a lot worse considering what they were about to do. Still, this was as rough as anything he had ever done.

Mr. Dean's voice resounded in his head.

"The world has changed, kiddo. And so will we, in time."

"Remember, stay away from people."

Jonathan wiped his mouth and nodded as if he had indeed just heard Mr. Dean speak to him. All he wanted now was to get back to the warehouse. He stepped away from the dumpster, pivoted to his right and found himself face to face with the same three men again.

Instead of counting their blessings, as they should have done, they had gone after him.

He had come to the City to observe and gather information.

What he was learning from this incident would turn out to be the most valuable and most lasting bit of data he would retain from this long, sickening day: no matter what, and without fail, their kind would never give up. They would always come back. Always.

Hunger was no valid pretext for this type of conduct. It was pure luck they were still alive, having survived not one but two waves of the virus and yet, they were determined to attack, barehanded, a well-armed man in full army gear. Jonathan's state of mind transitioned from fear to anger in the blink of an eye. The switch was so organic he didn't notice it.

It was over in less than ten seconds. Not a word was spoken. The men marched toward Jonathan with confidence, looking quite upset he had ruined the fun night out they had planned.

He shot the three of them in the legs.

The two least belligerent ones fell on their butts, holding their shins. The leader, much taller, wasn't as lucky as his friends. Given his height, Jonathan had to adjust his aim; the bullets ended up shattering both his knees. The manner in which he collapsed made it look as though his legs had literally been cut from underneath him.

Jonathan's first instinct hadn't been to kill them. All he wanted was to make sure they wouldn't follow him again. They would also think twice before following anyone else from that moment on, if they ever recovered. It seemed improbable they would. By the time his third victim had hit the ground, he was already running back home.

He, along with most of the other survivors in the City, heard the three men express their pain and anger through a loud litany of threats and vulgarities.

The farther away he got from the core of the City, the

safer Jonathan felt. Not safe enough to let his guard down, but it was quieter and thus easier to focus on sensing danger. He found the warehouse still locked and saw no signs anyone had tried to break in.

While his ration of freeze-dried eggs and ham soaked in boiling water, he reviewed the events of the last twenty-four hours.

Yes, the latest infection had killed more people, but that didn't make venturing out there less of a hazard.

There were no rules anymore and so the simple minded had been lured into believing there were no consequences.

And it had taken little time for food to become the most coveted of prizes.

As these thoughts crossed his mind, he looked down and stared at the ration in his hands. He jumped to his feet in a panic.

What he held was but a fraction of a priceless treasure. He needed to protect the rest of it much better than it was now.

CHAPTER 13

Jonathan had been shocked out of his afternoon nap on the roof. It had happened again. These random gunshots had been driving him insane for three days. He had lost count after ten instances. Screams sometimes ensued but never for long, only until another round was fired.

More people now roamed the streets across the river, drawn to the area by their quest for food or perhaps a safer place to live.

Jonathan had been hearing more footsteps by the warehouse in recent days. Not many, but still a growing number. Each time, he had reached for his rifle fearing someone would attempt to break in. No one ever had.

The weapon discharges came from the vicinity of an office building across his bridge and on the opposite side of the road from the warehouse. The ten-floor structure was the tallest on the block. Jonathan had spent several hours on the roof of his home trying to ascertain the origin of the shots.

At long last he figured it out that afternoon; a young man had set up camp on a higher floor inside that building. Jonathan had caught a glimpse of the tip of the rifle peeking out of one of the circular holes cut in the windows. He spied on him with his binoculars.

The large trees behind which the warehouse was hidden obstructed his view of the streets in that area. He couldn't see the shooter's intended targets or what happened after he pulled the trigger.

Jonathan had been quite diligent thus far in adhering to his own rules: he stayed clear of people and did not meddle in their business. Aside from the one time he had helped the woman escape from the three men downtown, he was content observing the new world take shape from a distance.

His ethics had been on his mind lately. He wondered if he wasn't being selfish in hiding from the world while hogging all of these supplies. His deliberations had led him each time to the same conclusions: while it was indeed quite selfish, he wasn't hurting anybody and his own safety was plenty to worry about.

This questioning — this guilt behind his behavior — was precisely what separated from him the bad elements. He could live it, he decided. His trip downtown had shown him how terrible a thing it was to watch people being killed. It had also made him aware that killing wasn't in his blood. From what he had gathered, getting used to the former was no longer a choice. As for the latter, Jonathan didn't think he could ever bring himself to do it. Becoming invisible was the only way he knew to ensure he would never have to.

He remained in retreat, but it didn't mean he lacked curiosity. Now that he had where these shots came from and who was firing them, he felt compelled to confirm why. All he wanted was a first account, nothing else. He carried a weapon, and wore army issued fatigues, but to him this was not war. At the very least, it wasn't his war.

Before the sun rose the next morning, Jonathan put on his gear and crossed the bridge.

He entered a pillaged sandwich shop, sixty yards to the left and across the street from the building the young shooter occupied. He waited there for daybreak. It must have been near eight o'clock when a man carrying a backpack walked in front of his hideout's broken windows.

Jonathan whistled to get the traveler's attention.

"Don't go that way," he whispered with as much urgency as he could show. "There's a sniper."

The man got spooked at the sight of Jonathan's rifle. He picked up the pace but in the wrong direction. Jonathan repeated his warning, which again went ignored. Mere seconds later, a shot rang out. Jonathan's shoulders dropped in discouragement at the same time this latest casualty collapsed to the ground.

He then saw what hadn't been visible from the warehouse. Two men and a woman hurried out the office building's front doors. The men grabbed the body and dragged it to the rear of the building through an alley. The woman picked up the victim's belongings and ran back inside to her post.

Aside from the fact that they were murdering human beings, Jonathan was taken aback by the laziness of the group's tactics. No one was forcing them to kill these people. They could have pointed their weapons at them and demanded what they wanted.

Stealing from the dead was just so much easier.

He found the sandwich shop's side exit and walked in a wide half-circle pattern until he reached a narrow lane that took him back to the rear of the group's building, where he came upon a pile of what appeared to be at least fifteen bodies.

"Jesus," he whispered, incredulous.

As the hours passed the gang's scheme and composition became clearer. There was the shooter on a higher floor, the woman and the two men Jonathan had seen earlier. These last two were relieved by a different duo later in the day, bringing their number to a minimum of six.

Their MO was simple; shoot to kill, steal and then take the body out of sight so other passers-by wouldn't be tipped off to the danger looming right above their heads.

Jonathan hid nearby and saw them repeat these steps twice in the afternoon. After the second time, he decided he could no longer let this continue. Victims were being added to an already disturbing tally under his watch. The longer he waited, he thought, the more blood stained his own hands.

The men had just swung the lifeless body of a woman on top of the pile when they turned around and froze. Jonathan stood a few feet away from them, his steady weapon pointed at their heads.

Silence and immobility lasted awhile.

The two men didn't dare speak or move because they knew their lives were hanging by a very thin thread. Jonathan was silent because of the switch in his attitude.

The change was similar to what he had gone through in the seconds before he had pulled the trigger on the three men downtown. Only this time, and even in the midst of a tense situation, he had full awareness of the transition. He hated the idea of a clash, but acting upon it didn't bother him all that much. He was fine while it unfolded, it was the *before* and the *after* that affected him.

The certitude he was on the right side of the argument was powerful reinforcement in the moment itself.

"Go tell your little friends it's time for you to leave this area," Jonathan said in a firm voice. "If I see any of your faces around here again, I swear by God I will kill you all. Go on."

Jonathan watched the men move down the alley and kept his eye on them until they made it to the front of the building. He was about to turn and flee when all hell broke loose. A group of four people charged the two men. The sounds of screams, gunshots and glass shattering followed.

Others, having also reached their breaking point, had decided to attack.

The magnitude of the chaos made Jonathan wonder if perhaps there were more members in the murderous gang than he had previously thought. This was not the time for a census; he needed to bug out and fast. The fight grew in intensity and spilled into the streets with both groups running and firing their weapons in all directions. Jonathan's hastened escape was fueled by the fear of a stray bullet. No matter where he ran, it seemed he was caught in the crossfire. He found refuge on the first floor of a commercial building a block from the main street. He moved the few remaining pieces of furniture in a corner of the entrance lobby and crouched behind the pile.

By early evening, the area had been turned into a war

zone. Although he was not yet panicking, Jonathan was beginning to wonder when and how he'd be able to get back to the warehouse. The fighting continued well into the night and culminated when an armed man seeking protection entered the building in which Jonathan was hiding and stood by a window ten feet from him.

He rose, slowly to remain quiet, and aimed his weapon at the stranger's back. It was too dark and he was too busy watching the streets, so the man didn't notice the danger behind him. Since Jonathan was unsure which group this one belonged to, he did not fire. The man eventually climbed out the window and disappeared.

Shots were heard until just about an hour before sunrise. Silence had returned. Jonathan sensed it was a fragile silence, one that could be broken at any moment. He nevertheless seized on this opportunity and snuck out. He couldn't walk straight home, but he didn't want to go too far in the direction opposite of the warehouse either. As he had done the day before, he followed a circular path that would take him back to the main street.

He came across four bodies a few yards from one another. If his memory served him well, they were the men who had gone after those in the building. Jonathan was curious to know if that group had also sustained casualties or if they had heeded his advice to pack up and leave. In any case, from the looks of it, these thugs had what it took to fight back.

He was two blocks away from his bridge when he saw the shadow of someone sitting on the curb. He stopped and looked through his binoculars. It was a child, a boy it seemed, and he appeared to be in distress.

His hesitation disgusted him. Yes, he had a rule about avoiding people, but this was just a kid, likely alone and in trouble. How could he live with himself if he just walked away?

As he got closer, Jonathan heard the boy's sobs. He had strapped his weapon to his back to make the kid feel at ease and show his peaceful intentions. He went down on one knee, leaned forward and put a hand on the child's shoulder.

He never saw it coming.

The pain from the blow to the side of his head was atrocious.

Then there was darkness.

CHAPTER 14

Anna kept a close tab of her progress on the map, which was high motivation. In the three days since she had left the garage, she had managed to cover four times the mileage she had prior to her interlude there. A red dot now marked her approximate address on the far-north side of the City as her ultimate goal.

Although she hadn't seen her atelier in months, it was still home to her. Making it there, which would come with the sweet benefit of sleeping in her own bed, had become a fixation that lit her will on fire when she climbed a hill. Some of those were at an angle so steep that if she needed to stop for a breather, she had to park her chair sideways and lock her wheels to avoid rolling backwards.

Her food situation was on her mind. She was careful with her supplies, but the way she traveled drained a tremendous amount of energy out of her.

She found she had to dig deeper in her bag every time she slipped a hand in it.

The sky was clear that night. Thanks to the half moon, Anna could see what was around her. Animals such as rabbits or foxes sometimes crossed the road ahead of her. The only creatures for which she had paused and waited before resuming her trip were a few skunks and a family of bears. On four occasions she had been forced to throw herself in the ditch to avoid being seen by motorists.

For the rest, the longer she spent out in the wild, the less intimidated she was by it.

She was nowhere near the City, but its outskirts would soon be within reach. Already, the pavement under her wheels was newer, a blessing in that it made her chair easier to operate. Higher-end enterprises, all with access ramps, had also replaced the industrial outfits and garages she had been rolling by for days.

She let her gut pick the one she would try and enter.

Bio-Dhall Inc. stood at a reasonable distance from the road. Its parking lot, hidden behind aged trees and lush bushes, was empty. Anna did a quick tour around the three-story building and went up the ramp. As with most corporate offices, all that stopped her from entering were doors made of thin sheets of glass. She knocked on one of them. No one came. After a long hesitation, she reached inside her bag, retrieved the hammer she had found at the garage and threw it at the door.

There was nothing of interest on the desk at reception. A security car reader guarded the main section of the building, but it had been disabled when the power had gone out.

Anna took the gun out of her bag, called out twice to possible occupants and then began exploring. The furniture and the decor were tasteful, modern, but useless to her. This company must have had a cafeteria. If it had one, however, it wasn't on this floor and it didn't look like it would be located on the floors above her either, which left the underground level.

She let herself slide down the stairs, one step at a time, with a firm hold on her folded chair next to her. At the bottom was a long hallway. The depth of the darkness down there was such that, even with her flashlight pointed in front of her, she couldn't see more than a few feet ahead.

The first door to her left led to what she had been searching for. The cafeteria hadn't been raided by anybody since the initial wave of the virus. Vending machines with cookies, bags of chips and granola and candy bars proved easy to empty after she broke their front glass. The last one, with beverages, was trickier because of its thick protective panel. She would have to return to it later if needed.

Anna located the pantry in the back room. The stench of rotting food escaping from the oversized refrigerator warned her not to open its doors. There was a lot to choose from on the shelves: cans of pudding as well as canned fruits and vegetables, countless packets, some with crackers and others with peanut butter or jelly. She dined on some of those and from a jar of pickles before chugging down two bottles of water from a stack she spotted in the corner of the room.

With her bag heavy again, she explored the basement further and found the restrooms. She dipped a ball of paper towel in one of the toilet tanks to wash her face. It felt so good she did her entire body.

At the far end of the hallway, Anna came upon a white

door with a red cross. She gasped at the sight of the narrow bed with clean sheets and a fluffy pillow. The room locked from the inside, which gave her enough confidence to leave her chair.

She lay down and closed her eyes for what was supposed to be a short, but well-deserved nap.

Her usual visions of Matthew woke her up fourteen hours later.

◆ ◆ ◆

Anna exited the infirmary with great caution, unsure if she was still alone in the building. It appeared so. The sun hadn't set yet, so she used the light seeping through the main lobby to study her map.

The halfway mark to the City was now behind her. She was upbeat; the last few days had been quite productive considering the mileage she had covered, the food she had found and the sack time she had been able to get.

She went by the bushes near the parking lot entrance to wait for darkness. This way she would be ready to hit the road as soon as the time came. It was a warm and windless evening, but far from a silent one. In the old world this concert put on by the birds would have gone unnoticed, masked by the loud synthetic makings of man. Anna closed her eyes to soak it in.

The crackling of branches nearby interrupted her meditation. She looked in all directions to see who might be coming.

The intruder soon appeared on the other side of the road and fed on high grass less than fifty feet away from her. Anna moved her chair to get an unobstructed view. When the deer heard her wheels roll over pebbles on the concrete, it raised its head, jerked back, but then froze just as fast upon seeing Anna.

What happened next was a mix of apprehension and delight.

The deer slowly crossed the road and walked with grace toward Anna. The sun was about to fade out on the horizon when the large animal came to a halt a mere six feet in front of her. She wasn't sure how to handle it. These looked majestic on television, but she was now realizing how intimidating they could be up-close. Still, Anna extended a hand as an invitation. Her visitor remained static.

"You're so, hum, so beautiful. Are you alone? My name is Anna and I'm, hum, I'm alone too you know."

The handsomeness of her new companion was mesmerizing. Aside from the image of her brother, Anna hadn't had a conversation with anybody in a while. It felt good to interact with a living being, though the deer barely reacted to the sound of her voice. She was sad when he eventually turned his back on her, walked in the building's direction and disappeared behind it.

Darkness had settled anyway so it was time to resume her journey. After this long rest, she was enthused and quite anxious to reach her destination. There were other buildings along this stretch, but since her bag was filled with supplies she didn't see the need to risk it all by trying to enter any of them.

Three hours after she had left the Bio-Dhall Inc. parking lot, Anna was deep in her thoughts. Apart from trees, grass and a few abandoned vehicles, this portion of her trip was mostly free of distractions.

She could still feel the deer's presence. Its image was

seared in her mind. She was so grateful for this lucky encounter.

"*What a stunning animal,*" she repeated to herself.

The calm of the night was shattered in a blinding flash. Her heart stopped, she raised her head and bit her lower lip; a car had just turned its headlights on after creeping up on her from behind.

Anna pushed her chair forward, hoping the driver would ignore her and pass her by. The car did make a move as though it was about to speed away, but once beside her, it slowed again. The two occupants stared at her through the rolled down window for what felt like an eternity.

"You can, hum, can keep going. I'm fine."

"You sure? You look like you could use a hand," the man in the passenger seat said.

"Nope. I'm, hum, I'm good. Thank you."

No amount of darkness could conceal from the two men the obviously heavy bag on Anna's lap.

"Now, that's just rude, Pete. We offer our help and look what we get for our generosity."

Anna's heart was now pounding hard in her chest. She tried to go faster but her chair was no match for a car.

"I don't want any, hum, any trouble. Please leave me alone, OK?"

At the last word of her sentence, the driver veered sharply in her direction. After the car's bumper clipped the side of the wheelchair, he pressed on the gas pedal and dragged the chair, with Anna still in it, over thirty feet before her front right wheel hit the curb. She was ejected and flew over the sidewalk. By some miracle, she landed on the grass and was able to hold on to her supplies while she rolled a few times.

The man who had addressed Anna got out, freed her chair and walked to her. He pulled on her bag to try and rip it out of her hands.

She needed those supplies. She needed them badly, and so she resisted. The man responded by delivering an explosive punch to her shoulder. The pain was sharp, but it was nothing compared to the heartbreak of losing her food.

Still, her safest bet was to just let go of it all.

The man returned to the car and emptied the bag on the hood. After his friend joined him, they both feasted on Anna's food in front of her. They threw the leftovers, which included the gun, on the back seat.

The one who had rip the bag from her hands tossed it back on the grass, by her head.

"Here, you can keep the rest of your crap. Next time, don't be so damn rude."

The extreme violence of what had happened had stupefied Anna. She didn't attempt to reach for her bag or answer the man. Perhaps it was better this way; any riposte from her could have sent these guys over the edge.

The two attackers had been gone for twenty minutes when Anna began moving again. She ran her hands along her legs to check for fractures. Aside from pain in her shoulder and inside her chest, as far as she could tell, she had sustained no injuries. Considering she had been hit by a car and thrown this far out of her chair, she had been lucky.

Her bag was nearly empty. The men had left her with one bottle of water, her sweaters, the blanket, her last catheter, the hammer, the map and the pen. That was it. The rest, all of her food, was gone.

While what had unfolded was terrible, it didn't surprise Anna. She had prepared herself to see more people as she closed in on the City. These two men were thugs. They had done exactly what they were meant to do. Thugs hurt. They steal and yes, sometimes they kill. As far as she was concerned, the nurses who had robbed her of her cookies were still worse than these men.

Anna crawled to her chair and sat in it.

Something was off.

The front right wheel was misaligned and wobbly after its impact with the curb. She could still go forward, but not as fast and not in as straight a line as before. This terrible setback made her sick to her stomach.

Food, however, was now back at the top of her priorities. She knew there would be fewer untouched buildings from that point on. The first two she circled didn't inspire much confidence. One had light coming from a basement window and the other showed signs it had been pillaged. The third was near identical to the one she had entered the night before. She spent some time observing it, knocked on the door and waited. She eventually broke in and found the cafeteria, but this was a bring-your-own-lunch kind of company. She took the bags of potato chips and the few remaining candy bars from the vending machines and headed back out.

At the parking lot exit, Anna stopped then looked both ways. The idea of retracing her path to where she had been at the beginning of the night crossed her mind. In her opinion, the buildings back there were better prospects than the ones now around her. In the end, she concluded that regardless of where she went it was only a matter of time before people showed up in search of supplies.

And the only way she would ever make it home was forward.

Her body and spirit were as beaten as her chair, but in the direction of the City she pushed.

CHAPTER 15

This night, which had begun in high spirits, had climbed its way near the top of Anna's list of bad ones. The awful night Matthew had been murdered took first prize, of course. The evening the virus had first struck was a close second. There was also the night of the furious storm after she had locked herself in at the Center. That one sure had been scary and long.

At the very least, she had a roof over her head then. And the dangers of being out on the road were foreign to her.

She was still reeling from her encounter with the two men who had robbed her hours earlier.

What she now called her *damned chair* was difficult to operate. Twice already she had sat on the ground to check and see if there was something she could do to fix the front right wheel with the hammer. Afraid she would turn a serious problem into a critical one, she had opted to leave it alone.

The sun wasn't up yet. She spotted a building that seemed promising not too far ahead. When the parking lot became visible, however, she declared a time-out to carefully plan her next move. That car by the entrance looked quite familiar.

Perhaps her two attackers were searching the place for more provisions. It was also possible they had chosen to spend the night there. Either way, to her this was an opportunity.

Next to the car, Anna stretched her neck to peek inside; the two men were nowhere in sight. What remained of her food was scattered on the back seat. The doors were unlocked, which made her believe the two had gone in the building with the intent of returning soon. What she reclaimed only filled a third of her bag, but a third was better than nothing.

She was about to flee, but stopped when she had an epiphany. Some expression of gratitude was in order. After all, the bullies had shown great generosity by allowing her to *keep the rest of her crap*. That crap included her pen, the tip of which she inserted in each of the tires' air valves to deflate them.

The bushes surrounding the parking lot were thick and far enough for safe cover. Anna found a spot with a good view of the car.

"Dinner and, hum, and a show," she whispered while munching on a granola bar.

The two men emerged half an hour later carrying boxes of supplies, which they dropped in the trunk. In the semi darkness, neither of them noticed anything suspect about the car. It rolled no more than five feet in reverse and then stopped. Anna held her breath in anticipation of the men's reaction. They got out and circled the vehicle, mad as hell and screaming at each other. One blamed the other for failing to mount guard as he was told, but received a salvo of insults as a response.

They calmed down and discussed what to do next. Anna heard them decide to still use the car to go as far as they could with it. She hadn't been able to put them out of commission entirely, but the screeching noise their wheels made as they left the parking lot was music to her ears.

"Welcome to my, hum, my world, assholes," she said out loud.

The car disappeared in the direction of the City. Anna went around the building and found a shed at the back with its doors wide opened. It was a fine shelter for a meal and a nap. She hid behind a snow blower and called it a night.

Sleeping in her chair didn't procure the kind of recovery she would have needed. Whenever the sky was clear enough, she preferred to drag herself away from the road to lie down in a field. She didn't mind it at all. The days were warm and high grass was fine camouflage. The result was ample peace of mind for uninterrupted rest.

Anna slipped in and out of consciousness while hugging her bag. Although her eyes were shut, she could sense it was now daytime. There was something else she could sense: a presence. She wondered if perhaps she was dreaming and even whispered Matthew's name. When she found the strength to open her eyes, she jumped at the sight of the man's silhouette standing by the shed's door. The sun was behind him; she could see the outline of his body, but not his face or the colors of his clothes.

The man noticed her look of panic and sought to reassure her.

"It's okay, it's okay. I'm not gonna hurt you, I promise."

Anna struggled to breathe and redirected what little energy she had to her arms so she could press her bag against her chest tighter than it already was.

"You don't have to worry, I swear I won't steal anything from you," he added with a soft voice. "Do you live here?"

"No, I just stopped to, hum, to sleep," she answered mortified.

He nodded and lowered his gaze to her wheelchair.

"We're heading east. Can we drop you off somewhere?"

"We?" Anna asked.

"My wife and my son. They're waiting in the car," the man said as he pointed outside.

"No thanks, I'm going to the, hum, the City."

The stranger appeared stunned. He tried to convince her to revise her plans.

"The City's a pretty bad place to be right now. There's a lot of violence, a lot of death."

Anna looked down, but then up again with assurance.

"That's where my home is so, hum, so that's where I have to go," she said in a tone that left no doubt as to her intentions.

The man respected her choice. He asked Anna permission to get closer so he could check the snow blower's gas tank.

She agreed and when he confirmed it was empty, he took a step back.

"Are you sure?" he inquired one more time.

"Thank you. I'm fine," Anna replied.

"Well, good luck to you, miss."

From where she sat, all she could see was the trunk of the man's vehicle, which remained stationary after he got inside. The car door swung open again seconds later and Anna heard footsteps coming back in her direction. The man walked to her with both arms extended in front of him. Scared, she held her breath, closed her eyes and winced in expectation of what was coming.

"It's not much," he said. "But it should help a bit."

Anna opened her eyes. The man was holding a can of stew in one hand and a can of ravioli in the other. She accepted his offering and thanked him for it.

A woman and a child stood in retreat. With this annoying sun still behind them Anna couldn't see their faces either, but based on their shadows' height and build, she guessed the kid must have been about seven years old, eight at the most.

"This is my wife Laura and my son North."

Anna waved at the woman and then turned her attention to the child.

"Hi. Your name is, hum, is North?" she asked the shy boy who nodded.

"North. Such a beautiful name," she said before pointing her index to the sky.

"My uncle used to say: *Family is the, hum, the True North of your life. Know where it is and you'll never, hum, never lose your way.*"

The boy seemed to appreciate and appeared to respond with a smile.

His mother, while handing Anna a bottle of water,

asked if she was certain she didn't want to join them. Though moved by their proposal, Anna declined once more.

"On your way here, did you see a car with, hum, with four flat tires?"

"Yes, we did," the woman answered. "About ten miles down the road. How do you know that?"

"They're bad people. They hit me with their car and, hum, and they stole my food. But I got some of it back and, hum, and I deflated their tires."

The man laughed.

"Well, you don't have to worry about them anymore. Someone shot them. They're both dead inside that car and there was no food left when we stopped and checked."

"Karma, right?" he added.

Anna nodded, but didn't say anything.

She came out the shed as the car drove away. North was on his knees on the back seat, looking back at her through the rear window, waving goodbye. Anna pointed her finger to the sky again.

North responded by doing the same.

She returned inside the shed and ate the can of ravioli for breakfast, which she opened with a chisel she found sticking out of a tool belt hanging on the wall.

The exchange with the family had left her with mixed feelings. There were still good souls in this world and interacting with them had given her some hope. Yet it hadn't escaped her that they hadn't seemed the least bit disturbed by the sight of the two men, shot dead in their car. How many scenes like this one had they come upon as of late in order to become immune to its effects?

Anna spent the day in her shelter and got on the road at dusk. The last twenty-four hours had been trying. Her backpack was too light and her chair now slowed her down to half her usual speed.

By her own calculations, she expected she would make it to the City in six days, perhaps a little over a week, a discouraging time frame even for someone traveling on two strong legs.

◆ ◆ ◆

Thanks to her artistic flair, Anna was able to descry details around her most wouldn't care about even if they stumbled upon them by accident.

Among other things, since she had left the Center, she had noted that no two nights ever produced the same type of darkness.

The moonlight sometimes painted everything around her different shades of gray, which made her feel as though she was the star of a black and white movie.

Other night skies gave the illusion the sun refused to go sleep, hiding instead mere inches below the horizon.

From the very start of her trip, she had always been able to distinguish trees and structures nearby regardless of the hour.

This night, however, was the darkest she had experienced until then. The wind rattling the bushes by the side of the road compelled her to pause at times. It sounded as though someone was following her. Since it was impossible to see, all she could do was take a moment to listen and then move on.

This was the second night of travel after her conversation with the couple and their son. She had expected she would eventually roll by her two attackers' car. Fate had picked that night for her.

She stopped by the driver's window and looked inside. The peculiar darkness was at least sparing her the clear image of their faces, but she could tell both men were sitting up straight and their heads were tilted toward her.

"Sorry," Anna said as she turned away and pushed her chair forward. She wasn't sure if she meant it, but she said it anyway, just in case.

A violent storm broke above her an hour later. Lightning brightened the landscape to the point she needed to avert her eyes because the flashes hurt the inside of her head. The resulting thunder was so loud and so sudden it drew screams out of her. During one of these flashes, Anna spotted a large tree beyond the gutter. She was aware it wasn't the best of plans, but it would be safer there than on the road, sitting on a bunch of metal rods.

She hid her bag under her chair to protect it and rested her back against the tree, stoic, ready to resume her voyage once nature would calm its fury. She removed the cap from a bottle of water and held it up to catch some of the rain.

At the first hint of the storm letting up, she got back in her chair. The rain was still quite heavy, but it was no longer enough to keep her from advancing. It was even a good idea she thought; in the middle of the night like that, and with such bad weather, the chances of crossing paths with other people were slim to none.

Night turned into day and Anna, exhausted, hungry and soaking wet, kept on going. There were no buildings in proximity anyway. The rain was cold and pushing her wheels in this much water made it feel as though she was climbing a steep hill when in reality the terrain was as flat as could be.

When potential shelters appeared on the horizon at the mid-day mark, she tried to pick up the pace but her arms refused to obey. Near the end of the afternoon, she pulled in front of the first building in the area. The glass doors and windows of the auto parts outlet had all been broken, so she knew she wouldn't find anything helpful in there.

All she wanted was to put a roof over her head for a short while. And if possible at all, rest a little.

The entrance was at ground level. She called out for people in a voice filled with such confidence it surprised even her. There was nobody, so she went in, turned her chair to face the parking lot and snacked while staring outside.

Her eyes were completely empty. At that moment, so were her heart and soul.

She fell asleep within minutes, a cracker pinched between her fingers.

CHAPTER 16

It had been raining for two days and Anna was still at the auto parts outlet. With her supplies depleted she wanted to disregard the weather and keep going, but her fear that in the long run water would damage her chair more than it was already had persuaded her to err on the side of caution.

She had explored the installations soon after she had arrived and found a room with a door that locked from the inside. This would be her fall back position should she ever need to leave her post at the entrance to hide.

She had also found a restroom with a mirror.

The image it had returned to her was appalling. The numerous times she had been forced to ditch into the gutter to avoid people, the days sleeping in fields or on the dusty and greasy floors of buildings and garages, the rain, the mud, the grass; every single inch of her body bore the marks of her trip.

Her reflex had been to bring her trembling fingers to her hair to try and fix it. She had stopped, stared at her reflection instead and then sobbed when she realized how pointless it would be.

It wasn't vanity. Anna had known she was a mess long before she had found that mirror. In the days leading to that moment, she had begun to sense that the world was not only leaving its impression on her, she was absorbing it, morphing into it. And the world wasn't pretty anymore. Confirming her suspicions in such a definitive manner had delivered a serious blow to her already fragile state of mind.

The rain ceased in the middle of the second night of this latest halt and she returned to the road, her backpack shielding all she had left to eat: six soda crackers.

Every building showed signs it had been raided and she went from one disappointment to the next in her search for food. In desperation, she turned to Matthew, pleading with him to reappear and give her strength. He didn't. Perhaps silence was his way of expressing anger at her for leaving him at the Center and, with every push on her wheels, getting farther away from him.

She begged for his forgiveness, hoping her tears and contrition would convince him to join her again. She eventually accepted she was on her own.

And so she decided not to take days-long breaks anymore.

At the very least, not until she had made it to the City.

◆ ◆ ◆

"Three days," Anna repeated over and over.

Three long days she had gone without any food whatsoever and her most recent meal had been the last of her crackers.

She still had some water, but that too was running low.

Hunger was making her delirious. Her brain kept showing her images of roasted chickens, juicy steaks and seafood platters. She had avoided fast food like the plague her entire life but now, her cravings for Whoppers and Big Macs and French fries were driving her to the brink of madness.

Since she had come out empty-handed from each of the buildings she had entered along her path, there was no point in scavenging anymore. It sapped too much energy out of her and finding something to eat in any of them now amounted to wishful thinking.

Traveling only at night no longer made sense to her either. If this was her new life, she wouldn't cower from it in darkness. Whenever she was awake, she was pushing that chair of hers. The more she did, she thought, the sooner she'd get to the City. There had to be some supplies left there. Maybe she would also find people willing to giver her a hand, although she conceded the effects of food deprivation were perhaps clouding her judgment on this.

She now sat at the foot of a steep and intimidating uphill stretch. The goal, however, was within her grasp. The City wasn't yet visible from where she was, but the smell of smoke still rising from it was all around her. Anna was certain she would roam its streets before the end of the day. After a short break and half a sip of water, she used most of her remaining energy to climb the hill. Two excruciating hours later, she had made it to the top.

And there it was.

Some sixteen days after she had fled the Center, she

had finally reached the last portion of a very long and trying trip.

This downhill stretch would take her to the south edge of the City. From where she sat, the streets down there seemed deserted; there were no apparent movements of cars or people. She would have to get closer for a better assessment. Her home was on the opposite side of town. At the bottom of the hill, she would need to head north and go across downtown.

Her final destination was still a great way away, but she did take a moment to savor the victory.

In eagerness, Anna pushed on her wheels with too much force and she gained uncontrollable speed in a matter of seconds. The chair then tilted to the right, came to an abrupt halt and flipped, sending her flying in the air with both her arms extended to try and break her fall.

The tumble knocked the wind out of her. Her hands, forearms and elbows were burning from the scrapes.

After a quick glance at the chair she figured out what had happened; the strong vibration had dislodged the already damaged front wheel. Anna managed to locate the missing parts and crawled on the pavement to recover them. She reattached the wheel with her bare and bleeding hands, although not as solidly as it should have been. It was now wobblier and noisier than before.

She resumed her descent. At the midway point, she stopped and observed again. There was a bridge above a river, to her left, leading to an empty field on one side of the road and to what seemed to be scarcely dispersed industrial buildings on the other.

It was already mid-evening when she made it to the bottom of the hill, turned and pushed toward the City.

The desolation was stunning.

Nothing, not even sleeping among corpses at the Center, had prepared her to the stench from the tens of thousands of bodies decaying in the buildings around her or scattered on the streets. It was rising from the earth itself.

"This is what war must smell like," she thought.

Darkness was fast approaching. She went up one of the main streets that would take her downtown. An uneasy feeling soon convinced her to leave this artery and use a back alley instead. She came upon garbage bags and bins and combed through them in the hopes of discovering something, anything that resembled food.

What she dug out was far from inviting, but she wasn't in a position to be picky; if it could be shoved down her throat, down it went. She sometimes managed to swallow whatever it was, but the reflex to spit it back out was so violent she couldn't always fight it off.

Anna found a space behind a dumpster to spend the night.

Although it had come fast, sleep wasn't enough to push her hunger to the back of her head. She dreamt of an outdoor dinner party, from years before, with dear friends. The delightful company, the smell of thick, perfectly aged pieces of meat searing above red-hot charcoal, the medley of fresh vegetables served as a side dish and the wine selection; it had been such a lovely evening.

Matthew was there, of course. It hadn't been planned and there was nothing special to celebrate. As is often the case, a spur of the moment gathering had turned out to be quite a memorable event. Anna had always cherished the recollection of that night because of the meal, the laughter and the simplicity.

The timing her mind had chosen to make her relive those glorious hours was as rotten as the garbage she had just forced herself to swallow.

Her bag moved.

She tightened her grip before it could be ripped from her hands. The two men trying to rob her teamed up and pulled on the bag with such force, they dragged Anna and her chair from behind the dumpster to the middle of the alley.

The surprise of the attack was such that she didn't say anything and rather saved her energy to hang on to the little scrap she had left.

One of the men, fed up with having to fight for the prize, yelled, "give me that bag, bitch."

He then took a swing and landed a punch across Anna's face. All strength abandoned her body and she was thrown out of her chair.

Before she hit the ground, while in mid-air, she thought she saw a shadow behind her assailants, far down the alley.

The second thug grabbed her chair and tossed it high in the air, away from her. None of it was registering. The terror and the pain had gotten so intense it was as though her brain was tricking her into believing this was all happening to someone else and she was but a witness to the scene.

She regained a fraction of her senses when one of the two men spoke.

"All you had to do was let go of the damned bag, lady. Come on Bud, let's get going."

"We can't leave her like that," his friend said. "That's just mean. We should put her out of her misery."

Anna was able to process these last words with the clarity they called for. This was how her life was about to end. It made her mad. She thought of the efforts she had deployed to get to the City. The grief, the sweat and the blood; it had all been just so she could die at the hands of two petty thieves over an empty bottle of water, a map, a pen and a hammer.

And on the first night she had reached her goal.

As one of the men stood above her, Anna summoned her brother and hoped he would be there to greet her on the other side.

"I'll be with, hum, with you soon, Matthew," she whispered.

But a fourth voice emerged amid the gloom of that moment.

"Don't touch her," Jonathan ordered.

CHAPTER 17

"Right, The Fur Ball," Jonathan said.

He walked to the corner of the room, reached inside a cardboard box and retrieved a tiny beige puppy dog from it. He landed a kiss on his head, rubbed his ears and put him back in his makeshift cage.

"Let's take care of you first," he told Anna.

While she was curious as to how on earth that puppy had managed to find its way inside that box, nothing could charm her at this point. She couldn't go anywhere. She was in pain and famished. The dirt that covered her from head to toe made her feel out of place in this clean, well-organized space.

"So Anna, what will it be? Jonathan asked. "Breakfast or a shower?"

The question was startling, to say the least. Food was tempting, but a shower had become a concept so vague Anna could barely grasp it.

Jonathan pointed to a red canister, courtesy of Great Mountain Coop.

"Fill it with warm water, pump the lever on top and voilà: shower-to-go."

Anna watched him grab a large pot and walk toward a door that seemed to lead to the roof. He returned and put the pot, now filled with water, on an induction cooktop plate. While it heated up, he gave Anna a packet of trail mix.

She limited her responses to Jonathan's inquiries to a few words. Uncertainty explained some of this abruptness. It was, mostly, a reaction to embarrassment; she knew she was filthy and smelled quite awful, which added to her already heightened sense of vulnerability.

He brought an army bag near the couch and unzipped it. He had found jeans, sweatpants, t-shirts and socks all over the City. These had turned out to be bad fits. He now only wore the fatigues anyway.

"I guess that's what happens when you shop in the dark," he told Anna.

He let her pick new garments from the lot. The ones she currently wore, beyond the point of salvage, would have to be discarded.

The water in the pot was now nice and warm. Jonathan took Anna, along with the canister, to the washroom. He sat her on a patio chair he had placed inside the shower and presented her with a *welcome basket*: a toothbrush, toothpaste, soap and shampoo.

With Anna washing up, Jonathan returned to the main room, sat on his bed and tried to put his thoughts back in order.

This woman represented a decision that broke every rule he had sworn he would never transgress: he had meddled, helped a stranger in need and brought her to his building. Minding his business had ensured his safety and comfort in the last few weeks. In fact, he hadn't spoken to anyone other than The Fur Ball since the incident with the boy. Not only had he become accustomed to the solitude; he was thriving in it.

Anna's arrival was about to turn his life upside down. He could sense it.

He had also killed two men earlier. This troubled him. It was the first time he had done so of his own volition. It mattered little that they had earned their fate; the burden was still his to bear. This was quite different than the night he had shot the three men in the legs a month earlier. They had likely died from their injuries, but since Jonathan hadn't seen their lifeless bodies their deaths, had they occurred, weren't on his conscience.

And there was that kid from three weeks ago.

The boy reappeared to mess with Jonathan's mind again. The sound of his voice was so clear he might as well have been standing by the bed, right this moment.

"Dad, I got one."

Jonathan began trembling at the thought of what he had done.

He needed to shake it off and focus. There would soon be a clean and hungry woman to feed. As he kept an ear out for her, he got busy preparing two meals: rations of dried eggs and ham, Pop-Tarts and coffee.

Twenty minutes had passed since he had last heard movements in the washroom. He called out to Anna and inquired if she was done. She didn't answer. He called out again, knocking on the door this time. Still she didn't respond, so he ventured in.

A sobbing Anna, now wearing the baggy clothes she

had picked earlier, was sitting on the floor, her face buried in her hands. Jonathan took her in his arms, carried her to the couch in the main room and sat next to her. He waited until she found the will to speak up.

"What am I going to do? I don't know what's, hum, what's going to happen to me now."

He wanted to reassure her. She was, however, well beyond the stage of customary words of encouragement. Such platitudes would have no impact on the kind of despair he had just heard in her voice. He settled on something tangible, something she could measure, instead.

"I'll tell you what, Anna. I'm giving you a two-week vacation. You'll have nothing to worry about except rest, heal and figure out your next move. What do you think?"

His words were faint. They had to fight their way through the powerful storm in which Anna was caught before they could reach her. But she did hear them and she accepted his offer.

"Let's get you breakfast," he said with a smile. "Plus, I have to take care of The Fur Ball."

With each bite she ate, Anna seemed to calm down a little. The sight of Jonathan, bottle-feeding his dog, was also quite soothing. If he were this gentle toward a defenseless puppy dog, maybe he would turn out to be a man she could trust.

After all, you can usually trust a man with a Golden Retriever.

◆ ◆ ◆

On Anna's second night at the warehouse, Jonathan had gone out to get the wheelchair he had promised her.

He had scratched the nearest hospital as an option. This had to be one of the most sought-after buildings to be raided, and by highly motivated looters, even this late in the game. A search in the Medical Supplies section of an old phone book left at the warehouse produced a good lead.

Jonathan had located Woodbourne Wheelchairs Inc. on Anna's map and let her in on what he was about to do. That night, he had told her that since she had trusted him until then he would do the same by leaving her alone with everything he owned in this world. He had also asked her to take care of The Fur Ball in his absence. She was tired and still hurting from the beating she had received from the thugs, but she swore to Jonathan she would look after his dog.

Getting to that small building, and breaking in, hadn't been easy. He had gone there and returned on foot, a nine-hour stretch on the road with no breaks. In the end, the reward had been as great as the risk.

Anna had been caught off guard by her own feelings when he had walked through the door: she had been as happy to see him back and unharmed as she had been about the top of the line chair he had scored for her. She had even smiled for the first time in weeks after she had sat in it. Jonathan had grabbed The Fur Ball, put him on Anna's lap and taken them both on a ride around the room.

He had lived up to his pledge. And so she began opening up after that night. In the course of their conversations, the bits and pieces she revealed about the story behind her survival grew in details and in lengths.

But this was now her fifth morning at the warehouse

and despite rest, care, food and clean water, her health had declined compared to the day she had arrived. She was no picture of well-being back then either.

Whatever the issue was, her attempt to hide it from Jonathan wasn't fooling him. He sat next to her on the couch, told her he was worried and insisted she came clean as to what was going on.

Anna began trembling.

"It's embarrassing," she answered while averting her eyes.

Jonathan's genuine look of concern convinced her to speak up. She needed a new catheter, as well as antibiotics she said, because she was feeling pain from what most likely was a urinary tract infection.

There was no way Jonathan would ever find a pharmacy with antibiotics. The catheters were just as long a shot. It left only one logical option: Anna's rehabilitation center.

It was too far, too dangerous, she objected. She didn't want him to risk his life as he had done for her chair. Besides she had tried, but never was able to enter the room where the supplies she needed were locked.

Jonathan was adamant; he wouldn't sit idle while her infection spread.

The Center was seventy miles away from the warehouse; making the trip on foot or on his bike was out of the question. He would have to break Mr. Dean's rule regarding the truck. He told Anna he would do all he could to be back as soon as possible, but if things went sideways, he would have to lay low and wait until the following night to return.

There was a favor she was dying to ask of him. She

almost raised the subject as she watched him make his preparations. It was enough Jonathan had offered to put his life on the line for medicine and catheters, she thought. Her wish, as burning as it was, would be an imposition. She remained silent about it.

At two o'clock in the morning Jonathan went to the roof to detect movements in the area. It was a moonless night, as he had hoped. All was quiet. Back inside, he sat by Anna who was lying on the couch with The Fur Ball sound asleep in her arms.

"Anna, listen to me very carefully. On the main floor below us, on the left side at the very front of the building, there is a fake wall. Something is hidden in there. If I don't come back, I want you to go and take it."

"What is it?" Anna asked nervously.

"Well, I'm not planning on you finding out," Jonathan replied with a smile. "I'll be back. But just in the very implausible case I'm not, you should know something is there."

"You're going to, hum, to come back," Anna said to reassure Jonathan as much as herself.

"I sure will. In the meantime, I have a task for you," he told her. "I'd like you to find a name for this bugger."

"You want me to, hum, to name your dog?"

"Well, we can't keep calling him *The Fur Ball*. Just think of what would suit him better. See what pops up."

Anna agreed to it. After he closed the door behind him, she regretted not bringing up the favor she wanted to ask, but she understood what the priorities were.

Jonathan doubted there was enough gas in the tank for a return trip.

His true concern with the truck, however, had to do

with the noise it made rather than with its fuel consumption. Still, halfway there, the needle had dipped a lot lower than he had anticipated.

Anna had told Jonathan about her rest at the industrial garage and the nurses who had abandoned her. He had a hunch and kept an eye out for that building, which he spotted without difficulty. He stopped the truck near the two bodies and got out to search their pockets. There they were; the keys he suspected opened the supplies and medicine room, the very set Anna had spent so much time and energy trying to locate but never could.

It was pitch dark and he knew nothing of the road, so he couldn't drive as fast as he would have liked. It must have been past four when he parked the truck behind some bushes two hundred yards past the Center's long driveway.

He observed the parking lot and compared what he saw against the information Anna had given him. The strangers' car, the ones who had forced her out of the building, was gone. What he assumed was Matthew's body was still by the entrance, covered with the blanket his sister had used.

Emotions washed over Jonathan as he stood by Anna's bed in the foyer.

Everything was exactly as she had described. So much so, he felt as though he was walking into her past and infringing on her privacy.

He had just seen the road she had traveled to get to him. Now at her point of origin, the scale of what she had endured was becoming clearer.

Jonathan was fit, armed to the teeth and up on two strong legs, yet he didn't feel safe at all there. He couldn't wrap his mind around how Anna had survived on her own in this building, and then on this dangerous trip, with nothing but courage and determination as her weapons.

"What an amazing woman," he whispered as he put a hand on her pillow.

The brown door that guarded the infirmary was near the middle of the hallway leading to the exercise room. Jonathan located it.

He was about to try the first key from the set he had found on one of the nurses when his heart stopped and the hair at the back of his neck rose.

"You have to get out of here," the voice said.

CHAPTER 18

It sounded like a young woman, perhaps a teenager. Jonathan looked in all directions. As far as he could tell, he was alone.

"There's nothing for you here," the soft voice added.

The possibility it was all happening in his head occurred to Jonathan. Isolation and stress, he knew, could activate odd sensory reactions. But since the voice was requesting rather than threatening, he ventured into a discussion.

"You understand this is a bit creepy, right?" he said.

"I don't care," she replied. "You have to get out of here."

"I mean you no harm, I assure you. But a friend of mine badly needs something from that room. I'm gonna take it and then I'll leave, I promise. Is that okay with you?"

"Take it and then go, please."

Jonathan tried one key after the other. He let out a sigh of relief when the very last one granted him access to the room.

Before he entered it, he had the good sense of blocking the door.

He found about fifty catheters on a shelf. He also bagged all the bottles of pills and glass vials with names ending in "cin" or "lin", along with syringes and everything else he could put his hands on like rubbing alcohol, swabs, feminine products and soap.

Jonathan retraced his steps to the foyer, rested his backpack on Anna's bed and retrieve the three army rations and the bottle of water he had brought.

"Are you still there? Hello?" he called out to the stranger.

"I've asked you to leave," the voice answered but with a much firmer tone this time.

"I am. I'm also giving you something to replace what I took from your building. You can come and get it when I'm gone."

On his way out he walked by Matthew's body again. He had an epiphany. He remembered the look on Anna's face earlier at the warehouse, which he had dismissed as an expression of her anxiety at the prospect of him hitting the road. He now knew what it truly was.

"You're such a selfish dumbass," he whispered to himself.

He kneeled by Matthew, peeled the white sheet off and turned him on his side to reach for his wallet. The driver's license read *Matthew Cobb*. Jonathan smiled; he had been unaware of Anna's last name until then.

Once he confirmed this was indeed the right body, he secured the wallet in his own pocket, did the same with Matthew's phone, but left Anna's letter where she had put it. Jonathan then wrapped Matthew tight in the blanket, sat him in one of the wheelchairs still lined up under the porch and walked away from the building with him.

Anna had told him about the few cars still in the parking lot at the time she had fled. He had hoped to refuel once he made it there. The gas tank cover of every single car was open, as great a disappointment to him as it was a concern.

He looked back at the building for one last glimpse just in time to see a shadow walk from the foyer and disappear into the hallway, holding the goods he had left.

With Matthew and the folded chair now in the bed of the truck, and with the sun about to rise, he hurried and got back behind the wheel.

The warehouse was less than twenty miles away when the "low fuel" warning light flashed red. The truck stalled, mere seconds later. Jonathan would have to spend the day in hiding and wait for darkness before he could finish his trip on foot.

Beyond mad, he pushed the truck into the gutter and walked at a swift pace with Matthew in the wheelchair in front of him. This was what Mr. Dean had cautioned him about. This was why using the truck was dangerous.

At least, he wasn't stranded near the City, where he would have been in a much more serious predicament.

◆ ◆ ◆

In the middle of the afternoon, Jonathan was resting in the high grass, away from the road, Matthew's body and the chair not far from him. He had won his fight against the urge to keep on walking and get back to Anna sooner. Better to make it a little later, but in one piece, than risk being seen by anybody. The car and the two groups of pedestrians that had so far passed by him were proof he had made the right choice.

He thought about the young woman, alone at the Center. Life was far from easy, but this was the beginning of summer so survival in the immediate future was possible. Fall would come and then, winter. How would she manage? How would others like her cope in such a harsh environment?

His concerns for a total stranger brought about his second enlightenment of the day: there was a conversation he needed to have with Anna, an important one they should have had already. He couldn't wait to get back to the warehouse, if only to put this matter to rest.

Time had slowed down after Mr. Dean's death. Jonathan had noticed it when he had become aware of the silence. The absence of noise, it seemed, had a great impact on time. *Silence the clocks*, they say? It was ticking even slower now, lying down in an empty field with nothing to do. A nap sped it up.

When he awoke he carried Matthew and the chair closer to the road and waited for complete darkness. This break had done him some good, although he was suffering the consequences of his outburst of generosity earlier at the Center. He hadn't had anything to eat or drink in a full day now.

He walked in the night and ditched in the gutter to hide from incoming cars a few times, just as Anna had done on many occasions. Jonathan was a brisk walker but the later it got, the more anxious he became to bring this trip to an end. He sat in the chair and carried Matthew on his lap. This was much more efficient, especially since long stretches of the road were at a soft down angle.

When he made it to the top of the long and steep drop from which he had first noticed Anna a week ago, he told Matthew to hang on and let the chair reach quite a high speed before slowing it down with his hands.

There were still a few minutes of darkness to spare when Jonathan made it to his building. He laid Matthew's body alongside Mr. Dean's grave and opened the warehouse entrance door.

"It's just me Anna, is everything alright?" he whispered.

"Yes, it's fine," she answered.

She was on the couch, two of the four rations Jonathan had left for her on the side table were untouched. The Fur Ball was sound asleep in his box next to her. The one lamp that lit the large room wasn't all that bright, yet he could see her health had deteriorated further in his absence.

"I'm sorry I took so long. I ran out of gas and I ended up walking the last miles. But it was worth it," he said as he revealed the fruit of his efforts by putting some of the catheters, antibiotics bottles, syringes and other supplies on her lap.

Anna's eyes sparkled as much as they could.

She remembered the prediction Matthew had made at the garage when he had told her she was going to be fine. There was now a real chance it could materialize.

While Jonathan chugged down a bottle of water, she rummaged through the lot.

"You found all of this at, hum, at the Center?"

"Yep. And that's just a sample. My backpack is full."

"How did you manage to get, hum, get in the room?"

"I'll tell you everything later, I promise. For now, let's make you all better."

The best course of action, he thought, would be for him to give her an injection of penicillin. Anna agreed, but since they had no clue how much of it would be enough they decided to play it safe; start with a small dose, switch to pills in four hours and monitor her reaction and adjust the treatment. He went to the roof to wash up a bit while she cleaned the infected area with rubbing alcohol and replaced her old catheter with a sterilized one.

From where he stood Jonathan heard heavy breathing, her response to the burning sensation when the alcohol made contact with her damaged skin and nerves.

With her care out of the way, he tackled the subject of Matthew. He kneeled by Anna, reached inside his pocket and presented her with Matthew's phone and wallet without saying a word.

Anna immediately recognized both items, grabbed them and pressed them against her heart.

"I have what you need to charge his phone."

"Thank you," she said in a quivering voice.

"Anna..."

He stopped talking, but kept looking at her, his sentence cut short by his own emotions. It hadn't occurred to him this would happen upon informing Anna of what came next. The realization of how big a deal this was going to be for her hit him hard.

"I brought him back. He's by the river," he finally said.

While Anna was caught off guard, she understood exactly what Jonathan had meant.

"Could I please, hum, please see him?" she begged.

He took her in his arms, then to the roof and stood by

the edge of the building that faced toward the river so she could see the white sheet that outlined her brother's body at the foot of the oak. Amid her sobs, all she could do was repeat Matthew's name over and over again.

Back inside, Jonathan helped Anna settle on the couch and sat next to her while she composed herself.

"Listen. On my way back here, it occurred to me that I have yet to ask you something. I should have done it sooner, and I apologize for waiting this long."

"What is it?" Anna inquired.

"Would you consider staying here with me? Being my roommate? I think we would make a great team. We could help each other."

After what had happened to her on the night she had reached the City, Anna had come to the harsh conclusion that making it to her old place would be a long shot at best. And even if she did manage to get there in one piece, what would she do after? How would she survive on her own? This had been on her mind since the night Jonathan had returned with her new wheelchair.

His offer was quite a relief. A hug sealed the deal.

"So today we'll take care of you and we'll both get some rest. Tomorrow afternoon, I'll dig a grave and after dinner, if you wish, we could have a proper burial for your brother."

They had a quick breakfast together after which Jonathan went to crash on his bed. He passed out in no time, but woke up on a regular basis to go touch Anna's forehead and give her water or more antibiotics.

"I thought they took good care of, hum, of me at the Center, but this, hum, this is VIP treatment," she joked.

Near the end of the afternoon, Jonathan woke up as

hungry as he had ever been. Anna was no longer on the couch. Her wheelchair, parked by the exit to the roof, was empty. He found her sitting by the edge of the building, her elbows on the ledge, looking down at her brother's body. Despite her weak state and many different kinds of pain, she had managed to crawl outside, push one of the patio chairs in the right position and climb on it. Jonathan went to her. Anna's complete trust in him was confirmed in the most powerful of ways; when he put his hand on her shoulder, she wasn't startled by his touch and even tilted her head to hug his fingers with her cheek.

Her mood had improved. No doubt the medication played a role in her newfound energy. Fresh air seemed to be doing her some good too. But knowing she had found a safe place to live with food, water, clean clothes and the company of a kind man also helped raise her spirits. Hope, as always, was a potent tonic.

"What do you say we have dinner out here tonight?" he suggested.

Along with a ration of beef ravioli, Jonathan brought Anna a hoodie in case it got cold. After every few bites, she couldn't help but lean over and stretch her neck to get a glimpse of her brother.

Jonathan gave her the details of what had happened during his trip, from the stranger at the Center to running out of gas and using the chair to carry Matthew on his lap.

When he revealed how he was able to get inside the medicine room, how he had retrieved the keys from one of the dead nurses, Anna's reaction was to burst into laughter and slap her thigh. She apologized profusely for this reflex. They both resumed eating their meal but

Jonathan started laughing again, which set Anna off once more.

The irony wasn't lost on them. The two nurses dying at that exact location was what had saved her life in the end.

"I can't believe you did, hum, did all of this," she said with gratefulness in her eyes after they regained their composure.

After his dinner, Jonathan prepared The Fur Ball's meal, which in recent days had evolved to dry food softened in warm puppy replacement milk he had found at the Take Paws store next to Great Mountain Coop. The dog devoured the entire bowl in less than two minutes.

Jonathan took him in his arms and rocked him while he inserted his name in movie titles.

"How are you, huh, The International Fur Ball of Mystery?"

"Did you eat well, The Fur Ball Always Rings Twice?"

"Guess Who's Fur Ball Came to Dinner?"

Anna looked on and laughed at every title, her favorite being "A Fur Ball Named Desire."

"I thought of a, hum, a name for him," she announced.

"Oh my, I completely forgot about that," Jonathan answered. "So? What did you come up with?"

"From now on, The Fur Ball shall, hum, shall be known as Charlie."

CHAPTER 19

It was as beautiful an evening of mid-June as it could have been. The sky was cloudless and the sun was warm. The winds, strong early in the morning, had slowly lost their will throughout the day and completely vanished by dinner. The thin layer of dust that had formed in the ensuing calm now hovered, undisturbed, above the high grass guarding the banks of the river.

Had it not been for a handful of inconsiderate crickets and birds, the soothing murmur rising from the river nearby would have been the only instrument featured in the soundtrack to Matthew's burial.

Anna had kept an eye on the road from the roof in the afternoon, ready to alert Jonathan at the sight of travelers as he cleared an area and dug a grave by the oak, not too far from Mr. Dean's plot. Once it was done, he had rolled the wheelchair — the one he had used to carry Matthew — at the foot of the hole. He cleaned up, changed his clothes and had dinner with Anna upstairs.

She was nervous. Although the grave was only a few

yards from the warehouse, she was about to venture outside of it for the first time since she had met Jonathan.

She was also about to bury her brother. The trauma of his brutal death hadn't dissipated. Her mind was still recreating the same morbid scene every night while she slept. More than once she had awakened in shock only to see Jonathan sitting next to her on the couch, telling her that it was just a bad dream, that she was safe. Anna hoped the evening to come would bring peace to her own soul, now that it knew Matthew's was resting so close to her new home and at the foot of such a majestic tree.

After dinner, Jonathan carried her in his arms to the chair by the grave and told her that if she preferred to be left alone, he could stand in retreat and mount guard for her. Anna declined, insisting he had earned the right to be a part of this moment.

An hour or so later, she nodded to signal she was ready, but asked Jonathan to help her to the ground so she could sit next to her brother one last time. With her fingers on Matthew's chest, she closed her eyes for a minute then dragged herself to his feet so she could assist in lowering him inside the grave.

While Anna settled back in the chair, Jonathan unfolded a gray army blanket. The abruptness of dark dirt hitting a white sheet, he thought, shouldn't be part of the very final instants between siblings.

Before he covered the upper body, he went on his knees, reached inside the grave, put his hand on the side of Matthew's head and mouthed a few words.

He then stood, plunged the shovel in the mound of dirt and handed it to Anna as a way of involving her in the burial.

She was quite familiar with this ritual, having been through it too often in her life already.

The flow of her tears was steady, but she made a conscious choice to absorb as much of this event as possible. She also set aside the anger spawned by the waste that was Matthew's death to focus instead on the kindness of the man now burying him.

They stayed a little while longer, in silence, before returning inside. Jonathan pushed Anna's chair past the stairs and to the front of the building on the main level.

"What are you doing?" she asked.

"You'll see," he answered with a smile.

He aimed his flashlight toward the left corner, removed a bundle of two-by-fours and pulled on a cord.

A panel covering a ten-foot-wide portion of the wall swung open without making a sound. He moved Anna in front of the opening so she could see what was hidden inside the mysterious space he had already told her existed.

"Oh my God," she whispered, incredulous.

Weapons, ammo, explosives, fatigues and more army rations and freeze-dried meals than she could have ever dreamed of were all neatly stacked.

"We should be fine, right?" Jonathan said half-serious and crouched by his new roommate.

"This is all ours, Anna, but it comes at a price. For now, this is why we can never let anyone know we're here. Some people wouldn't hesitate for a moment cutting us to pieces to get their hands on just a fraction of what's in there."

Anna agreed and they went upstairs.

Jonathan opened Mr. Dean's bottle of Whisky and

poured two glasses while Anna unplugged Matthew's phone, now fully charged and operational. She swiped through the many pictures and videos to show Jonathan exactly who it was he had worked so hard to lay to rest. For hours, he listened with great interest as Anna recounted some of the most important events of her life with her brother including their car accident and its aftermath.

At about three in the morning, Jonathan declared it was time for bed. He gave Anna antibiotics and helped her to the couch. She seized on that proximity to ask the question that had been burning her lips all night.

"What did you whisper to, hum, to Matthew?"

He made sure she was tucked in and comfortable before he answered.

"I made him a promise. I promised him I would do my best to step in, to be him for you."

She smiled and nodded. By the time Jonathan had come back from the roof after his usual round to secure the building, Anna was already asleep. Her face showed a relaxation he hadn't seen until then.

His phone's silent alarm was set to vibrate at eight o'clock for Anna's next dose of medicine. It was his turn to feel less than good upon waking up.

The last few days had been trying.

The walk back from the Center on an empty stomach, the sleep deprivation, the constant care for his two companions and the work on Matthew's grave, all of it had finally taken its toll.

Still, he handed Anna a pill and a bottle of water.

Her forehead wasn't nearly as warm as it was when he had returned from his trip. Her external injuries were healing well, and the treatment of her infection seemed to be working.

"One small victory at a time, right?" he told her.

"How about some *Eggs in a bag* to celebrate?" he suggested.

He made fun of it, but some of these meals were quite tasty. The morning menu consisted of oatmeal, scrambled eggs mixed either with ham, bacon, or sausage and cereal with powdered milk. Jonathan had figured out that by adding hot water to the cereal, instead of cold as indicated on the pouch, the result was one of the best breakfasts he'd ever had. Those, however, were available in limited numbers. They would have to pace themselves if they were to make them last.

For dinner, they alternated between sausage patties, shredded beef or pork and a few choices of pasta and chili.

Anna would have been fine with one ration per day split in two servings but Jonathan insisted she had two full courses, at least for the time being. The stronger she would become, he thought, the faster she would heal.

He saw to her every need. Food, water, medicine, trips to the bathroom; he was there for it all and she rarely had to ask for any of it.

His dedication, while inspiring, wasn't out of character for him. Before he'd met Anna, and before the virus, laziness, daydreams and nonsense ideas had always been for others. Jonathan wasn't rich but he wasn't poor either. He had never relied on anybody to do, get or achieve anything. He had taught himself to use intricate computer programs, saw to Kat's car maintenance and even cooked her a fancy meal now and then.

Meeting Jonathan Foster for the first time meant being lured in by his charm and simplicity and then disarmed by his extensive knowledge on subjects ranging from current events to mechanics and everything in-between.

Those who knew him best, however, had long identified his greatest flaw. The one issue that had poisoned his adult life had to do with commitment.

Every single woman he had ever dated had dumped him. Some had left in desperation, though quietly. Others had been more vocal about it, their exit accompanied by a level of decibels matching that of their frustration. All had fled for the same reason: his refusal to explore a deeper and a more meaningful relationship.

Kat had just moved in his building when she initiated a conversation with him in the laundry room. Until she had come along, he just didn't seem to care for a future with someone. It was fate; she was in no hurry either. They took it slow at first. Their love grew to the point where they decided it was time for him to move into her apartment a little over a year before the virus.

Although the core of his family lived hundreds of miles southwest and they had seen Kat in person no more than on a handful of occasions, they adored her.

Jonathan was thirty-three at the time he had moved in with her so they were relieved to see he had found such a great woman with whom he appeared ready to settle down.

They saw his parents on Facetime every Sunday morning after breakfast. His mother, Patricia, had even taught Kat how to prepare Jonathan's favorite meal during a secret chat session.

It was while the chicken potpie had simmered in the oven that the two women had their most significant conversation to date. The topic had been a traumatic incident Jonathan had experienced when he was ten years old, something he was keeping not only from her, but also from everyone else he knew out east.

Not even Mr. and Mrs. Dean were aware of it.

On a hot Saturday afternoon of August that year, the family had gathered at the farm owned by Patricia's brother to celebrate his son William's fifth birthday.

It was chaos, of course, with a dozen kids screaming as they played, fought and ran all over the property from the backyard's underground pool to the barn and the stables. When William's parents brought out the cake, the guests sung Happy Birthday as prescribed. William was nowhere to be found. The search for the boy, casual at the onset, had grown more worrisome when it remained fruitless.

Jonathan was the one who had located him, motionless, at the bottom of the pool.

After he'd called for help, he'd jumped in and brought the tiny body back to the surface. He had held on to the edge of the pool, his face inches from William's and his sobs growing more violent as he had grasped the scope of the tragedy.

"I can fix this. I can fix this," William's father had repeated as he had desperately tried to revive his son.

He couldn't.

As is often the case in small towns, rumors had circulated regarding the events of that terrible day. The most persistent involved Jonathan. Legend had it the only reason he had known to look at the bottom of the pool to find William was because he had been the one to push him in there in the first place. Morbid details were added to the lie each time it was repeated.

It got out of hand in a hurry and evolved to face-to-face insults and threats. An old man had walked up to Jonathan in church, pointed his finger at his face and yelled: *Murderer*. This had only happened once, though. His father had seen to it by making an example of the old man in front of most of the community.

His family knew the truth. Jonathan hadn't been near the pool all day and those present had taken good note of the bravery in his reaction. They had all chipped in and bought an ad in the local newspaper to set the record straight. The town's population, incapable of satiating its hunger for such juicy gossips, kept on talking anyway. Jonathan endured the looks and heard the whispers for nine interminable years after the incident.

At thirteen he had begun warning his parents he would move as far as he could, as soon as he'd be of age. They knew him well enough to know he meant it. They were devastated, but understood and respected his need to get away.

Kat had listened to the tale with a heavy heart. In the end, however, she had promised Patricia she wouldn't speak of it unless Jonathan brought it up first.

He never did. She was fine with his silence. It's not always necessary to talk about everything.

Perhaps words weren't the balm his kind of wound required.

As for comfort, well, it comes in many disguises.

Her chicken potpie had been a triumph that night.

CHAPTER 20

Jonathan had already grown fond of breakfast with Anna and Charlie. She asked the dog be brought to her, sat him on her lap and had long-drawn-out conversations with him while she fed him some of her food. The pup stared up at Anna, mystified, as if in the presence of a glowing blond angel. In return, she scratched his chin after each tiny bite she gave him and rejoiced at his appreciation and his begging for more.

Jonathan observed and smiled, quite amused by their interactions. Moments like these could no longer be taken for granted. He was aware of it. Along with food and clean water, minutes of innocence had become the luxuries of the times.

And yet it was such a moment he chose to interrupt that morning, cutting short Anna's cuddly session with Charlie.

"It was a bad day," he said.

Anna turned to Jonathan, sunken in Mr. Dean's big chair. She didn't know what he had meant by that, but his somber look called for her silence. And so she waited.

His eyes were locked in Charlie's general direction, but he wasn't really seeing him. He appeared to be digging deep in his own head, though not for the memory. That, much to his sadness, was readily available. He was searching for words, searching for a way to express a thought that made absolutely no sense.

"The day I found him... It was a bad day."

Jonathan's hesitation between the two sentences worried Anna she was about to hear a story she might not like.

"He's one month old today. I brought him here, at about this hour, thirty days ago. I had spent the night trapped in the building where you and I stopped for a breather on the morning we met. I was there, pinned down between two groups shooting at each other and hiding because I didn't want to be seen. I never want to be seen. People lay their eyes on a clean man nowadays and they put two and two together real fast; he must have a lot to offer.

At dawn, when it quieted down, I went back out and rushed to get here. I left the main road at some point and used the backstreets although they had been so unsafe the entire night.

I saw a child in the distance, a boy sitting on the sidewalk, alone and he looked in trouble. He couldn't have been more than twelve. I hesitated, but this was a child in distress. What was I supposed to do?

I walked up to him with my rifle strapped to my back to show him, you know, that I wasn't a threat. I put a knee to the ground and a hand on his shoulder. Just as I was about to ask him what was wrong, he took a swing at me and hit me with a rock on the side of the head.

I never saw it coming.

After he struck me, everything went dark and I fell on

all fours. I was conscious, I could hear, but my sight was gone.

The kid yelled, "Dad, I got one."

I heard his father running toward us from across the street. Somehow, the only thought that popped into my head was to focus and order my hand to reach inside my pocket to grab one of the discs I always carry in there.

The father said, "Give me the rock, I'll finish him."

My lights were still out, but the sound of their voices helped me gage their positions. I threw a disc in their direction. The boy screamed and the man said, "What the f-" but he never finished his sentence. The second disc I had thrown hit him in the abdomen so hard it went all the way inside.

My sight came back in a flash at the same time the man was taking a step toward me despite his injury. Again, as a pure reflex, I threw one last disc. That one landed deep on the right side of his face and took his eye out."

Jonathan paused and took a deep breath. He needed it for what came next.

"I got up on my knees and looked at the kid. My first disc had sliced the side of his neck. He was down, barely conscious and bleeding to death."

Anna pressed Charlie tight against her with one hand and used the other to cover her mouth. It was difficult to believe that the same kind man who had risked his life three times in the last week alone to save hers could be responsible for the death of a child. The memories of her own experiences out there, however, convinced her he was telling the truth.

She knew enough about Jonathan by then to trust that whatever he had done was nothing more than what he was forced to do. She did suspect it had to be unbearable to him. Such a decent heart couldn't possibly beat without aching given the results of his actions.

"So I stood up. The father was trying to scream he was going to kill me, but he obviously didn't have long to live. I had to get away from them and fast because it was just a matter of minutes before other people stormed in. I felt so dizzy after that blow to my head. I couldn't keep a straight line and I threw up every ten yards. My face, my neck and my shoulder were covered in the blood that was pouring out of this deep gash.

I had made it a few blocks from our bridge here when I heard faint cries. I don't even know why I went to see what it was. To this day, it still doesn't make any sense to me. I was in such bad shape I should have just kept on walking.

I found his mommy underneath the fire escape of a building. She was weak, so thin. She was so weak that when I leaned over her she didn't even raise her head. When the survival instincts don't kick in, all hope is gone.

I could tell she had given birth no more than a minute or two before I got there because her puppies were still wet. Three of them were already dead. This bugger over here looked like the stronger of the two alive. He had managed to drag himself away from his mother and he was crying the loudest.

I did the humane thing and I ended it for the mother and the weaker puppy. You don't do that every day.

Add what had happened the night before plus my run-in with the young boy and his father, and it was turning out to be one massively screwed up morning.

I put that fur ball in the palms of my hands and walked back here, bawling my eyes out. It must have been shock or something. I remember telling myself over and over: *if I could just do this, if I could just save him. If I could make it home and save this tiny little thing, then maybe I can build on that. Maybe the rest will be fine.*

I didn't care anymore about being out there in the open and in broad daylight; all I wanted was to get back here."

Anna raised Charlie near her face and pressed her lips against the top of his head. Hearing the story of his birth and that of his unlikely survival was only deepening her love for him.

"When I finally got here, as I was coming up the stairs, I recalled I had found evaporated milk while scavenging. I wasn't going to take it at first since I didn't know what use I would have for it. Good thing I had because I once read somewhere that it can work for puppies. I put a bed sheet on the table, laid him on it and placed the lamp above him to keep him warm.

After I washed him up a bit, I dipped my pinkie in the milk and rubbed it on his lips. He appreciated the taste and began eating like a horse."

Jonathan loved Charlie, obviously. The dog, however, was a reminder of a terrible day. Anna's reaction to the tale helped him put it into perspective. He still didn't feel any better about the outcome of his face-off with the boy and his father, but since Anna didn't appear to condemn him for what he had done, he was relieved of some of the burden.

He told Anna how, a couple of days later, he had found all he would ever need to ensure his tiny friend would live and grow strong. He had gone back and forth between the Take Paws pet store and the warehouse twice a night, four nights in a row, collecting enough food to last for years to come.

"Not an hour goes by I don't think of that kid, though," Jonathan said.

"I think of that father of his. How he was using him as bait. I think of how well they executed their plan; this wasn't their first time, they had killed before. Imagine that; he had trained his own child to maim people so they could steal their stuff.

Anything is possible now I guess.

It's even possible one day I'll make peace with what I had to do. But I know for sure I never will with what that man did."

◆ ◆ ◆

"You think that's, hum, that's what caused it?"

"I don't see what else it could be," Jonathan answered.

Nine days before the first wave of infections, NASA had released images of the largest ice shelf — three times the size of Texas — to ever break off Antarctica. The fracture itself should have been enough to occupy newsrooms around the world for many cycles. The media and the science community, however, were more baffled by the now exposed black hole estimated to be dozens of miles long and up to three hundred feet high.

Infrared stills from satellites showed vapors, a gas of some sort perhaps, pouring out of the seemingly hollow strip in massive quantities.

All communications were lost with the group of researchers dispatched to investigate.

When the rescue team sent after them also went silent, most of the countries on the planet reacted with proportional concern and the UN called for an emergency assembly.

An unmanned drone flew over the breach and scooped samples. They were never analyzed. Three of the four scientists that had been charged with the task froze upon entering the lab despite wearing state of the art protective suits. There were no volunteers to go anywhere near the samples after that. The one man who had survived exposure became a pincushion for a few days, but then fled and went into hiding when the tests performed on him grew increasingly invasive. He contacted the New York Times, which in turn published the article that alerted the world to the toxicity of what was pouring out of the earth in Antarctica.

The WHO and the CDC held joint daily press briefings during which they prescribed "life as usual" until more was known. It did little to calm the general public's anxiety.

In the United States, the President saw the crisis and the fear in the population as an opportunity.

His administration had been embroiled in heavy turmoil since November. He had won re-election, popular vote and Electoral College, by a crushing margin despite devastating late October polls and approval ratings in the low twenties, a level of dislike from the electorate never before seen.

His numbers had taken a steep dive toward the end of the summer as a result of his handling of the COVID-19 pandemic.

He had dismissed the virus as nothing but a hoax from its onset. It quickly became impossible to deny it was indeed real, so he promised it would all go away on its own, as if by magic. It didn't. Governments around the world implemented drastic lockdowns and sanitary measures to contain the spread. They also voted on plans to help their population cope financially. The President, despite having been briefed early on about the severity of the virus and its likely consequences, refused to follow in their path.

The number of deaths in the US skyrocketed. The economy cratered. Tens of thousands lost their jobs and their homes. Lines in front of food banks extended for miles.

Elected officials in the President's party fell in line behind him, some out of devotion others out of fear they'd be mentioned in one of his mean tweets. Through it all, the President's supporters were also more than willing to ignore reality. And why not, inside the media bubble where they lived the weather was beautiful.

In September, six months into the pandemic, the death toll had surpassed two hundred thousand. On the same day this sad milestone was achieved the White House announced a series of three Presidential Addresses to discuss the end of the pandemic and celebrate the millions of lives the President had saved with what was described as his swift, decisive and early actions.

These rallies, disguised as Presidential Addresses to entice the networks to broadcast them, had been held inside arenas in Michigan, Pennsylvania and Wisconsin. Tens of thousands of his supporters had shown up despite calls from local authorities to avoid such large indoor gatherings. Given the President's aversion to them, protective masks were forbidden. The staggering number of hospitalizations and deaths among the people who had attended the events had finally managed to erode his popularity, especially within his base.

When the President himself was diagnosed with COVID-19, he insisted on remaining at the White House. Thirty-eight people on his staff were infected in the weeks after his diagnosis. Ten of them died, including two of his doctors. The administration had tried to cover it up, but failed.

Only then did his numbers hit rock bottom.

Still, he had won the November election. Since his party had also taken the House and the Senate, every attempt by his opponents to investigate these baffling and seemingly impossible results was dead on arrival.

A month before the situation in Antarctica, the President had tweeted he was firing his entire Cabinet. By then he had beaten the infection, though it was said he was highly unstable and reeling from the effects of not only the virus itself, but also the potent experimental cocktail of medications used to treat him.

Family members as well as shady individuals from his entourage and the media filled the Cabinet positions a week later. His youngest son became Chief of Staff and his oldest daughter Secretary of State.

A grossly unqualified TV host was appointed National Security Advisor.

His new Secretary of Education had once said on the record that those who believed in evolution should either repent or be crucified.

The new head of the EPA, a coal industry lobbyist, had sued the Agency he now controlled a dozen times to argue America's God-given right to pollute in the name of profits.

There were no confirmation hearings. The appointees showed up for work one morning with armed security teams and took over.

The unraveling hit an unthinkable low on the day the President arrived unannounced at an afternoon press briefing to rollout a slew of reforms in Education, Transportation and Defense.

He walked to the podium and remained silent while journalists from most news organizations were forcefully, and in some cases violently, removed from the room leaving only friendly networks to broadcast the event and offer their undying praises afterward.

The reforms were a giant step back into the Dark Ages.

"The Word of the Christian God" would now be taught for two hours at the beginning of each day in every public and private school in the country.

Fuel efficiency regulation was a thing of the past since it had been implemented as a response to the hoax that was global warming.

And because he now intended to make good use of it, the United States would triple its nuclear arsenal.

So the country was already in chaos when the breakage in Antarctica was announced. Amidst the confusion and apprehension that followed the release of the images by NASA and the article in the New York Times, the President paid a surprise visit to the hosts of his favorite live morning TV show.

He proclaimed he had proof there was no truth to the reports from Antarctica. It was fake news, an elaborate mise en scène orchestrated by the crooked media and political opponents in an effort to distract from the good he was doing for the country, and thus for the entire world.

He would reveal his evidence at a later date, but in the meantime he had signed an Executive Order suspending the licenses of most major networks in America. All but a few were to remain on the air. The others had proven they were "the enemy of humanity."

The announcement had rendered him so giddy, and he put such emphasis on the last two letters of the word "humanity," that his top dentures had flown out of his mouth and landed on the lap of the already freaked out female anchor seated next to him on the couch.

When the head of the FCC refused to pull the plug on the networks, the President fired everybody at the agency, including the support staff. He was about to install a team of loyal followers in their stead when the virus first struck.

In an ironic twist, after the initial wave of infections, the countries that had addressed the situation with the seriousness it called for did just as bad as the United States. Everywhere, it seemed, the rich and the powerful had hijacked the supplies for themselves. In the fourteen days that separated the two waves, the remaining populations around the world had organized and attacked their leaders.

By the time the virus had circled the globe a second time, most of the food and the fuel had been consumed.

In the end, it didn't matter where on the planet people lived. It didn't matter how deep underground they went or what suit they wore, bio or business. The virus managed to find those it wanted to kill and survival of the fittest took over as the new way of life.

Jonathan had always made a point of voting and he followed politics, though he had never been actively involved. Guys would sometimes argue about it at work. The intensity of their exchanges had increased with the last President, so Mr. Dean had signed his own Executive Order banning all political talk on the premises.

Anna, for her part, leaned more to the left of the spectrum. The practicality of politics, however, amounted to an aggression on her artistic mindset. She hated the lack of flexibility pundits showed and she couldn't stand the screaming matches often seen on cable TV. Politicians seemed to make good use of their power, connections and money, but never of their imagination. That bothered her.

None of that mattered anymore.

Whatever it was that had escaped the ice in Antarctica couldn't have cared less about politics, allegiances or beliefs. If it had defeated entire governments and the best scientists in the world at such a speed and in such a definitive manner, anyone's theory on the matter was as gaseous as the substance that had poured out of that hollow strip.

This was where they were. It was real. There wasn't a thing they could do to change it.

"There's no point in rehashing it. All I know for sure is this damned thing happened. And it happened the only way it could have," Jonathan told Anna.

"Fast and deadly."

CHAPTER 21

Charlie's potty training was long overdue. Jonathan had even taken to calling him "The Little Poop Engine That Could."

He built a sandbox at the far end right corner of the roof, away from where Anna and him sat every day. It was made of wood beams already piled up on the first floor when he had moved in at the warehouse. The sand came from the banks of the river.

His phone's silent alarm was set for just before dawn. After he put on his gear, he would walk to the roof to listen for noises and gage the quality of the air before taking Charlie to his box. The smell of death from the City, although it was subsiding, could still reach them across the river on the days the wind blew south.

Anna insisted Jonathan wake her up so she too could witness and assist in their dog's milestone. They put Charlie in the middle of his sandbox and repeated "go potty" to him a million times. The pup, excited, stared at them with his tail wagging at an incredible speed.

Then, on the fourth morning, he discovered not only the joy of doing his business in the sand, but also the sweet taste of the crunchy treat he received as a reward just for doing so. With Anna cheering on, Jonathan carried Charlie high in the air for a victory lap around the roof.

The training was done within a week, which meant Charlie could now sleep with his humans. It wasn't rare for him to begin the night with Jonathan, but wake up the next morning in Anna's arms.

Jonathan was suspicious as to how this could be since Charlie wasn't yet tall enough to jump off his bed and on to Anna's.

He was in awe of how fast the dog was changing. He had long and light-blond hair, a big belly and oversized paws. His face showed hints of what he would look like once fully-grown.

Charlie, however, could get restless on occasion. He was six weeks old and the only one of his kind. At times, his instincts appeared to trigger a frantic search for something specific in nature, as if an inside voice was telling him he wasn't meant to be unique.

His universe until then had consisted of his cardboard box, the top floor of the warehouse and now whatever he could see from the roof. Jonathan had warned Anna that, in a few months, he would take him outside for a walk. He needed to move, run, smell the world and experience how big it was. She didn't like the idea, but she also understood how unfair it would be to restrict Charlie to a single building for his entire life.

On a Saturday night, with a clear sky and the area peaceful, Jonathan headed to the pet store. Maybe there were a few items left that could occupy Charlie when he became agitated.

It had been a while since he had ventured in that direction. He was stunned by how much the scenery had changed. The grass was high and the trees fully leafed so his view wasn't as unobstructed as it had been before.

Once he made it to where the army vehicles had veered off the road on the night Mr. Dean had been infected, he stopped and got off his bike. He had camouflaged them pretty well and erased their tracks. Both trucks had been there and untouched six weeks earlier when he had gone to the pet store after rescuing Charlie.

They were gone, now.

He could see tire marks leading to their resting spots on each side of the road. All that remained were the bodies of the six occupants, stripped of their fatigues, face down on the grass.

Those trucks were heavy machinery, relieved of their cargo or not. Jonathan wondered who had managed to flip them back on their wheels and get them out of the gutter.

Whoever it was, they were probably far by then, he thought.

He reached the Take Paws store without having to hide from anyone. After his usual stakeout of the building, he entered it and found there were still plenty of supplies available.

He got a giant dog bed, a blanket and some chew toys. While at it, he added flavorful treats of all sizes and a fury teddy bear to the lot.

The Great Mountain Coop had been looted and emptied of what he and Mr. Dean had left behind. All that remained were books on the subjects of hunting and survival, which Jonathan deemed more relevant than ever so he took them.

He was about to head back to the warehouse when he stopped in front of the arts and crafts store. He smiled and turned to address the teddy bear in his trailer.

"I hear you, buddy," he said before he went in.

With the last of the supplies secured in his trailer, he rose, faced up wind and took a deep breath. He immediately detected the subtle fragrance, but it was so improbable he dismissed it as his imagination playing a trick on him.

He did remember a conversation he had with Mr. Dean on the day they had inspected the warehouse prior to its purchase. While they had gone for a drive to survey the neighborhood, his boss had told him that, a long time ago, this entire county had been made up of farms growing fruits and vegetables.

Jonathan rode his bike to the back of the renovation depot that sat at the edge of an empty field.

When the wind picked up again, the pleasant aroma drew a smile from him. This was no hallucination. The deeper he walked into the open space, the stronger the smell became. He knew he was on to something big. He stopped, crouched and switched on his flashlight.

"Good Lord," he said.

In the old world, he would have missed it. Most shoppers back then probably did. Good thing he always carried an empty plastic container in his backpack, which he filled with his precious discovery.

It was still early, but Jonathan decided to call it a night when, from his position in the field, he heard a car drive at high speed. Pushing his luck was no longer an option, not with all he had waiting for him at the warehouse. If he saw people on this road, they had either passed by his home or were about to do so. He had to go back and make sure everyone was safe.

Jonathan and Anna had worked out a code. Whenever he went out, upon his returning to the warehouse, he would open the door and call out her name. If everything was fine upstairs, her response was to be "I'm up here, Jonathan." If she didn't include his name or remained silent, it meant there was a problem. He would then get out of the building, and try to enter from the roof to neutralize whatever the threat was inside.

He received the good answer so he went up, leaving the supplies he had found on the first floor.

It was still night. He convinced Anna to sleep some more and wait until morning to see what he had brought back.

◆ ◆ ◆

Jonathan had turned his back on religion years ago. Decency inspired solely by the promise of heaven or the fear of hell bordered on hypocrisy, he had long decided. Kat's death, and then Mr. Dean's, had made him revisit his views. He often spoke to them, looking up to the sky for Kat and down at the grave for his old boss. It felt right. It felt good. The essence of such wonderful people couldn't have just vanished into nothingness. A part of them — a soul he was now willing to concede — had to have remained somehow.

Regardless of his current beliefs, he wanted Sundays to be meaningful and dedicated to rest as it had been when he was a child.

The Sunday lunches of the summers of his youth were some of his fondest memories. Sitting on the front porch of the family house after mass. His mom carrying a tray filled with sandwiches and vegetables from their garden. The sound of ice cubes dancing inside the glass jar and then falling in red plastic cups as his dad poured lemonade. His parents slowly rocking on the porch swing while he sat on the steps a few feet away. It was all so simple.

It was that simplicity he was longing to recreate. This new world desperately needed the Sunday-feel. One day only. One day to try and forget about the hard work the other six demanded for mere survival.

It wasn't too much to ask, was it?

And so on Sundays, after he got out of bed, Jonathan shaved then took a shower, groomed his hair and put on fresh clothes before breakfast. He reserved the premium coffee — the stash from the camping store — for these mornings. The pots of instant he had found while scavenging and the numerous packets from the army rations were for the other six days of the week. Anna, of course, received her equal share of the good stuff.

She was quite moved the first time she had witnessed Jonathan observe his Sunday routine. There was something reassuring about it. If this man, so well grounded, had enough faith in the present to maintain traditions of the past, it had to be good omen for the years to come.

Early on the Sunday morning after he had gone to the pet store, Jonathan finished washing up and found Anna already sitting at the table with Charlie on her lap and waiting for him. She was anxious to discover what he had scored the night before.

He flipped his backpack upside down over the table.

The treats and toys landed in front of Anna who raised her arms in the air to declare victory. Jonathan went to retrieve the large bed from the trailer and then laid it on the floor by the wall between his and Mr. Dean's bunks.

Charlie seemed to find it comfortable and got busy smelling it and rolling on its entire surface.

The teddy bear drove him to madness. He scratched, licked and bit his new toy with such fury Anna worried perhaps this was too much. Jonathan had to bring the dog back on her lap so she could calm him down.

"Can you give me one second? I'll be right back," Jonathan said.

He carried his backpack to the roof and used some of the rainwater to rinse and prepare his harvest from the night before. They looked as delicious and ripe in daylight as he had hoped.

With the container hidden behind his back he returned inside and made the announcement.

"Charlie's not the only one getting a surprise this morning."

He put the container on the table in front of Anna and removed the lid.

Strawberries.

He had come upon a field of wild strawberries.

Anna's disbelief was such that, given the expression on her face, Jonathan thought she wasn't interested. It took her a moment to decipher the information.

"Do you think that maybe, hum, maybe I could have a few?"

Jonathan was confused by her question. She didn't seem to understand he had picked them for her.

"Anna, you never have to ask," he said as he crouched

by her side. "Whatever I bring back here, whatever is already here, half is yours. Always."

No words came to her mind after his statement. She did manage to put a trembling hand on his cheek. It was more than enough for him.

"But in this case," he added while he pointed at the container, "these are *all* yours."

Every sweet and juicy explosion in her mouth was followed by "Thank you, thank you, thank you" and "I love them, Jonathan" and "I absolutely adore them."

CHAPTER 22

Their evenings were quiet. Weather permitting they had dinner on the roof and adjourned inside after dusk. Jonathan read books while Anna flipped through the different moments she had immortalized on his iPad during the day.

She insisted she was only documenting their survival. Jonathan wasn't fooled. Most of the dozens of pictures and clips were selfies of her, him and Charlie taken at her incessant requests. He was more than happy to oblige.

Daytime was much busier. It was, for him, anyway; tending to his roommates and to the building kept him on his toes. He was up before the sun, beginning each day the same way the previous one had ended: standing on the roof with an eye and an ear out for signs of activity nearby. He served breakfast at about nine o'clock and then worked on improvement projects or planned future scavenging trips.

People still drove by the building, although more had caught on and now chose to move on foot to attract less attention. It was an exhausting way to get around, but sweat and blisters were a small price to pay for greater safety. It also meant that, every once in a while, Anna and Jonathan had to stop whatever it was they were doing on the roof to avoid alerting those traveling on the road to their presence.

All things considered, since the bridge by the warehouse was the only link to the City from the south, it was relatively quiet.

Anna was inching toward a full recovery. Her time, however, was split solely between the warehouse's top-floor room and the roof. Aside from holding Charlie and looking at Jonathan work, there was little for her to do or to occupy her mind.

This calm came with an unexpected side effect.

In their downtime, both Anna and Jonathan were preyed upon by memories of their past. Any reminder of what they had lost to the virus held tremendous power over their mood. A word, a sound, a fragrance; the triggers abounded. There was no need to alert the other when one was affected. The tall wall of silence behind which they retreated signaled their longing for space.

Those days hit Anna like a freight train. She would ask to be taken outside, on the roof, and stared at the horizon above the empty field across the road for hours. Jonathan would check up on her, bring her water or a cup of coffee, and squeeze her hand to give her strength before returning to his chores. He could see, at times, that she had wept.

Charlie sensed her sadness too.

He carried his teddy bear outside, dropped it at her feet and looked up at her. Anna would pick him up, sit him on her lap and scratch his head. Her mind remained miles away, though.

Jonathan never dared to ask where it went.

Some paths must remain secret to preserve the comfort the destination brings.

The day after they had moved to the warehouse, Jonathan had gone to the building next door with Mr. Dean to steal the dumpsters they wanted to use to hide the entrance to their new home. They had walked through a patch of trees and high grass behind the oak to avoid detection. Jonathan had been struck by the strongest of déjà vu episode. The smell of the trees there, a mix of maples and pines, had taken him back to the summer camps of his childhood.

Whenever he had a heavy heart and a need for solitude, he would walk past Mr. Dean and Matthew's graves, continue a few yards further and sit with his back leaned against the largest of the maples. This way, he could meditate while keeping an eye on his building.

There were plenty of subjects to reflect upon: Kat and Mr. Dean's losses. The sick violence he had witnessed from people downtown and from those in the building across the bridge. And this damned nightmare the boy and his father had forced him into. That would forever be on his list.

The guilt over his parents consumed him.

He hadn't been able to go to them as he had promised because of the chaos early on and then because he couldn't leave Mr. Dean on his own. The morning he had returned to the warehouse with Charlie in the palms of his hands, covered in blood and traumatized by his encounter with the boy and his father, he had come to the conclusion that a nine-hundred-mile road trip in a world like this would amount to a suicide mission.

He still held hopes for his folks, though. They were so strong. If one or both had survived the virus, they stood a chance. One day, maybe…

Soon after he had surprised her with the strawberries, Anna had been floored by one of those spells. She had now climbed her way back to happier dispositions; the timing was perfect.

Jonathan told her he needed help preparing dinner. He carried her from the roof to her wheelchair in the main room and pointed at the table, which was covered with an army blanket.

"Do me a favor, will you? Please remove the blanket and clear that crap off the table so we can eat," he said in a firm voice.

Anna, in shock, watched Jonathan walk away from her. She wondered where on earth the tone and the words he had just used came from. Ever since they had met, he had never asked her to do anything. He had always spoken to her with great empathy and had been an absolute angel of patience. This kind of talk was so unlike him. She lifted one corner of the blanket and as she began discovering what was underneath, Jonathan turned around so as to not miss her reaction.

She hadn't yet seen half of the lot and already she was nearing elation. No longer able to control his own excitement, Jonathan rushed to give her a hand so she could lay her eyes on the rest of it.

No one, it appeared, had shown interest in what was inside the arts and crafts store near the Great Mountain Coop.

"I got you these on the night I brought the treats and the toys for Charlie. I just hope I didn't fetch you a beginner's set," Jonathan joked.

Although he couldn't carry as big a load as he wanted, he had managed to score five rolls of canvas and a wooden box that doubled as a tabletop easel. Its drawers were loaded with palettes, brushes and paint tubes of all colors. Not knowing if that would be enough he had also filled two large bags from under the cash register with a bunch of items from the shelves.

Some of what he had brought had nothing to do with her craft, but he figured that since Anna was an artist she would know what to do with it.

She inspected the box easel first and announced it was far from a beginner's set; it contained all she would ever need to be able to work again. Every item she took out of the bags triggered an "ah" or an "oh" of amazement. Her mind was exploding with ideas.

Jonathan had to remind her to eat before her food was cold.

This excitement had gotten Charlie restless and crying for attention. Anna took him on her lap while Jonathan prepared the dog's usual meal.

"I feel so, hum, so lucky," she declared.

"Funny you should say that," Jonathan answered.

"What do you mean?"

"Because I thought about it a lot. I thought about you and the word *luck*. You're not lucky, Anna. I've seen where you come from. I've seen the road you've traveled. You kept yourself alive in the face of tremendous adversity. You're here because you're strong, because you fought, because you made the decision to live. And nowadays, it is a decision."

Jonathan pointed his finger at her to add more weight to his argument.

"There is no luck in your survival. There is some in mine; Mr. Dean helped me make this place what it is now and all this food pretty much fell in my lap. But I still don't think we should call ourselves lucky. I had to go get that food and I had to protect it. You? You suffered to stay alive. You suffered to get here. Privileged, yes. We're privileged, that's for sure. We should appreciate what we have. But we're not lucky."

Anna looked down at Charlie and took a moment to reflect upon what she had just heard.

She nodded approvingly.

"Yeah. We're privileged," she concluded.

◆ ◆ ◆

Anna's injuries to her hands and her face had healed. Her infection would soon be a thing of the past. Now that she was up to it, Jonathan saw it a priority to show her some defensive moves. If anything were to happen while he was out scavenging, he wanted to know she could put up a fight.

She had her own rifle, which he taught her to use. Every morning from the roof, she shot a few rounds at targets he planted by the river or in the field across from the warehouse. A small pouch containing some of his discs was also tied to the side of her chair, by her hip.

Anna's skills were nothing short of impressive. She could hit any target with as much accuracy as Jonathan with either the rifle or the discs. She was a fierce opponent in the competitions they staged; he never held back and she won her share of contests fair and square. The winner was awarded an extra treat such as a candy bar or a pack of Pop-Tarts from the rations.

Nevertheless, Anna confessed she didn't think she would ever be capable of using her weapons against people.

"I hope you never have to," Jonathan answered. "Keep an open mind, though. Look around you. We have so much to protect."

◆ ◆ ◆

"I think I would like to, hum, to paint."

It was the first time Anna had voiced this desire since Jonathan had given her the art supplies. He hadn't pressed her on it early on because she wasn't feeling well enough. Her health was fine now and he had begun to wonder if she would ever let this creative side of hers speak again.

He had already assembled five frames by attaching squares of canvas to folded metal laths. The result could have fooled the most experienced of observers. Those had been resting against the wall by the couch, unsolicited for weeks.

"Sure! Where would you like to set up?" he asked excited.

"Maybe the, hum, the roof?"

With the easel set outside, and Anna seated in front of it, he informed her he'd be working on a project of his own.

The door to the roof sat on half a step that prevented Anna from passing it with her chair. Jonathan didn't mind carrying her outside in his arms, but he wanted to give her the freedom to come and go as she pleased.

The plans for platforms raised flush with the step on both sides of the door had been taking shape in his head for some time already. With ten feet-long ramps leading up to these platforms, the angle would be soft enough for Anna to go in or out with ease. In just a few hours, the parts were assembled and ready to be installed.

This day could have deluded both of them into believing they had resumed their former lives. Painting, a home improvement project and a dog to push out of the way were things of the old world. For the first time since Mr. Dean's death, Jonathan had regained a certain sense of normalcy.

The minutes had lapsed so slowly since his passing, every day had felt like a month. No wonder he had the impression the events that had brought him and his two current roommates to the warehouse had occurred years ago already.

The wind picked up as dinner approached. Anna was afraid her canvas would fall off the easel. She reminded Jonathan it was time to eat and asked if it would be appropriate for her to have the hot cereal.

"Cereal? At night?"

"Yes," she answered with a grin. "They taste like the, hum, the strawberries you brought me."

He returned soon after to the roof with her food and offered to take her equipment inside. She agreed, but insisted he was not allowed to look at the painting before it was finished. Jonathan played along. He lifted the canvas from behind and went inside.

After he prepared his own meal, he walked to the door to go join Anna, but stopped and looked outside, puzzled.

Her chair was empty, her food spilled on the ground.

"Anna?"

"Don't come outside Jonathan. Someone is, hum, is shooting at me."

CHAPTER 23

The bullet, fired by a suppressed weapon, whizzed by her ear and exploded on the brick wall behind her. Another bullet followed a similar path a few seconds later. When she realized what was happening, Anna dove to the ground in time to see a third projectile tear through the backrest of her chair. She crawled toward the side of the roof that faced the City, the direction from which the shots had come, and hid alongside the three-foot ledge.

Jonathan had just made it to the door. He too put two and two together when a fourth shot landed a few inches behind Charlie. The door blocked his view of Anna, but he knew where she had disappeared.

"Good girl. Stay right where you are, they can't hurt you there. You hear me?" he said in a calm tone.

"Yes," Anna cried. "But, Charlie, Charlie…"

The dog was dining on the food Anna had dropped on the ground. Jonathan had to act fast; he jumped out in the open and grabbed him. A bullet sliced through the roof where Charlie had been just standing.

Jonathan turned around and ran back inside. He put Charlie on his bed, took his weapon and his emergency backpack before he headed back to the door.

"I'm going out, Anna. Don't move. I'll come back to let you know when this is over."

"Oh my God," she whispered repeatedly as an answer.

Jonathan exited the warehouse and slid the door shut behind him. He walked to the rear and then to the side that faced the City. Through the trees, he knew exactly which building and which window to look for with his binoculars. Sure enough, the same young man from weeks earlier was there, holding a silenced rifle.

There were footsteps and voices on the bridge. Two men were headed in the warehouse's direction. They too looked familiar; they were the ones Jonathan had confronted in the back alley after they had dumped a fresh body.

"They always come back," he mumbled. "Always."

There was no point in trying to reason with these guys anymore. They had their chance and they had now blown it in spectacular fashion.

Given how close already they were to the warehouse, Jonathan guessed they had left their post on the other side of the river before he had emerged on the roof to grab Charlie. In their minds, they were about to attack a woman in a wheelchair and no one else.

The element of surprise could play in his favor, but he had to make sure not to send a signal to the others across the bridge that something had happened to their partners.

He crouched and hurried behind the oak where he hid and waited for the men to find the entrance. On that side of the building he would get them quickly and out of the shooter's view across the river.

There they were, by the entrance.

He had one of them in his crosshairs. His finger was on the trigger. He removed it.

A better plan had just presented itself. There was less than an hour of daylight left; all he needed was one of these two men to walk with him in semi-darkness to make it to the group's base unharmed. The shooter, or anyone else mounting guard, could be tricked into believing the two shadows moving in the distance were that of their accomplices returning.

As the men tried to roll the dumpster by the entrance, Jonathan snuck up behind them.

"Don't turn around. Hands where I can see them. First one who speaks gets one in the head."

"Okay, calm down, we can talk about this…" the one on the right said.

Jonathan's rifle, also suppressed, gave him the freedom to act whenever he saw fit. The shoulders of the man on the left jerked as his friend collapsed to the ground.

"How 'bout you, lonesome? Wanna give a speech too?"

The man shook his head. After he surrendered his weapon, Jonathan searched him and renewed his order not to speak, giving his directives loud enough so Anna could hear him and know he was in full control.

The sun took its sweet time going down. During this entire time, Jonathan stared the man in the eye with an anger he never knew he could muster.

It wasn't rage, though.

Rage is dangerous. Rage is difficult to manage and it

clouds reasoning. This confrontation was revealing to Jonathan; he could tweak the intensity of his own anger. He made the conscious choice to hold it at high level.

"I told you I'd kill you all if I ever saw any of your faces around here again," Jonathan said.

The man shrugged, as if his current troubles were nothing more than *occupational hazard*.

Dusk had now arranged for them to still be visible, but impossible to identify in the distance. They kept a sustained pace and crossed the bridge without a glitch. Jonathan looked up at the building's windows; the shooter's perch was on the sixth floor.

There was nobody in the entrance lobby. He asked his prisoner where the others were.

"It's just me. I'm the last one left," he answered.

He was lying, of course. Jonathan knew about the shooter and at least a few more members in his posse. He hadn't expected full collaboration, but a little help in locating the group would have made things easier.

The man's fate was sealed anyway when, coming from the floor above, a burst of laughter echoed throughout the lobby. The stranger had outlived his usefulness, so Jonathan shot him.

Midway up the stairs, he paused and listened. The sounds were muffled; he could hear people talking, but not quite make out their words. The door giving access to the second floor had a narrow rectangular window. The opposite end of the dark hallway, about eighty feet away, was lit by a weak source of light escaping from a room. Jonathan counted the voices as he moved in closer; five people, maybe more if some were just keeping quiet in there. His steps were long, slow and silent.

He stopped near the room's entrance, remained still and listened some more. Each time someone spoke, they revealed their exact location.

A minute later he raised his weapon at eye level, took a deep breath and walked in.

The room, about twenty feet by twenty feet, was lit just enough for Jonathan to notice the shock on the faces of those inside when he burst in.

Men playing cards at a table set near the door were the first to go. He was at such close range he required only six bullets to eliminate the four of them. He then turned to his right and pulled the trigger again. Five more bullets ensured the three people sleeping there, on the floor by the wall, would never see the sun rise again.

One last man stood at the very back, by a stash of food and supplies, his hands high in the air. The expression of terror on his face puzzled Jonathan. How could a man responsible for the death of so many others be this afraid of his own in the end? He was about to scream for help when the bullet silenced him.

While he removed the empty clip on his rifle, Jonathan counted eight victims. None of them had reached for a weapon. It had all happened so fast there hadn't been time for words, let alone returned fire. The dead included the woman and the other two men he had seen on his first stakeout of the building. The rest of them didn't look familiar and there were no signs of the shooter who was probably at his post on the sixth floor.

Jonathan didn't like the two choices he had: climb all of these stairs to finish this in complete darkness or wait until morning.

For his own sake, he decided on the latter.

♦ ♦ ♦

Anna seized on the darkness to crawl back inside, leaving her wheelchair behind. Her only movements in the last five hours had been to cover her mouth after she had heard Jonathan shoot one of the two men, a reaction not only to the fear, but also to the graveness of what he had just done. She had come within less than half an inch of her own death and yet, she couldn't process that of one of her aggressors. Not then and there anyway.

She grabbed her rifle, as well as a few discs, and climbed on the couch with Charlie to wait for Jonathan. She had already begun to worry about him soon after she had heard him leave with the man whose life he had spared. But now, in the middle of the night, she had switched to wondering if she was ever going to see him again.

Hours passed.

The hypnotic rhythm of Charlie breathing in her arms made it impossible for her to fight exhaustion.

Not long after she had fallen asleep, at about five o'clock in the morning, she was shaken by the sound of a loud deflagration on the other side of the bridge. She dragged herself out on the roof, crawled alongside the ledge for cover, and raised her head just enough to look up on the horizon.

Smoke and dust were escaping from the sixth-floor windows of the building in which the thugs had set up their camp, but silence had returned. She stared at the sky until the smoke dissipated and then lowered her gaze to the bridge praying for Jonathan to appear. He didn't.

She crawled to her chair. Before she folded it and pulled it inside, she looked at the cereal spilled on the ground. The previous day had been so incredibly beautiful. It had played out in such nonchalance, in such good company and with her favorite thing in the world, painting. It had all crumbled in an instant.

Jonathan and Anna had discussed at great lengths the bad people they had met on their paths in recent months. Both had agreed that in this world, just as it was in the old one, maintaining decency was a decision they needed to make. But not everyone had reached that conclusion. They would have to be forceful, if not merciless, against those who would try to steal their supplies. It couldn't possibly be a sin to protect each other as well as what they owned.

Disserting on such a scenario was one thing. Acting upon it was another one altogether. Anna had witnessed violence and been on the receiving end of it. Inflicting it, however, wasn't in her DNA. This would require a major shift in her personality. Jonathan had obviously already been through his. This fresh nightmare was showing her how ill prepared she truly was. She vowed to ask for his help in making that change after his return.

Once inside, Anna took Charlie on her lap and made both their meals. It seemed inappropriate to eat at a moment like this, and she hesitated at first, but she hadn't eaten in almost a day.

She ate with her eyes locked on her weapon and remembered what a torment it had been to wait for Matthew to return to the Center after he had gone to the City.

She had known Jonathan for a month and a half and yet he had made his way so deep into her heart already, her fear for him was the same as the one she had felt for her brother.

Her food could barely pass the knot in her throat as she realized how fast Jonathan had fulfilled his promise to step in Matthew's stead.

If he hadn't come back in another fifteen minutes, she would go look for him.

No doubt she was willing to do it.

She hadn't reached the end of that thought when the main entrance door on the floor below her slid open.

Anna tightened her grip on her weapon.

CHAPTER 24

The shock from what Jonathan had just done went to his knees and he collapsed on one of the chairs amid the dead bodies. His throat was burning from the heavy breathing and sweat fell in a steady stream from his chin. His mind was stuck on idle.

The first man he had shot upon entering the room tried to crawl to a gun that had fallen near him on the floor. His movements shook Jonathan out of his torpor. He stood, picked up the gun himself and searched the room for other weapons so he could empty them of their bullets.

Though the man was the only member of his group still breathing, it was obvious he didn't have long to live. Jonathan used his foot to roll him over and look him in the eye. His face was lit by the glow of an oil lamp, still intact on the table and soon-to-be sole survivor of Jonathan's assault.

Even as he struggled to cling to life, the man found it in him to mouth the words "Goddamn you."

"You're gonna be an asshole 'till the very end, aren't you?" Jonathan asked him in disbelief.

The stranger attempted to say something else, but couldn't. His head tilted to the left. His eyes, squinting with anger toward his assailant at first, opened wider and then relaxed to confirm his death.

Jonathan left the room and found an unlocked office a few doors down where he sat to wait for the sun to come up. He hated having to drag out this dirty chore, but this was his safest bet.

There had been no shootings since the day he had confronted the two men and their group had been attacked. A plausible scenario was that, after that night, they had retreated to another area, but decided to come back. As Jonathan saw it, this building was prime location for their routine. Any survivor using one of the three major paths on the south side to either enter or leave the City was bound to fall into their trap and become an easy target.

It was a horrific scheme, but an efficient one.

It was also proof that a ruthless heart pumping blood to a brain capable of critical thinking was a terrifying mix in a society where people didn't have to answer for their actions.

"They're all a bunch of Kevins," Jonathan mumbled.

The very fact that Kevin had popped in his head at that moment took him off guard. Kevin also worked for Mr. Dean. Before the virus, every single shop in the world had at least one dumbass like him on the payroll.

Why Mr. Dean had kept him for so long was a mystery to Jonathan.

Kevin, it appeared, was never as happy as when he

stirred the pot. Calling his co-workers faggots and dipshits, sticking his wet and dirty index finger in their food at lunchtime, even throwing punches every now and then; not one week went by he didn't do something that forced Mr. Dean to intervene. It inevitably ended with their boss yelling: "I'm going to retire, shut this place down and you'll all be out on the street."

If by some unfair wonder Kevin was still alive somewhere out there, Jonathan was certain he had joined a gang like the one in the other room. He would have to leave the critical thinking part to others, though.

The enormity of what Jonathan had done was affecting his train of thought. His mind veered toward a more sensitive topic.

Nearly three months had passed since Kat's death. She remained a painful subject for him to reflect upon, albeit a much more attractive one than Kevin could ever aspire to be.

The concept of her, alone on the bed in their apartment, was eating him inside. No matter how hard he tried to convince himself that fleeing on the night of the first wave had proven many times over to be the right thing to do, the image felt wrong.

He didn't expect a reprieve from this feeling in the near future either.

Guilt and *regret* are relentless for a reason; they stain the soul. That stain may fade in time, but it never really washes away.

"Focus," Jonathan whispered.

Returning to Anna regained the top spot on his list of immediate priorities. He knew she would worry about him and he wished he could tell her he was still fine.

The best way for him to reassure her was to complete the task at hand and make it back to the warehouse in one piece, he thought.

His heart rate reached rapid pace again as light began to surge on the horizon. He climbed the metal stairs on the opposite side of the building from where he knew the shooter was, stopping at every flight to listen. On the sixth floor, he crossed the hallway one long and slow step at a time. At the very end of it, two doors giving access to some sort of conference room devoid of furniture were wide open.

Jonathan stood outside the room, staring at a stash of food, bottled water and an empty sleeping bag set below the windows that overlooked the main street.

Silence lured him into believing he was alone but after he walked in, from the corner of his eye, he saw the young man waiting for him at the very back, his rifle pointed straight at him. Jonathan took a swift step back.

The first bullet missed his nose by little. The second bullet exploded inches from his face on the concrete around the doorframe. Fragments from the wall hit him so hard on the cheek and jaw he thought he had been shot in the face. Concrete dust now blinded his left eye.

He panicked and pressed the trigger on his weapon multiple times. His first two rounds finished their run in the ceiling. He adjusted his aim and saw the shadow of the shooter running to take cover behind one of the columns in the middle of the room.

Jonathan retreated in the hallway, dropped his backpack to the ground and pulled a grenade out of it.

He had never used one of those before, having been unable to find a location remote enough to test them.

He had no clue how long it would take to detonate. Still, he pulled the pin and aimed at the wall beneath the windows. Since he was at an angle compared to his target, he hoped the grenade would slide on the floor, ricochet off the wall and get close to the young man behind the column.

He almost hit his mark.

Jonathan had to re-enter the room to throw the grenade. His instinct had been to stay and confirm where it had stopped. It did bounce off the wall and reached behind the column, but it rolled a little farther than he had anticipated, reappearing in his line of sight and leaving not only the shooter as a possible casualty, but him also.

He realized how stupid his reflex had been, pivoted, and grabbed the doorframe with all of his strength to add speed to his exit. Most of his body was out of harm's way when the deflagration shook him to his very core. Every window in the room was reduced to dust.

Pieces of shrapnel hammered his hand and tore the skin on his forearm. Jonathan held his arm in front of him; there wasn't much blood yet, but the burning sensation was excruciating.

He looked inside the room and saw the shooter was face down on the floor, his weapon out of reach. The fraction of a second it had taken him to figure out he was next to a grenade had proven fatal; it had gone off as he had tried to get away and his entire backside was ripped to shreds.

Jonathan went to the young man and stood above him. He was just a kid, barely in his twenties.

"You know why I did this, right?" Jonathan said.

The sniper was concussed and couldn't answer him.

Or beg for his life for that matter. Jonathan positioned the tip of his suppressor above the young man's forehead. The anger he had felt the night before had made way to a disgust split in equal measures between these people's actions and his own.

He couldn't bring himself to pull the trigger. He waited instead for the young man to draw his last breath, which he did less than a minute later.

With his mission now completed, Jonathan went to the window to get a look at the warehouse.

The roof was almost entirely hidden behind the trees that edged the building. A small portion of it was made visible only when gusts of wind bent the largest branches downward. It was sheer bad luck the shooter had gotten a glimpse of Anna, about to enjoy her meal.

He noticed an industrial heater in a corner of the room. Even at a moment like this, he thought of ways to add to the comfort he could give Anna and Charlie. He'd have to come back for it later.

With his arm and face bleeding, and his left eye closed shut by the swelling, he exited the building through the front doors.

There were people, five or perhaps six of them, waiting for him on the other side of the street. One of them took a step forward. Jonathan dropped his bag and raised his weapon in the man's direction.

"Wow, no, I'm not armed," he screamed with his hands in the air.

Exhausted, and too weak to hold his rifle leveled anyway, Jonathan stood down.

"Are they dead? Did you get the sniper too?" the stranger asked.

Jonathan nodded, though hesitantly.

He was surprised to find out there were still survivors in the area. And it seemed they had been living in fear of the threat he had just neutralized.

"Thank you," the man said.

"There's lots of food on the second floor," Jonathan answered in a shaky voice. "You can thank me by sharing it instead of killing each other for it."

He grabbed his backpack then carried on toward the bridge.

"And don't you follow me," he added with force.

During the ten-minute walk to the warehouse, Jonathan was able to put aside his pain thanks to the prospect of a reunion with Anna and Charlie, and also because of what he had just witnessed. There were others nearby and they didn't appear to be violent. He wanted nothing to do with them, of course, but the sheer knowledge of their existence stirred half an ounce of hope in his heart.

At the sound of the door opening below her, Anna held her rifle tight and waited while she kept Charlie quiet. When she heard Jonathan's voice calling her name, she closed her eyes in relief and took a deep breath before answering.

"I'm up here, Jonathan."

Afraid of how Anna would react at the sight of this much blood, Jonathan tried to find some words to lighten the mood when he reached the top step.

"Don't be alarmed. It's worse than it really looks. Or something like that."

His poor attempt at humor had no effect.

Anna, sitting in her wheelchair parked by the couch, had to contain her screams when he collapsed on his knees in front of her. She extended a hand to touch his face, but the fear of causing him more pain stopped her.

"Everything is going to be fine. I'm here now. Wink, wink."

On his way to the warehouse, he had pulled out the largest of the pieces of shrapnel lodged in his arm. His blood loss had been significant. At the end of his sentence his good eye rolled and he fell backward, landing on his behind.

He dug deep to find the strength to crawl in the direction of the door leading to the roof.

"What are you doing?" Anna asked.

"I'm making a mess in here. I should go outside," he answered.

With the portable shower and the bag containing the medical supplies Jonathan had brought back from the Center in tow, Anna dragged herself through the door to join him on the roof. They both sat on patio chairs, facing one another. She sprayed water on his head and arm to remove as much dirt and blood as she could.

"I killed them all, Anna. I killed them all," he kept repeating.

The stress and the loss of blood had flushed the colors from his face and his injuries were significant, but it was his one good eye that worried Anna the most.

It looked different.

Jonathan had the kind of eyes that could reassure her in her darkest of moments. There was a spark in there, something she had noticed the morning they had met. It was highly contagious and one virus she didn't mind contracting at all.

She was no longer seeing it.

She worked fast to clean Jonathan's face so she could move to his arm, which was in bad shape. His hand was bruised and swollen. His forearm had deep cuts, closer to the wrist, which by chance left the muscles near the elbow untouched.

"This is going to, hum, to sting," Anna said, showing the bottle of rubbing alcohol to Jonathan.

His breathing accelerated when the liquid flooded his gaping wounds and he bit his other hand to keep quiet. Anna put two fingers under Jonathan's chin to turn his head toward her.

"Oh well, look at you. The spark is, hum, is back."

She was wrapping gauze around his arm when he noticed her food spilled on the ground. He was sad she hadn't been able to enjoy the cereal she loved so much.

"You must be so hungry," he told her.

◆ ◆ ◆

Jonathan lay on his bed while Anna prepared a meal for him. She then went and got Charlie. That dog was a potent shot of comfort. Jonathan held him on his chest with his good arm and closed his eyes. The shock was subsiding and the consequences of what had taken place in the last twelve hours were becoming clearer.

He wasn't the pretentious type, nor had he ever been one to overanalyze things. Still, deep down he knew he was a good and decent man.

This assessment, however, was based on metrics valid before the virus. The new world wasn't even three months old and already his body count stood at fifteen, with an option on the three thugs he had shot in the legs early on. How many more lives would he have to end just so Anna, him and Charlie could keep on living theirs?

"I didn't want any of this," he said.

"You saved us," Anna answered. "We wouldn't be here now if it weren't for, hum, for what you did. I can't wait for the Army or the Police to, hum, to regroup and, hum, and bring back order," she added.

He looked away as Anna spoke. This last day should have tempered her hopes, if not erase them altogether. Help wasn't on the way and it never would be. He had no energy for exasperation, so he chose not to object.

Jonathan drifted in and out of sleep throughout the morning. Each time he awoke he saw Anna sitting by his bunk, gazing either at his iPad or Matthew's phone.

It was while he slept that she stared at Jonathan.

She recalled all he had done for her and wondered why. Why had he saved her? Why had he risked his life for a complete stranger and treated her to strawberries? Why had her destiny wrapped itself so tight around his and in such a hurry?

A light drizzle fell later that afternoon. Jonathan rose from his bed and went outside to make sure the water collecting system was intact and in good working order. He walked to the far end of the roof and turned toward the City, staring at the building across the bridge and its broken windows on the sixth floor. The image of the dead young man inside was seared in his mind.

He then looked at the spot where Anna had been sitting the night before when the initial bullets almost hit her. The terror in her voice when she had warned him not to step outside gave him the chills.

For every situation, it seemed, there was an appropriate Mr. Dean recollection. He went to the side of the roof that faced the river, looked down at his boss's grave by the oak and heard the old man's voice again.

"Some of the choices we're going to have to make will scare the hell out of us, but I trust us. I trust you, kiddo."

Jonathan shook his head. He had done the right thing, this much he knew. But did the right thing really have to be killing eleven human beings between sundown and sunrise?

"Do you still trust me?" Jonathan mouthed.

Anna sat by the door and allowed him a few minutes of reflection in the rain. His fighting spirit made her feel safe. But it was the sorrow that tore his soul apart after he had ended the lives of horrible people that gave her hope.

"You should, hum, should come back inside."

He turned around, smiled and walked to her. After he lay back down, they heard footsteps near the warehouse.

Anna was terrified, but Jonathan saw an opportunity. He knew he had locked the entrance below them and that climbing on the roof would be quite a challenge. He remained on his bed, unarmed, and whispered to Anna to get her rifle and back off a bit to maintain a clear view of the two doors that gave access to their hideout from the ground level and from the roof.

Anna kept signaling "no". Jonathan insisted, mouthing the words "stay calm," "focus" and "raise your weapon."

The footsteps eventually grew faint and disappeared. Anna, still trembling, lowered her rifle and began breathing again.

"I know this is difficult Anna," he said. "But you have to be prepared. I'm not always going to be here when that happens. You may have to protect our home. You may have to protect yourself and Charlie."

She hesitated, but nodded.

She was about to go rest her weapon against the wall where it belonged, but took long good look at Jonathan holding their dog in his arms.

She kept the rifle on her lap.

CHAPTER 25

A week had passed since the attack. Anna had taken great care of Jonathan, but two days in bed with her catering to his every need was all he could bear to impose on her. Once he regained enough strength, he used his one good arm to finish his project of giving Anna unassisted access to the roof.

The morning it was completed, he invited her to give it a try. She stopped at the foot of the ramp and stared at length at the door. Instead of pushing her chair up the ramp, she returned to the table in the middle of the room, her back turned on Jonathan.

After what had happened, she no longer felt safe out there.

They both loved spending time on the roof with Charlie. Their most meaningful conversations had been held inside, either after sunset or on rainy days. The roof, however, with its open air and the sense of security it provided had been for their leisure. The shooter had robbed her of that peace at the first pull of his trigger.

Although he showed no signs of it to Anna, Jonathan was devastated.

Rather than insisting, he spent that same night crafting five screens made with the thickest and largest rectangular metal sheets he had. He screwed them to the ledge on the side of the roof that faced the City. This not only protected them from bullets or unwanted eyes, it also shielded them from the wind.

Anna rewarded his effort by agreeing to join him outside. She was nervous at first, but they resumed spending most of their days there.

An intense heat wave engulfed the area the third week of July. The room on the top floor felt like a sauna. They slept out on the roof three nights in a row.

At the peak of this trying stretch, Charlie was boiling hot and so lethargic it worried Jonathan. He held the dog on his lap while Anna sprayed water on his fur with the portable shower. Charlie showed an immediate positive response to the treatment.

When the water stopped flowing abruptly, Anna inspected the showerhead and then turned to Jonathan.

"I think it's, hum, it's broken. There's something here, look."

Jonathan leaned forward, within inches of the nozzle, to examine it. The water exploded out of it again. He wiped his face and looked at Anna in disbelief. She was laughing so hard tears were rolling down her cheeks.

"Well, I guess what's good for the Fur Ball is good for me too," he said.

A violent storm cooled the temperature down a bit and they resumed their previous sleeping arrangements with Anna still crashing on the couch. On their second night back inside after the heat wave, Jonathan suggested she used the other bed they had at their disposal. The idea made her uncomfortable, she said; this was Mr. Dean's bunk.

"Nonsense," Jonathan answered. "If he were here, he'd sleep standing up if it meant giving one of us better rest."

Anna pushed her chair next to the bed and then sat on the mattress. A few simple movements became a significant moment. Sleeping on the couch implied temporary accommodations. Settling down on a bed, her bed now, confirmed their agreement to be roommates. She smiled and looked at Jonathan who nodded in approval.

Jonathan had about fifty movies on his iPad, but they chose to pace themselves and wait for bad weather days or winter to watch them.

He was a fan of older flicks. His collection included *The Odd Couple, The Sunshine Boys* and *It's a Wonderful Life*. He also had the whole *Ghostbusters* series and other comedies like *Groundhog Day* and *The 'Burbs*.

Anna had become addicted to the puzzles and word games Jonathan had downloaded on his tablet a while back. He let her play whenever she wanted. She was so competitive. He liked her reactions when she achieved a level, but even more so the faces she made when she failed at the next one. For his part, he had begun reading his books on survival, which Anna noticed.

"Are you going to, hum, to hunt?"

"Yes, I'll have to. We can't just eat those rations. We have to make them last. And we need variety."

"I don't know if I'll ever be able to, hum, to eat an animal that you kill."

"I get what you mean," Jonathan replied. "But you realize the meat in the rations comes from somewhere, right?"

"Of course," she answered with a sad tone. "But please don't shoot anything like, hum, like a deer."

"Agreed. Just small game, whatever we can consume without waste, I promise."

Throughout the month of August Jonathan and Anna saw an increase in the number of people passing in front of the warehouse, all traveling in the direction of the City. Small planes also flew over their heads. June and July had been quiet, but the flow now was constant.

It then dawned on Jonathan: the remaining population was migrating south. It made sense. Starvation was one thing, but facing it in the bitter cold of winter was another one altogether. People were betting that hitting the road to a more welcoming climate was their best chance at survival. Those passing in front of the warehouse most likely came from the neighboring towns to cross the bridge and scavenge in the City before they reached the highway to follow it to their new destination.

"What about us?" Anna asked.

"We'll be just fine," Jonathan reassured her.

They had plenty of food and would have a bit of heat after he had gone back to the building across the bridge to retrieve the heater he had seen. While he was there, he had also searched the young shooter's bags and put his hands on another item of interest.

This migration was good news to Jonathan. The fewer people there were in the area, the safer the three of them would be.

◆ ◆ ◆

At Anna's suggestion, the Sunday ritual now included spending time by Matthew and Mr. Dean's graves after dinner. Jonathan, already sold on this kind of observance, had loved the idea.

He had worked on a project on the ground floor in the days leading to their first Sunday visit. Anna had asked him what he was doing down there. He had smiled and pointed at her unfinished painting, which was still facing the wall because he had yet to receive authorization to lay his eyes on it.

"You have your secrets, I have mine," Jonathan had told her with a grin.

So that Sunday, after their evening meal, he took Anna in his arms and carried her to her brother as planned. Army blankets covered bulges at the head of Matthew and Mr. Dean's graves. Once Anna was in her chair, Jonathan removed the blankets to reveal two fairly large stones he had found by the river. Each stone was fitted with a metal plaque.

Anna read the inscriptions on them out loud.

"Joseph Dean."

"Matthew Cobb."

Jonathan had made good use of his tools, which included a metal stamping kit, and crafted the tributes. They were all it took to transform a small patch of land with unmarked graves into an oasis of peace guarded by the majestic red oak. Dressing up the scenery — any scenery now — no longer required much. A flower here, a picture frame there; everyday garnishments, often ignored until then, were getting their due attention. These stones and plaques, by old or new measures, made a strong impression.

He took Anna in his arms again and kneeled by Matthew's stone so she could run her fingers over each of the letters in his name.

"After what happened a while ago, I felt the need to focus on good men," he said referring to his storming of the building across the bridge.

"You picked two, hum, two great ones. Thank you, I love it, I, hum, I adore it."

On their second visit, after Jonathan took Anna to the graves he went back inside and reemerged seconds later with Charlie in his arms. The dog panicked and tried to escape from Jonathan's grip as soon as they stepped outside. Only when he was sitting on Anna's lap did he calm down. There was much to see and his head went from side to side the entire hour they were out.

Anna's brother had been buried for a little over two months. The visits to his grave were already less of a reminder of the terrible circumstances of his passing and more of an opportunity to just talk to him, to let him in on all that what was happening inside the warehouse.

Anna called it the Weekly Gazette.

While their proximity to the road forced them to be mindful of the noise they made, whispering was allowed.

And so she did.

◆ ◆ ◆

The temperature remained comfortable at the beginning of September with the exception of one cooler day followed by a cold night.

Jonathan had reassured Anna about their odds of making it through the winter. This temporary chill had alerted him to how they were, in reality, ill prepared for it. He had some warm clothes but she didn't. The stores, even in the unlikely chance they hadn't been pillaged, were a no go. The summer collections had already replaced the spring apparels on most of the racks at the time of the first infections.

Jonathan could only think of one place where he would find everything he and especially Anna could ever need, but he dreaded going there. He took a full day to reflect on it and came to the conclusion he couldn't let Anna face the upcoming cold season with only what she currently had on her back.

He used the last hours of daylight to make sure his bike and the trailer were in good working order. At about two in the morning, he sat at the edge of Anna's bed, gave Charlie a long kiss and handed him to her.

She knew he was about to walk back into his former life, the last segment of which had left him in pieces.

"Are you certain that's the, hum, the only way?"

"No. But I know it's the surest way. And I know I have to do this."

He gave her a hug, went to the roof to survey the area and then exited the building.

He hadn't been on this road since the initial wave of the illness five months earlier. The night was fresh, but not cold. Aside from the sounds of his breathing and pedaling, there were no other noises. The desolation was striking. The windows of most houses were shattered. Their doors were either wide open or hanging from their hinges, warning wannabe scavengers there wasn't a thing left inside to take. Alone and in the dark like that, it should have been a frightening sight.

Jonathan's nervousness, however, had less to do with

the décor along the journey and more with what awaited him at his destination.

He made it to his old apartment complex without seeing a single human being or moving car, not even in the distance. While he was convinced there were still people in the City, it appeared the east outskirts where his building was located had been all but abandoned.

The back entrance wasn't locked. He hid his bike, stood in the lobby to listen for a while and then headed for the stairs. With each flight he climbed, the pounding of his heart grew heavier. By the time he made it to the third floor, he had to put a hand on his chest and apply pressure to try and calm down. His floor, the seventh, seemed to take forever to reach.

At least, the moonlight that peered through the small windows in the stairwells gave him a bit of confidence.

As he had done when he had fled, he opened the door leading to the hallway with great caution and took long and slow steps forward to get to his apartment. There were no signs of activity anywhere. Some of the units he walked by had their doors broken down but the others were just unlocked and ajar, as his was. He went in and made sure he was alone.

On the night he had left Kat behind, he had shut the bedroom door to give her some peace and privacy. It wasn't anymore. She was still on the bed, her arms extended in front of her, the position in which she had frozen when she had been infected.

Jonathan kneeled next to her and looked down, like a teenager would after being caught coming home way past his curfew. He put a hand on the bed by his girlfriend's shoulder and took a deep breath.

"I'm so sorry Kat," he whispered. "I wish I had better words. I swear that's all I've got. I'm so sorry."

There were many tears. His pain was as sharp as the night he had lost her. He hadn't had time to mourn, not unlike Anna who had only been able to do so after her reunion with Matthew at the warehouse.

He wrapped Kat's body in the thin comforter underneath her and carried her to the couch in the living room. He then locked the entrance door so he could move around the apartment without worries.

The food had been taken except for the spices Kat loved so much. Other delicacies like molasses and brown sugar had also been ignored, so he took those.

Their warm clothes were still there as he had suspected. His apartment had most likely been looted in May or June; winter items weren't in high demand then. Anna appeared to be close to Kat's size, but since he had never seen her standing up, this was more of a guessing game. A tight or a loose fit was some sort of a fit after all, so he shoved everything he could in his backpack.

The sun was rising. There was a solid nine hours to kill before he could head out again.

His old place put out an awkward vibe.

He felt was as though he was trespassing on someone else's property. The warehouse, of all places, now felt much more like a home. This was so confined he wondered how two people had ever been able to live there without stepping on each other's toes. He had to open the windows and the patio door leading to the balcony to try and create the illusion of greater space.

He stood at the juncture of the living room and the kitchen, looking for anything that would revive a sense that this had once been his home. The uselessness of most of what he and Kat had owned was mind-boggling. Sure the appliances and the furniture were nice, but not much else was of any importance. Did they really need these bookshelves with all these knickknacks? Or this area rug, or these fake plants, or this incredibly annoying cuckoo clock?

It all seemed petty. Everything had been so easy to get that none of it held any real value. He never had to fight to protect this place or hide in darkness to go get food. No one had ever taken shots at them on the rare occasions they sat out on the balcony either.

Anna's medicine and supplies, which he had carried on his back for miles, now that was priceless. The empty jugs he had found on his scavenging trips, the same ones filled with the precious water keeping them alive, now those were real treasures.

And these warm clothes he was about to bring to Anna? She would cherish them forever.

In the afternoon, Jonathan slept seated on the floor, his back rested against the couch to avoid falling into too deep a daze. When he awoke, it was dark again. He had a late meal and put on his heavy backpack. After he made sure the hallway was clear, he took Kat in his arms and brought her downstairs, into the trailer behind his bike.

This night was cooler than the one before and he did come upon survivors walking in groups, getting close enough to some of them to hear their conversations.

The few terrible things he had been forced to do in the preceding months had rewarded him a generous dose of confidence, but this was not an evening for confrontation.

Whenever he saw people, he hid behind bushes or houses and waited for silence to return so he could resume his trip.

He crossed the bridge well past two in the morning and expected Anna to be sound asleep when he got off his bike at the back of the warehouse.

His mind went blank.

The entrance door was wide open. Its lock had been broken. He walked inside and saw the door at the top of the stairs was also ajar.

Jonathan called out the code in a shaky voice.

"Anna?"

The next few seconds of silence were the longest of his life.

CHAPTER 26

Anna's clock inevitably came to a standstill whenever Jonathan was away. It only resumed ticking at the sound of his voice calling out her name from the ground floor.

Ever since the shooting incident in the summer, she no longer ventured out on the roof by herself for extended periods of time. Inside and by the door, on the platform Jonathan had installed, was far enough. With her weapon on her lap, she could get a bit of fresh air and listen for noises around the building.

On the morning Jonathan had gone back to his old place, Anna had sent Charlie out to his sandbox after their breakfast. She then used her alone time to wash up.

A few weeks prior, she had expressed her desire to help out more and had asked Jonathan to give her something useful to do. Since she was now able to access the roof, Anna was assigned to Water Management duty, a responsibility she took rather seriously. The jugs were kept filled with the water she filtered, the supplies rationed from one rainfall to the other. And she hadn't shied away from reminding Jonathan to keep his consumption in check.

"Save it for, hum, for rainy days," she told him.

So in the afternoon, she did go out on the roof, but solely to get water from the barrels. She then returned to her post by the door to filter it.

The temperature had cooled down by the evening. Anna kept the door open and put on a hoodie, determined to mount guard until Jonathan came back. She hadn't slept since he had left in the middle of the previous night. With Charlie on her lap and a firm hand on her rifle, her intention had been to close her eyes to rest them, nothing more. Exhaustion had decided otherwise.

It was well past midnight when she was awakened by Charlie's first growl, his response to the sound of footsteps by the building. She held the dog tight to try and keep him quiet.

Whoever was out there found the side entrance behind the dumpster and began hitting at the lock.

Anna and Jonathan had practiced defending themselves without ever discussing how to deter people from attempting to enter their home in the first place. Asking the person to leave, she thought, was the logical thing to do at this point.

"This building is occupied, please, hum, please go away."

"Do you have any food?" a man's voice inquired.

Anna took a deep breath.

"No, I don't. No one around here has, hum, has food."

"Well, if there's no food, then why the hell do you live here?" the man mumbled.

After a moment of silence, he hit at the lock again. His effort was more motivated now. The lock broke and

Anna heard the door slide.

"Don't come in, I'm warning you," she said with what she hoped sounded like confidence.

The man ignored her order and soon found the stairs leading to the second floor.

"Look lady all I want is a bit of food and I'll be out of your way, okay?" he said as he slowly went up.

She had the presence of mind not to answer, which would have tipped the man to her exact location in the room. She rolled her chair in the left corner at the very back. This way, she would have more time to decide what to do once he was in sight. Perhaps this would give her a chance to reason with him. The door swung open and he walked in. Anna pointed her weapon at him.

"Stay where you are. Don't, hum, don't you come any closer."

The intruder once again ignored Anna's request and advanced toward her as he spoke.

"Come on, girl. No need to get feisty. I'm not gonna hurt you. I told you, all I want is a bit of food."

He then took two giant steps.

"And by the looks of it, you have plenty of it, you lying bit…"

Anna closed her eyes, held Charlie tight with one hand and fired two rounds of three shots with the other. Four bullets missed their mark, but two hit the stranger in the upper chest.

He collapsed to the floor, by her feet, an arm's length from her.

She went into shock.

Charlie's aggressive barking drew her back to reality. She rolled her chair away from the intruder who was still alive, but injured badly enough to no longer be a threat to her.

Anna didn't have the will to shoot him again, so she decided to wait for Jonathan. For more than an hour, the man moaned, coughed and cried for help. He couldn't get up, but managed to flip on his back. With her weapon aimed at him the entire time, she hoped to God he wouldn't force her to pull the trigger.

When she heard Jonathan's bicycle outside and then his voice call out the code, she was so relieved, it took her a while to get the words out in between sobs.

"I'm up here, Jonathan."

He flew up the stairs and saw Anna in the corner of the room. Her head was down, her arm extended with her index finger pointing to the opposite corner.

Jonathan first went to see the man to check on his condition and then to Anna.

"He wanted our, hum, our food. I didn't have a choice. I swear I didn't, hum, didn't have a choice."

"You did good, Anna. You did the right thing."

"He was about to, hum, to attack me…"

There was no point putting off what came next. Jonathan drew a scream from the man when he grabbed both his arms to drag him downstairs and all the way across the road to the empty field.

He aligned the stranger next to the remains of the thug he had killed on the night he had stormed the building on the other side of the bridge.

When the man saw the body, his breathing accelerated and became heavier. He begged for mercy by raising his hands toward Jonathan who shook his head to show his resentment at what he had tried to do.

He then finished what Anna had started.

With his bike now parked on the ground floor and the door secured behind him, he went up to be with Anna. She was frozen by fear and hadn't moved an inch since she had rolled her chair away from the man after she had shot him.

Jonathan walked to her and took her in his arms for comfort.

"I can't believe I, hum, I did this," she said.

"You only stopped him from hurting you, Anna. He didn't come up here to shake your hand and discuss the weather."

He went to the roof with a bucket to get some water and rags to clean the blood off the floor and erase all physical traces of what had happened. He then took Anna to her bed and crashed on his own afterwards to try and rest.

She wouldn't stop crying.

Jonathan rose and went to her bed again. He lay down behind her, pressed his chest against her back and wrapped his arms around her.

She fell asleep within minutes.

So did he.

◆ ◆ ◆

Anna awoke in stages. She hadn't slept this well since before the accident with Matthew.

At first she thought Jonathan was there, behind her, because she could still feel him holding her. Only when she opened her eyes did she become aware he was no longer inside the building.

The door to the roof was ajar and she could hear the

sound of a shovel hitting the dirt by the river. This was odd because there was no way he would bury the man from the night before, let alone bury him anywhere near the warehouse.

Jonathan had emptied his backpack on the table. A part of her rejoiced; although she was too polite and grateful to say it out loud, the clothes she had been wearing for the last few months didn't do much for her. Some were too tight, others too baggy. These beautiful and neatly folded garments would be welcome additions to a limited wardrobe. Yet, she was reluctant to touch any of them. She knew these were Kat's and felt it would be disrespectful to lay so much as a finger on them without a formal invitation from Jonathan.

Anna went to the roof and looked down by the oak. The scene unfolding there was so poignant she needed both hands to cover her mouth.

Jonathan had laid Kat's body alongside the grave he had just finished digging between the plots occupied by Mr. Dean and Matthew. He was now kneeling by her, his forehead rested against hers with nothing but a thin comforter separating them.

After he got back on his feet, Anna whispered his name. He looked up, smiled as much as he could and took a few steps toward the building.

"Did you sleep well?" he asked her.

She nodded and then moved her eyes to the body.

"Is this Kat?" she asked even if she already knew the answer.

He nodded.

"Are we going to have a burial like, hum, like we did for Matthew?"

"That would be nice. We can do it later. After dinner, if you're up to it," he answered. "You hungry?"

While they ate, Jonathan asked Anna if she liked the clothes he had brought for her. They seemed lovely, she said, but she didn't feel comfortable trying them on just yet. Perhaps later, when Kat was resting in peace by the oak, she would look through them more thoroughly.

In truth, she was most anxious to put on the running shoes. She could no longer stand the sight of her own. They were dirty, worn out and the only leftovers from her long road trip. Putting them on every morning was an ugly reminder of her past struggles.

At noon, Jonathan walked by the river to look for a stone he thought suitable to mark the head of Kat's grave and then worked on a plaque, but needed a pause after he stamped each of the letters in her name. The same had also happened for Mr. Dean and Matthew. This, to him, had become the toughest part of a burial. It ratified the death of someone who had mattered. He could never get used to it. Nor did he ever want to.

Something else was on his mind.

While he had worked on Kat's grave in the morning, and then on her tribute in the afternoon, he had also thought about how easy it had been to end the life of Anna's attacker. The man had deserved his fate, just like all the others he had fought had deserved theirs. Killing a human being, however, wasn't supposed to feel this casual. It wasn't supposed to be guilt free. Jonathan decided this lack of a burden on his conscience would eventually warrant some sort of reflection.

Just because most of humanity had vanished, it didn't mean his had to follow course.

After dinner, he carried Anna to the oak. She gasped again when she saw the plaque Jonathan had made.

Ekaterina "Kat" Laslow, it read.

Anna had flipped through the pictures and videos on Jonathan's iPad during his numerous absences, so she had seen how beautiful Kat was. Her delightful personality jumped right out of the screen. She had dared to imagine that, had Kat escaped the effects of the virus, they could have become the best of friends. Instead, she now sat at the foot of her grave, her eyes locked on a broken Jonathan.

They followed the same steps they had for Matthew. When she noticed Jonathan couldn't cope with the moment, Anna grabbed a handful of dirt.

"I have looked at your pictures so, hum, so often, I feel like I have known you for a long time. I don't. Not really. But I feel like, hum, like I do. If you were with Jonathan, then you must have been an, hum, an amazing human being. Because he is."

"You would be so proud of him," she added, chocking up as she let the dirt fall on Kat's feet.

Jonathan walked to Anna, put his left hand on the side of her face and rested his cheek on top of her head. On the roof, Charlie had begun barking for attention at the sound of Anna's voice. Jonathan took her upstairs so she could calm him down and he returned to the oak to bury Kat.

He stood by the grave until the sun was just about to set and offered a silent goodbye to his girlfriend. Anna watched him the entire time from the roof, with Charlie on her lap. Before Jonathan went back inside, he looked up at her.

"So much pain. So much death. And by such a beautiful tree," he said.

He was grieving. Anna understood it, so she nodded and gave him a pass. Deep down, however, she was offended by that statement. Her brother was buried there. It was a magnificent, peaceful setting. The essence of those resting there enriched the soil that nourished the oak at its roots.

And so their loved ones lived on through it.

This, to her, was now sacred land.

The evening was not as grand an affair as it had been following Matthew's burial. They were both still reeling from the events of the night before and Anna kept looking and listening outside, as if she was constantly hearing something suspicious.

As for Jonathan, he had no energy left. The return trip to his old place had taken a physical and emotional toll on him. But along with exhaustion, he felt an intense sense of relief as a result of this day.

Kat was not alone anymore.

At long last, he could stop blaming himself for leaving her behind.

CHAPTER 27

The morning was crisp, typical of the early hours of a mid-October day. The temperature had taken a steep dive overnight. With any luck, it would begin to climb back up with the rising sun.

This had always been Jonathan's favorite month of the year. He loved everything about it: its calm, its colors, its cooler air easily defeated by a thin extra layer of clothing, not to mention its fragrances.

October had its very own bouquet of aromas.

As a child, on weekends, the comforting smell of the baked beans or the chicken potpies his mom prepared filled the entire house. Outside, it was as though the earth was exhaling one last giant time before its long nap through winter.

Even now, despite his age and the critical obligations of his new life, Jonathan couldn't resist sliding his fingertips on the brown aluminum that protected the ledge around the roof to write Anna's and Charlie's names in the thick and cold morning dew.

He had awakened a few times the night before to check on the building and his two companions. In the second of those rounds he had covered Anna's sleeping bag with an army blanket in fear she would get cold. He was cautious not to wake her up, but she had nonetheless opened her eyes and thanked him before closing them again.

At first light, he had gone to the roof, sat on the ledge and was now waiting for Charlie to relieve himself. His business was interrupted. The dog raised his two front paws on the low brick wall and growled. Jonathan held his weapon up, believing he had sounded the alarm on someone walking by, but Charlie was staring at the river. Jonathan did the same just in time to catch a glimpse of the shadows of ducks flying in formation a few inches above the water.

He had warned Anna that if this were to ever happen, he would have to leave in a hurry to keep on their tail.

She understood the need to complement the army rations with other types of food and, like Jonathan, she longed for a home-cooked meal. The idea of killing defenseless animals, however, gave her the chills. They had reached an agreement: only small game that could be eaten in one or two servings.

"Please don't shoot, hum, shoot a deer," she begged of him again and again.

Jonathan came from a town where hunting was as natural as breathing, walking or screaming at the TV during the Super Bowl.

His father was somewhat into it, but his mother's side of the family counted several enthusiasts.

"If you want your car fixed, ask your dad. But if you want to eat, talk to your uncle Giles," she had once said.

He had gone duck hunting with his uncle as a young teenager and had gotten lucky on occasion, returning home with trophies held with pride. The firearms they had used then were different than the weapons and ammunition he had found in the army trucks. Jonathan would have to make do with what he had now, which was far from ideal for shooting birds.

He walked alongside the river for an hour before he heard the ducks quacking from hundreds of feet away. He slowed his pace to be quiet and when he got within reasonable distance, he spotted a patch of sand by the water where he could lie down and keep an eye on them. They were floating near the steep bank on his side of the river but they were too far apart and the current was pushing them downstream. He had to reposition himself every minute or so, but his patience was eventually rewarded.

When the ducks moved closer to the ground, and to one another, Jonathan peppered them with bullets. The ones that had been spared flew away as he ran to retrieve the two he had hit. Uncle Giles's teachings resurfaced. He sat behind bushes to skin the ducks, keeping the meat attached to the breastplates and discarding the rest in the water.

On his way back home, he was thinking about the meal he would prepare Anna. His attempt to reverse engineer his mother's baked beans recipe was cut short by a commotion and frantic voices coming from the road, not too far from where he was.

He crawled from the banks of the river get a look. It was a group of seven people heading toward the City and probably migrating south like so many had done before them. The cause of their distress quickly became obvious; three of them had just frozen. The others were reacting to the shock of their sudden losses.

The virus had struck again.

Jonathan went back down to the river and ran to the warehouse. Inside, he stood at the bottom of the stairs and tried to call out to Anna but he was so winded, no sound came out of his throat. At this point, he couldn't have cared less about their code and he hurried up. Anna was in bed, facing away from him. Jonathan kneeled behind her and whispered her name while he put a hand on her shoulder.

She jumped, startled by the touch of his cold fingers. He fell back on his butt, let out a loud sigh of relief and helped Anna get in her chair. He tossed her a hoodie and instructed her to go to the roof.

While his behavior was troubling, she didn't raise any objections. They both knew by then that if one asked the other to do something there was a valid reason. Time was always of the essence; none of it was to be wasted in doubts or arguments.

Jonathan went outside the building, stood halfway between the warehouse and the graves and waited for Anna to appear.

"I just saw people get infected, Anna. I ran back here as fast as I could because we may not be safe."

Anna brought her hands to her mouth, in part because of the seriousness of what she had just heard, but also because she now understood why Jonathan had chosen not to stay upstairs with her; if the virus got him, he didn't want her to be trapped there with his body.

"It may have passed already and spared us, but if it's

coming toward us… You remember where the food is stacked, right? And the ammunition too?"

"Oh my god please don't, hum, don't do this. We're going to be fine."

"We don't know that, Anna. We have to accept it. You see, it occurred to me on my way back: maybe it's been happening all along. There could have been many more infections before today and we just don't know about them. It may happen to us, we can't ignore that."

Anna looked down while she tried to digest it all. Both remained at their position, waiting, but each also praying the other wouldn't be taken in this wave. Jonathan sought to reassure Anna by lightening the mood.

"I was able to get two ducks earlier. When it's safe, I'll come up and make us a meal you're not about to forget. Wild duck on baked beans."

She smiled. Not a smile so large it would be inappropriate at that moment, but it was enough to reward his thoughtfulness.

"I don't know if I can eat, hum, eat wild duck."

"You'll see. It's not going to be as good as what my mom made, but I'm feeling quite confident."

As Jonathan finished his sentence, a gust of wind made him fear the virus might be swept their way. He braced for it.

Nothing happened.

Charlie raised himself up and put his front paws on the ledge so he too could see Jonathan.

"You and Charlie, you make my life so beautiful. I can't even begin to imagine what it would be like without the two of you. Everything I do, Anna, everything I plan and everything I wish for, has the two of you right in the center of it."

"Don't do this, please," she begged of him.

"It's okay. This isn't goodbye, far from it. Pretty soon I'll be up there with you guys. It's just that we never say these things. What we've been through so far has been so intense we act as though it's all implied. I need to say it out loud at least once. How much time is there to do it, really?"

Jonathan's words forced Anna to acknowledge they were indeed living in a world where time might constantly be running out on them. He had a valid point. How much of it was there?

"When you first brought me here, I wasn't sure if, hum, if I wanted to stay with you. But now, there's nowhere else I, hum, I want to be."

"I'm glad you feel that way. Everything is going to be fine. I'm here now. Wink, wink," he said drawing another smile from Anna.

"That's so, hum, so corny," she said with a grin.

"What? Corny?" he said before turning his attention to Charlie.

"What about you Fur Ball, got something to say?"

Charlie barked twice as a response. Anna picked him up and sat him on her lap to keep him quiet. He was getting so big, so fast, there were but a few days left of her being able to do this.

Jonathan signaled to be silent and then rested his back against the wall of the warehouse to hide. The group of people he had seen on the road earlier, the same one that had alerted him to this latest wave, was now walking by the building.

While only four of them remained, he was dismayed at the level of noise they were making. The rattling of what they carried in their backpacks alone announced their presence, but they also spoke loudly and dragged their feet on the pavement. How could they not have learned by then that the number one rule of survival was invisibility? After they crossed the bridge, Jonathan kept an ear out because he suspected there would be trouble for them. He heard nothing.

He let two hours pass before he deemed it safe to re-enter the warehouse and go upstairs. He gave Anna a long hug. They had cheated death again, but they had been served with a powerful reminder. The last month had been quiet, and so both had forgotten what had brought their paths to meet in the first place. Danger didn't come solely from people. It was also lurking in the air they had no other choice but to breathe.

Jonathan began working on the meal he had promised Anna, but warned her it wouldn't be ready until the next morning. The beans had to soak all day and the duck breasts would have to simmer on top of them overnight.

Mr. Dean, in his usual wisdom, had included a family size slow cooker in what he had brought from his home. Jonathan had no clue how much power it would draw from the solar system's batteries. The preparation of his meal would serve as a test to see how much strain he could put on them. Much colder days were just weeks away and he needed to know how long it took before the power was depleted.

Anna awoke twice during the night. And twice she got in her chair, went to the cooker and lifted the lid to smell the beans.

On her way back to her bed, she stopped to check on her roommates who were sound asleep together.

The second time around, she stole the dog and took him to her bunk.

In the morning, Jonathan walked out on the roof with Charlie. He was treated to quite a sight; the trees by the river, including the oak by the graves, had gone through quite a transformation in the last day.

Back inside, he checked on the batteries. They were still over three-quarters full, but he wondered if this would be enough to get them through the winter. The cold, mixed with less sunlight, could make it too close a call for his liking.

He was curious about how his meal had turned out. He plunged a spoon inside the cooker and brought it to his mouth. His beans weren't anywhere close to the feast his mother used to make, but this simpler recipe worked and the duck was so tender it fell apart when he touched it.

He woke Anna up to give her a taste as well. She was hesitant, but after this one spoonful she asked if it would be appropriate to have a full bowl of it for breakfast.

"That's the thing with our lives now; we can break these old rules and not feel one tiny bit guilty about it!" Jonathan answered.

Before they ate, he invited Anna to follow him to the roof. The vista took her breath away; the tips of most of the leaves on the oak, green from top to bottom the previous morning, had been painted a bright shade of red in less than a day.

They had their first home-cooked meal outside while they marveled at the tree. Anna tried to thank Jonathan for the food and comment on the view, but she couldn't stop eating. One bite followed the other, at the last of which she declared herself full.

This success was all the motivation Jonathan needed to step up the frequency of his scavenging trips, which he also used to hunt.

There were a few days of rain left before December and he wanted to keep as much of the water as he could. Winters had been deprived of heavy snowfalls in recent years and he feared they would run out of water at some point. Anna had stored close to one hundred gallons of it, but there was no way of telling if or when they would have the chance to replenish their supplies.

He walked the downtown area in the City, entering office buildings in search of empty jugs from water dispensers. As always, discretion was his main defense, though with most survivors gone to the south, he wasn't expecting many encounters. Still, he couldn't wrap his mind around how deserted the core of the City was. The streets appeared wider, the buildings bigger, in the absence of a crowd. This lack of activity was beyond strange.

Fewer people meant he was able to venture in neighborhoods he hadn't dared visit before. He got lucky on most of his excursions and found more containers, including some of the larger jugs he wanted. Now all they needed was more rain.

Some mornings Jonathan would show up at the warehouse with canned food and treats like bags of potato chips or packaged cookies.

Other mornings, and this was happening more and more, he would tell Anna he was going to the roof and she shouldn't follow him. This warned her there was a dead animal in his backpack and he was about to skin it.

Anna was too sensitive for this part and he respected

she didn't want to witness the preparation. Early on, she had gotten curious and questioned Jonathan as to what he had in his bag. When he informed her it was a rabbit, she had insisted on seeing it. It was so beautiful, and its fur so soft when she ran her fingers through it, she had categorically refused to eat any of it.

While Jonathan was out scavenging at night, Anna kept herself awake by painting at the glow of the small lamp. She had resumed working on her project a month after the sniper had brought to it a halt.

Her physical limitations, mixed with the low light, slowed her progress. This reduced pace didn't bother her, though. In fact, she welcomed it.

She wanted the piece to be perfect.

And she knew exactly when she would finally let Jonathan see it.

CHAPTER 28

The first three weeks of November had been unseasonably warm. The sun had remained hidden behind clouds so dark and thick, however, that Jonathan and Anna wondered if perhaps it hadn't disappeared from their lives altogether.

No one walked by the warehouse anymore. The migration south seemed over, so whoever was left would have to try and make it through the winter where they were.

Acting on his wavering confidence on the solar system's capacity, Jonathan took advantage of the desertion and the comfortable temperature to pile up a bit of wood on the main floor.

Some of the houses near the City had logs stacked against their sidewalls or in their backyards. He used the trailer attached to his bike to carry what he could back across the bridge. Anna and him had come to the decision to wait as late as possible in the winter to fire up the stove. Even then, they would only do so at night to avoid detection and preserve the wood.

Charlie was six months old. He had never been anywhere farther than the graves by the oak during the Sunday visits. He was now mature and obedient enough to be put on a leash. Jonathan had begun training him for an upcoming short walk. They practiced a few commands in the week ahead of the big day and, while Charlie was confused at first, he got the hang of it.

Anna was far from excited about this milestone. Jonathan was often out scavenging and thanks to Charlie she had never really been alone at the warehouse. Over time, he had become much more than just a presence; he was her companion, her confidant. The daily grooming sessions to which she subjected him were in reality excuses for long monologues filled with confessions of hopes and worries.

Some of those she also shared with Jonathan. Most, however, were meant solely for Charlie.

So when the moment arrived, she went to the roof to watch her two roommates leave at sunrise. Even if she knew they would remain within a few hundred yards from her, she was a nervous wreck and couldn't contain her tears after she lost sight of them.

Aware that Anna would welcome them back with a barrage of questions, Jonathan had brought his iPad to document their dog's very first escapade.

Charlie stopped every ten feet or so and looked up at Jonathan, uncertain, as if to ask permission to keep on exploring.

They soon reached an empty field.

Jonathan unhooked the leash, stood back and held the tablet in front of him to immortalize the instant Charlie would finally run free of any restraint. The dog sat down, cried and trembled. While Jonathan kept filming, he talked to him in the hopes the sound of his voice would carry enough comfort to reassure him. It didn't work, so he ran in circles around Charlie who soon forgot his fear and eagerly chased him.

They returned to the warehouse an hour later, both out of breath, Charlie holding his leash in his mouth. Anna, though cold and shivering, had remained on the roof to wait for them.

While they ate breakfast, Jonathan showed her the footage of Charlie's new adventures.

She watched and analyzed the short clips for hours.

◆ ◆ ◆

December brought much colder weather. Anna declared a strict rationing of the water. It hadn't rained in some time and it was safe to assume it wouldn't in the foreseeable future.

The water from the river was off limits; with scores of manufactures built along its shores, they could only guess at what had been dumped in there before and after the virus had struck. This was also where Jonathan emptied the bucket in which they both relieved themselves. Other survivors upstream likely did the same. As he put it, even boiling that sewage for hours wouldn't convince him to drink it. Perhaps he would reconsider in a few years.

The power situation was under control. The days were cold but the sun had returned and the system's batteries were responding well.

Jonathan still went out two or three times a week to hide in the field across the road and hunt while Anna guarded the fort with Charlie who was not invited on these outings because they sometimes extended until sundown. They made the most of the cold temperatures and stored his catches in a camping cooler they kept outside, by the door, on the roof.

On a gray and windy afternoon, Jonathan asked Anna if she wouldn't mind assisting him on a home improvement project. He teased her by not telling her what it was they were assembling.

Anna played along. She enjoyed watching him work, thinking up his plans and acting upon them. His ability to build pretty much anything from scratch, with nothing but the few tools he had and his naked eye, was profoundly reassuring. He was focused and the precision in his execution was jaw dropping. These traits explained so much about him; how he could locate useful things, how he had turned a dusty warehouse into a real home and how he was able to put so much food on the table.

For his mystery project, they transformed thick metal sheets into a box with a front door. They then fitted four tubes underneath to keep it up and leveled. A few hours of work later, Jonathan announced it was ready. Anna, still unable to figure out what it was, looked at him and shrugged.

He carried the apparatus and positioned it on top of the stove with the box hovering three inches above it.

Anna stared at it for a moment before she clued in.

"We have an oven," she proclaimed while clapping.

◆ ◆ ◆

A startled Anna awoke to the sound of Bob Seger's *Little Drummer Boy* playing in the room.

She called out Jonathan's name.

"Rise up and look," he said.

The two had never discussed their respective Holiday traditions, but Jonathan saw no valid reason why they shouldn't make Christmas a day to remember. Anna laughed when she noticed two presents under a tiny tree Jonathan had set on the table. She put on warm clothes and he aimed the heater toward the middle of the room.

"Welcome to our first Christmas together," he proclaimed. "Special breakfast, entertainment and a few surprises await!"

The breakfast wasn't really that special; just the hot cereal they liked so much. It was the atmosphere that was different. They ate while watching *Scrooged*, one of his favorite movies for this time of the year.

"I love Christmas," he told Anna. "Once a year, I get to hear Bill Murray say the words *the bitch hit me with a toaster.*"

After the credits, Jonathan handed Anna her present. It had been wrapped by a man and after civilization had ended. He apologized many times over for how terrible it looked. She couldn't have cared less. The word *surprise* had taken on a whole new meaning since last April. It was refreshing to know for certain that what she now held in her hands would be a pleasant one.

She removed the paper and discovered it, still sealed in its original packaging.

"Oh my goodness! It's my, hum, my very own iPad!" Anna screamed. "Where did you get, hum, get this?"

"During one of my scavenging hunts," he answered.

Jonathan hated lying to Anna, but he didn't want to ruin the moment by telling her it belonged to the sniper he had killed in the building across the bridge. He had found the tablet among the young man's personal effects on the day he had gone back to retrieve the heater.

"And since it's Christmas for everybody, this one's for Charlie," he said as he gave the second present to Anna.

Upon hearing his name, Charlie rushed to stand by the table. Anna unwrapped his gift with the same eagerness she had shown for her own. She looked at Jonathan and let out a loud burst of laughter. Charlie had never received a treat like this before. There were only a limited number of these left at the pet store, so Jonathan wanted to wait until he was a bit bigger to give it to him.

"Are you ready, Charlie? It's a, hum, a giant bone you lucky dog!"

Anna ripped the bone out of the packaging. After a few whiffs, Charlie clenched his jaw around it, ran to his bed and began chewing away.

"Wait here," Anna told Jonathan.

She rolled her chair by her bunk, where she kept her unused canvasses, reached behind those and retrieved the painting on which she had been working for so long.

"I finished it last month and I, hum, I saved it for today. Merry Christmas, Jonathan," she said before handing it to him.

When he realized what he was looking at, Jonathan covered his mouth and sobbed.

The painting was a depiction of a rear view of Anna, Charlie and him by the river, at the foot of their oak turned bright red. Anna was in her chair, looking up at Jonathan who was gazing back at her. Each had a hand on Charlie, sitting between them.

The piece was titled *"Life by the Red Oak."*

It was her response to his statement, after he had buried Kat, that there was *so much death by such a beautiful tree.*

The rendering was impressive, but beyond the message and the accuracy of the re-creation itself, Jonathan was moved to tears by the fact that she had chosen their little unit as the subject of what he knew to be her very first painting since her accident. He was also hearing her message loud and clear; there was indeed life by the Red Oak. He faced away from Anna to hide his reaction, but she got closer and rubbed his shoulder to give him comfort.

He quickly composed himself and they returned to their joyful selves to celebrate the rest of the day.

Jonathan synched Anna's new iPad on his laptop in the afternoon. She flipped through the pictures of the three of them she had captured since they had met. He asked if she was happy with her present.

"Of course!" She answered. "I can look at our, hum, our pictures whenever I want. We make such, hum, such a cute family," Anna declared as she held her iPad up to show the screen to Jonathan.

"It's nice that you think of us in that way. I like that."

"Family is the True North of, hum, of your life. Know where it is and you'll never, hum, never lose your way," she replied.

At the end of her sentence, she frowned and turned to look intensely at the closed door leading to the roof.

"What's wrong, Anna?" Jonathan asked.

"North," she said. "I wonder where, hum, where North is now," she added before pressing her index finger against her lips.

"North? It's always been there," Jonathan said as he pointed his hand in the right direction.

Anna smiled. "Forget it," she said to Jonathan who looked at her, puzzled.

They spent the evening by the tiny tree on the table while they each recounted their happiest holiday memories from their childhood. Anna had to think hard and dig deep to find hers.

Good thing the Christmas spirit filled the inside of the warehouse, because the scenery outside wasn't even close to looking the part. The sky throughout the day had been as dark as it had ever been. The ground was frozen, but the grass was still visible because it hadn't snowed yet.

And then it did.

◆ ◆ ◆

Jonathan sensed a change in the weather after Christmas. It was cold but damp. He warned Anna the first snowfall of the season might be imminent.

He had never been so right.

Strong winds crashing against the side of the warehouse that faced toward the City woke them up late in the night before New Year's Eve. Jonathan opened the door; a thick layer of snow covered the roof. About two feet of it had fallen, or enough to hide the bottom half of the solar panels.

He got dressed and went to clear them, harvesting some of the snow in a large pot, which he brought back to Anna so she could melt it down to water and then filter it. He repeated these steps every two hours until exhaustion stopped him late in the afternoon. The storm was gaining in intensity by the minute. It seemed by the time he was done digging a panel out, the previous one had been buried again.

On top of tending to the water, Anna had to go up and down the ramp to let Jonathan back inside. She was exhausted and her hands were freezing and hurting.

Since the system's batteries were taking a pounding, and given the situation, they both agreed it would be safe to fire up the stove. No one could ever follow the smoke to its origin, not with this much snow falling and not with these strong winds. With more water stored and a fire roaring, they paused for dinner. They were famished and beat, although an evening toasty warm by the stove with Charlie sound asleep on his bed next to it was quite enjoyable.

They were again awakened in the night, this time by a loud impact noise coming from the roof. Jonathan went to see what had happened. The wind, now blowing snow with extreme fury, had dislodged one of the solar panels. It had hit the ledge then flown away.

He put his gear back on and ran downstairs with a flashlight to try and retrieve it.

The snow was so dense, he couldn't see beyond a foot in front of him and he had to cover his mouth to be able to breathe. He found the panel by the graves and hurried back to the top floor. The solar system was of the utmost importance to their survival. He couldn't risk losing more parts of it to the storm.

"Remind me to go back down and lock the entrance later," he told Anna with great urgency in his voice. "I have to secure the other panels. I may need you."

Jonathan got the tools he and Mr. Dean had used to install the system in the spring. As he headed out on the roof, he did what he had always done to hold the door open, which was to shimmy a piece of wood under the middle hinges. Anna followed him as far as she could. The snow stopped her midway down the ramp. She aimed the flashlight at Jonathan, who had walked to the far end of the building. It did little to help, but at least she could see his shadow.

During a brutal gust of wind, Anna turned around at the sound of a cracking noise behind her. The piece of wood holding the door open had split in half under pressure and fallen off.

The door, now loose, swung and slammed shut.

They were both trapped outside.

The loud, persistent noises from the storm drowned Anna's frantic calls to Jonathan who couldn't hear her at first. When he did, he stood and took a few steps forward. One of the thick metal sheets he had installed in the summer to help Anna feel safe out on the roof detached and flew straight at him. It hit him flat on the shoulder at such a velocity it shoved him four feet to his left.

Jonathan fell, hit his head on the ledge and was knocked unconscious.

"Jonathan," Anna screamed. She jumped out of her chair then crawled to him in the snow. She yelled his name and shook him, but he wouldn't wake up. She dragged his body across the width of the roof and positioned him against the ledge, below the remaining sheets of metal. They were now somewhat protected from the wind and if another of those sheets ever came loose, it would fly over their heads.

Anna knew they wouldn't survive out there very long. The bitter cold would kill them within an hour at the most. She remembered Jonathan had told her he had left the main entrance door unlocked after he had returned upstairs holding the missing solar panel.

There was only one way she'd ever be able to get back inside. And it had to be done now.

She grabbed the ledge with both hands and looked down. The wind had carried a lot of snow against that side of the building. She searched for a spot where it had piled up the thickest and found it at the front corner. She fired up the flashlight and let it fall to get a sense of how long it took to reach the ground.

She climbed on the ledge and lay on it, face down.

Without the slightest of hesitation, she rolled and threw herself off the roof.

CHAPTER 29

Jonathan smiled. It was just what he did. It was embedded in his DNA, like he had brown hair and blue eyes. He smiled while he spoke to her, when he brought her food or watched her play with Charlie. The night they had buried Matthew, he had listened to her speak about her brother for hours. His smile then had been as wide and as genuine as the one he had two weeks later the morning he had surprised her with strawberries. The mood or the moment mattered little to him; he always managed to slide in a grin.

Every single image that had flashed in Anna's head after she had thrown herself off the roof had been of Jonathan looking at her, a large smile on his face.

She wasn't injured and the snow had somewhat softened her landing. The impact was still violent enough to knock the wind out of her. She opened her eyes and, after a few painful attempts, took a deep breath.

She had ended her fall on her back as she had hoped, but after a near twenty-foot drop from the ledge her body had dug quite a hole underneath her. Trying to get out of that of that position without the use of her legs made her feel like a turtle flipped on its shell. She cleared the snow on her left side then rolled before she began to crawl.

The spot she had picked to hit the ground was indeed the best one. Now, in order to reach the entrance, she had to cover the entire width of the warehouse, make a turn then keep going alongside the building for most of its length.

Anna struggled to pull herself forward in fresh and loose snow. She made it to the entrance in twenty minutes and she was about to lock the door behind her, but thought better of it. She still had to go back out on the roof to rescue Jonathan. What if something went wrong and she was forced to jump again?

Charlie greeted her upstairs with long licks in the face. He then ran to the door leading to the roof and barked. Anna opened it and used a hammer and a wrench to block it this time. Charlie hopped down the ramp, found Jonathan and continued barking until Anna arrived.

He was almost entirely buried in snow and in the same position Anna had left him. She grabbed him from under his arms and pulled him toward the door, half a foot at a time. It was another twenty minutes before they were both safely back inside. She dragged Jonathan near the stove, threw a couple of logs in it and removed his frozen coat.

The toque and hood he had been wearing weren't as good as a helmet, but it was still better than a clean impact with the ledge. Anna confirmed he was breathing, covered him with his sleeping bag and, with great care, raised his head on a pillow.

After her trip down the stairs to go lock the entrance and then up again, she had no energy left to go retrieve her chair, still outside. She took her own sleeping bag from her bed and laid it next to Jonathan. Charlie settled between the two, his chin rested on Jonathan's chest.

Anna was mortified.

"Don't you dare leave me," she told him out loud.

In the morning, following a night spent putting cold compresses on Jonathan's forehead and tending to the fire, she went out to the roof to retrieve her wheelchair. The wind had decreased, but it was still snowing quite heavily. Her chair, which she had pushed off the ramp to make way for Jonathan and her, was buried up to the middle of its backrest. After much effort, she was able to clear it and bring it inside.

Charlie refused at first to go outside to do his business. The impatience in Anna's tone finally did the trick and he agreed to face the elements. While she waited for him, she dug out the cooler that contained the meat and picked two partridge breasts, which she laid to thaw while the beans soaked. This wouldn't be for her; she wanted Jonathan to have a large meal upon waking up. Until then, she would stick to the rations.

She stayed warm by the stove, keeping a close eye on her patient. Every once in a while he moved an arm or a leg, but showed no response to the sound of her voice when she called out his name.

Before the sun went down, Anna opened the door to look outside. It had finally stopped snowing. The solar panels and the water system had disappeared under what she estimated to be five feet of snow.

It then hit her.

Had Jonathan not taken her in as his roommate after he had saved her from the two thugs on the day they had met, she would be dead at this point. If by some miracle she had survived the summer, the fall and the bitter cold of the last four weeks on her own, this storm would have been the final nail in her coffin. Every cell in her body was screaming at him to wake up at once so she could remind him of that.

Anna did her best to replicate the baked beans recipe Jonathan had prepared in front of her a few times already. She mixed the ingredients in the pot from the slow cooker, which she then placed inside their handmade oven above the stove.

She checked on Jonathan and the food once an hour during the night. The fourth time she awoke, she was about to throw a log in the fire when she was startled and dropped it on the floor instead.

"Anna," Jonathan whispered in a weak voice.

She looked at him, unsure if he had regained consciousness at long last or if he was being delirious.

"Everything is going to be fine. I'm here now. Wink, wink."

His words lacked their usual assurance, they were still very corny and he had never finished that sentence without a smile, but it was good enough for her.

He was back.

◆ ◆ ◆

In the days after Jonathan regained consciousness, Anna kept a tight schedule. She was up at dawn to prepare his breakfast, which she fed to him because he was too weak to raise his arms. She also tended to Charlie before eating her share. Then it was off to the roof to collect snow.

At first, after she had filled her bucket, she was forced to climb back up on the ramp in reverse. The process was arduous, but this was crystal clear snow and wasting it was not an option. Once she made it farther onto the roof, she was able to make a path wide enough to turn around and go back inside the right way. Three days into this routine, Jonathan told her she needed to put the water aside and focus on digging out the solar panels. The system's batteries were dead and he worried about leaving them in that state for a prolonged period.

He was frustrated. He only left his bed to go to the bathroom. Even then, when he rose, he felt nauseous and the pounding in his brain was excruciating. Anna knew too well how debilitating a head injury could be. She had experienced the same ordeal upon emerging from her coma.

"Time is the only, hum, only remedy in a case like this," she warned him.

"I'll be good as new in a few days," he answered with what he thought sounded like confidence. Anna wasn't buying it.

"Oh, Jonathan, it will be, hum, be longer than that."

She then went for the kill and used his own words against him.

"I'm giving you a two-week vacation. You'll have nothing to, hum, to do, and nothing to worry about."

He had no recollection of being hit by the panel.

The last thing he remembered was realizing they were trapped on the roof.

Anna told him how she had managed to re-enter the warehouse. Jonathan didn't know how to process that information. On the one hand, her actions were nothing short of heroic. But on the other, what she had done was pure insanity. He held her hand, kissed it and promised her he would come up with a plan to make sure she would never have to take such a risk again.

"Good. Because I'm not throwing myself off the, hum, the damn roof in the middle of July!"

Ten days into his recovery, he asked Anna for help getting dressed so he could go out for some fresh air and see how much snow there was. She agreed, though it would have to wait until dusk. The sky was free of clouds and the sun's reflection on the snow would be too painful for him.

Just before dinner, a frail Jonathan slowly made his way outside. The temperature had dropped after the storm and none of the snow had melted. He couldn't believe how deep under the white stuff they had been buried.

He went to the corner of the roof where Anna had jumped and looked down. He then walked along the ledge, following the trail she had crawled to save his life. This was the real reason he wanted to go out. He had been dying to see for himself ever since Anna had told him what she had done. Had it not been for the fear of adding to his discomfort, he would have shaken his head.

The air was crisp. The snow, the cold and the absence of pollutants gave it a smell that reminded Jonathan of the inside of a snow fort he had built as a child during a visit with distant family members in Canada.

"We should come back out again tonight, you know, to look at the stars," he said.

"Sure," she answered. "But for now, let's, hum, let's eat."

Despite feeling miserable since he had awakened, Jonathan was able to appreciate and acknowledge Anna's dedication to his care. The food she prepared, in particular, was quite good. Her baked beans tasted so much better than his.

She assured him she was just trying to follow his recipe. Perhaps it was because they had simmered in their oven instead of the slow cooker.

"Maybe. It's also possible I've outlived my usefulness," he joked.

"Don't worry, we'll find something for you to, hum, to do around here."

"What about you, Fur Ball? Still need me for anything?" Jonathan said to his dog, lying on his bed.

Charlie raised his head, his teddy bear pinched between his teeth, and looked up at Jonathan wondering where on earth he had found the gall to interrupt playtime like this. Anna laughed so hard she almost choked to death.

It was an additional week before Jonathan could return to a normal schedule and one more for the headaches to subside. That last week, a cold front blanketed the area. Jonathan estimated the temperatures to be around minus twenty-five. Some days, Anna refused to come out of her sleeping bag in which she was wearing her full winter gear.

The solar system's batteries were working fine, though the heater was struggling to warm up the room and drained them fast. Despite their hardship, Jonathan was sticking to the rule of using the stove at night only to avoid detection. They hadn't reached the end of January yet and already their supply of wood was at critical level.

As soon as he felt up to it, he reinstalled the solar panel that had detached during the storm and then headed out of the building to find some wood. The thick snow made it difficult to go far. It also left traces leading back to them. Still, he managed to score enough logs to keep the second floor at a survivable temperature during the crisis.

More would have to be done to get through the next two or three months. He fought the temptation of taking down some of the trees around their building. These worked as camouflage and provided some much-needed shade during the summer. He was outside every day with an axe and a saw. The snowshoes and the sled he crafted with sheets of metal helped him stack up some reserves. Even then, they had to make sacrifices to make them last.

On a positive note, this also meant he was out hunting more often. The camping cooler on the roof was overflowing with meat, which Anna made sure to inventory and prepare for the both of them, an arrangement that made Jonathan uncomfortable. He felt her responsibilities with the water were plenty, but Anna insisted she didn't mind. Plus, whenever he got back inside he was so tired he usually collapsed in the big chair and dozed off. Depending on the hour, Anna would either let him sleep or wake him up with a steaming bowl of food.

A second major snowstorm raged in the middle of February. The winds weren't as strong as they had been six weeks earlier, but heavy snow fell for four full days. Jonathan made sure the solar panels remained clear, shoveling the roof once an hour during the day. Anna stayed inside by the door this time around.

This episode turned out to be a test of Jonathan's physical and emotional limits. Going out in the cold to cut wood and hunt for food was trying enough, now this blizzard would make it all but impossible to walk anywhere. The three of them were going to be trapped inside a cold warehouse for a while.

This lack of preparedness was a terrible failure. His failure, he thought. Anna, seeing his mood inch toward desperation as the storm progressed, did all she could to raise his spirits each time he came back inside from the roof to warm up.

On the third morning, after a two-hour shift clearing the accumulation of the night before, he finally broke down.

Before he knocked to signal Anna to let him in he fell to his knees by the door and sobbed. Not even when he had witnessed the worst of what humanity had to offer or when they had been under attack had he ever felt this hopeless. For the first time since the start of this mess there was a doubt in his mind on their odds of making it.

The only thought with the power to pull him back up on his feet was that of Anna. He reminded himself of what she had endured before and after they had met. She had lost so much and yet, her sheer will to live had pushed her to travel seventy miles on her own in a damaged wheelchair. She had had the courage to throw herself into nothingness in the middle of a snowstorm. And her resilience alone had pulled her forward as she had crawled in the snow to save both their lives.

So surely he could find it in him to face the challenges ahead.

He rose, wiped the tears off his face and knocked on the door.

CHAPTER 30

The early days of spring were a thing of beauty. A thick layer of snow sill covered the ground, but the sun was flexing its muscles. On some afternoons, Anna and Jonathan sat on the roof, wearing nothing but a sweatshirt. This, she said, made her feel as though they were taking a break from the slopes on the upper deck of a ski chalet somewhere in the Alps.

Warmer days followed by freezing nights hardened the snow's surface, helping Jonathan in his constant quest for wood. Every afternoon, he walked alongside the river or at the far edge of the field across the road to cut the biggest branches he could find. His efforts paid off; should a late-season storm occur, he now had enough wood to ensure their comfort.

On the first evening of April, he sat at the table in the middle of the room on the second floor, fiddling with pieces of metal. He crafted two cones, four inches long, fitted with hooks underneath them. Anna got curious and asked what he was doing.

"It's a surprise," he answered. "Let me rephrase that. It's a sweet surprise."

The following morning he disappeared in the patch of trees behind the graves where he normally went to reflect, carrying his cones, two buckets and a drill.

He had once watched a video of people tapping trees on YouTube. He was certain the maple against which he leaned when he needed to be alone could sustain two taps. As soon as he pulled the drill bit out of the bark, he knew he had done the job right.

Two days later he went back to collect the sap and found enough of it in the two buckets to fill a larger one. Upstairs, Anna inquired as to what he had in there. Jonathan winked at her, plunged a glass in the bucket and raised it. The liquid looked like water, but his expression after he took a sip led her to believe it was something else. He handed her the glass so she could have a taste too. She was reluctant.

"Trust me," he said.

She was caught off guard in the most pleasant of ways when the glass touched her lips. Jonathan leaned forward and smiled.

"Let's try our hands at maple syrup, shall we?"

The sap boiled on the stove in the biggest pot they had and the intense fragrance filled the inside of the warehouse. Anna, who had been a bit of a sweet tooth in the old world, was elated even if in the end the pot's content was reduced to a little less than half a Mason jar worth of syrup.

Before he transferred it, Jonathan went to the roof and covered a dinner plate with snow. He then poured some of the steaming hot golden liquid on it, gave Anna a fork and instructed her to stick it in the frozen syrup and to roll it.

"Voilà. Instant maple taffy!" he proclaimed.

Jonathan repeated the process until he filled two jars he planned to use to make maple flavored baked beans. Anna didn't need to mix it with anything else; after her evening meal, she'd dip a spoon in a jar before shoving it in her mouth and closing her eyes to better savor the moment.

◆ ◆ ◆

The ground was becoming visible again. Before the snow melted completely, Jonathan thought he would go to the City to get a feel for how winter had transformed it. He also wanted to know if there were survivors left.

He picked a cold night with a clear sky and walked his usual route, weapon in hand. Everything was indeed different in that it was utter desolation. The silence was absolute and he saw no signs anyone had spent the recent months there.

The surrounding calm convinced him to venture all the way past midtown to a mall where Kat had dragged him from time to time.

Jonathan despised shopping, even more so in large settings such as this one. Kids screaming and crying, adults wandering aimlessly and bumping into each other like lost souls; Mr. Dean had once compared it to purgatory.

"Some also call it *life as a couple*," he had told Jonathan.

His boss had earned himself a heartfelt slap on the shoulder from Mrs. Dean for that one.

Now that it was abandoned, he couldn't resist and went

inside the mall. Countless bodies, along with broken glass and trash covered the floors. Most of the dead had fallen victim to the virus, but a few showed signs of violence. Those were at different stages of decomposition; some of these deaths had obviously occurred as recently as when the temperatures had dipped below the freezing point in December.

The stores had all been looted, although he did find a dark t-shirt and a pair of track pants for Anna. He also scored a blue bandana Charlie would perhaps accept to wear.

There was plenty of time remaining to make it back to the warehouse before sunrise. Jonathan left the mall with the intention of heading straight home with his light findings. Outside, he rested his rifle against a mailbox and walked a few steps away from it while he adjusted his backpack.

After everything he had been through in this last year, few sounds held enough power to scare him anymore.

These aggressive growls stopped his heart.

The pack of six coyotes slowly moved closer, forming a half circle in front of him.

They were about to push on their rear paws and charge him when shots fired from suppressed weapons took them down two at a time.

Jonathan, too busy thinking of a way to escape from the beasts, hadn't seen from where the bullets had come. He was so stunned his only reaction had been to raise his hands as a sign of surrender. Two shadows jumped out of a store's broken windows across the street and advanced toward him.

His life, he now knew, was hanging by a thin thread.

The two strangers looked at the coyotes and then at Jonathan with puzzled expressions.

"You don't need to raise your hands, sir. We're not gonna hurt you or steal from you."

He wasn't falling for that one; something was about to go down. But the second man insisted they meant him no harm and the two strapped their weapons around their shoulders to prove it.

"No really, it's OK, sir. We promise."

Both were in their early twenties. Jonathan also noticed they were clean and owned impressive equipment. These guys were doing quite well for themselves.

They asked him if he was from the area. He was careful not to reveal too much about himself, but he did tell them he had spent the last fifteen years near the City. The men were not as secretive. They told Jonathan they were with a group of seventeen people that had set up camp on the side of the City opposite from where he and Anna lived.

Sensing the boys were well-meaning, Jonathan apologized for his reluctance to give them more details about his current situation.

"I'm not alone. There's someone else with me and I can't risk her safety."

"No worries," one of them answered. "Things got messed up real fast at first. We've seen our share of pretty bad stuff happen. So we understand."

The three spoke for a while and compared accounts of the latest wave of the virus they had witnessed. Theirs, a few days before Christmas, was more recent than the one Jonathan had come upon in the fall. At the end of their conversation, he thanked them both for saving his life and shook hands with the young man near him.

The other moved in closer and did the same.

He looked deep into Jonathan's eyes.

"Oh my God, I recognize you," he said.

"What do you mean?" Jonathan asked, thinking these kids had been pulling his leg this entire time and now trouble would be coming his way. He was wrong.

"You're the one who took out that bunch of guys, those jerks, with the sniper in the building. You spoke to my dad when you came out of there."

Their group, much smaller back then, had found a place to settle down near the building across the bridge at the same time the ruthless gang had returned for their second round of murders. No one had the guts, the skills or the equipment to do anything about it and so they had spent days in fear of being killed every single time they stepped outside. It was Jonathan's actions that had convinced them to find weapons and teach themselves to use them.

They asked what had prompted him to storm the building on his own.

"They shot at my friend," he shrugged.

"You would be a great addition to our group, sir."

"Thanks, guys. I have to get back to her now."

As they walked away from him, one of the young men turned around and asked for his name.

"Jonathan," he answered. "Jonathan Foster."

He watched them disappear into the dying hours of the night. This had been his first positive interaction with strangers since he had come out of that building and exchanged all but a few words with this young man's father. This gave him a boost and he walked back to the warehouse with renewed energy.

But that encounter would also serve as a test of his character.

Would he tell Anna about it?

The certitude she had that the army, or some other level of law enforcement, would rise again and bringing back their old way of life was as strong as ever. The revelation of a meeting with good people could deepen what he saw as nothing more than wishful thinking on her part.

These two men with whom he had just spoken were in awe of his grit and yet, Jonathan thought of himself as a coward for lacking the courage to confront Anna about her beliefs and at the same time, risk crushing her hopes.

But he also hated even considering not telling her about this meeting. She needed to know that there were others who had retained a sense of decency, who hadn't lost their humanity.

If something ever happened to him, she shouldn't be afraid to observe and try and approach people like them to ask for their help.

◆ ◆ ◆

It wasn't Sunday. Yet before their evening meal, Jonathan shaved, had a shower and put on clean clothes.

Anna had noticed the long stretches of silence behind which he had retreated in the preceding days. She hadn't brought it up; her quiet days were more numerous than his and he never infringed upon them. Matching the patience and restraint he showed when that happened to her was no easy task. She had to fight the urge to invade his space, to try and comfort him.

On this night, however, it was obvious he was getting

ready for something unusual. She couldn't contain her curiosity when he came out of the bathroom.

"What's the occasion?" she inquired, upbeat and smiling.

"Today's April twentieth…" Jonathan said in a somber tone.

Anna put two and two together immediately. Her grin faded away as her eyes filled with sadness. A year had elapsed since the virus had first struck and almost erased mankind. That little bump in the history of the world, however, didn't matter as much to Jonathan as the fact that it was also the anniversary of Kat's death.

It was easy to lose track of time. It had slowed to the point where its notion had pretty much been erased out of their lives. Except for their weekly visits to the graves, their birthdays and the few holidays they continued to observe, there was no need to know what day or what time it was. Their calendars and clocks were different now; the date was sunny, rainy, warm or cold. The hour was either light or darkness.

"You want to come with me?" he asked.

By Kat's grave, Jonathan recounted what had happened the night she was taken from him. They had already been over it, but it only seemed appropriate to highlight the reason they were there.

Two weeks later, they commemorated Mr. Dean and Matthew's passing.

These were sad events, but they both acknowledged how privileged they were to be able to visit some of their loved ones whenever they wanted and in such a peaceful setting.

Not everyone was afforded that luxury.

Anna made sure to thank Jonathan once more for making it possible.

The month of May marked a return to a much more comfortable living. Anna was painting again and tended to the water when it rained.

Jonathan had learned the lessons of an abysmal winter. He vowed to be better prepared for the next one and spent most early-morning hunting while gathering wood. He let Charlie tag along on trips he knew wouldn't take them too far from their home and stacked the wood he brought back on the first floor.

His work to seal off the warehouse was relentless. Keeping intruders, and the cold, out of the building had become an obsession. Some nights, Anna saw him leave his bed and go out on the roof up to five times just to check on something he thought he had heard. There was never a reason for concern; the noises he'd heard were either from the wind, the rain or animals.

For the most part, Anna was happy. They had resumed their summer schedule, which, of course, included a Sunday visit to the graves. Since they felt safer, it was moved to earlier in the day so they could have brunch by the oak.

She was grateful for the relative peace of mind she had found at the warehouse, but it existed solely in Jonathan's presence. When he went out, she awoke in the night to see him off and stayed awake until he returned, which often meant midmorning or even past that. On rare occasions, he was forced to hide somewhere to avoid detection. He'd come home to Anna, still waiting for him with bags under her eyes.

She had retained her own lessons from the winter. Saving Jonathan's life, and the few weeks thereafter, was only the tip of a very tall snow bank. This long and cold stretch had been trying, and yet boring at the same time. Night after night they had sat by the stove, with little to do but stare at whatever was simmering in the pot. Boredom was a luxury at first. A few months into it and, despite the ever-constant uncertainty that plagued their existence, it had become a burden.

Anna was worried they were growing too isolated. She adored Jonathan and Charlie's company and she understood his reticence to let strangers inside their bubble, but surely they couldn't spend the rest of their lives just the three of them locked up in a warehouse.

How could the world be the world again if the survivors didn't speak to one another? Not now maybe, but perhaps when the time was right they could make an effort to reach out to others. How about those two young men he had met in April?

Jonathan listened as Anna calmly made her case while they sat by the graves during one of their Sunday brunches. He promised to give it some thought.

All in all though, despite the hard work their survival required, most of their days were spent in high spirits.

Fewer people meant less danger. They took random afternoons off during which Jonathan carried Anna downstairs, outside by the river, where she played fetch with Charlie while he mounted guard.

Their days were just fine.

The nights, however, had now become less peaceful.

They had for Anna, anyway.

CHAPTER 31

Well over a year had passed since power had gone out and Jonathan still didn't hold a firm opinion on the darkness of the night hours.

It was less of a debate for Anna; she hated it. She had from the very beginning.

Her experienced of darkness was quite different than his. The nights at the Center had been far from relaxing. She had been abandoned at the mercy of terrifying people and ended up isolated from the rest of the world with nothing but dead bodies for company. Matthew had also been killed there in darkness.

She had spent over two weeks alone on the road, often traveling after sundown. Obscurity hadn't been a friend to her then either.

Reasons to hate the night abounded.

It was easier for Jonathan to show confidence, regardless of the time of day, when he stood strong and armed to the teeth. With Mr. Dean's help, his transition into this new life had been smoother than Anna's. Most of what they owned at the warehouse had been found, and carried there in the old man's truck, thanks to the cover of darkness.

But he understood what Anna meant when she spoke of the creepiness of those hours. Most of the terrible things he had been forced to do since the onset virus had taken place at night. Every evening, as he watched the sun go down, the thought of being caught in a situation where he would have no other choice but to repeat these actions was on his mind.

There was one aspect of the night he knew he would love until his last breath; no matter where he was, he always took a moment to look up at the stars and marveled at the clarity of the spectacle. He could never tire of it.

Anna's nightmares began near the middle of June.

The ones recreating her brother's death had ceased after they had buried him by the oak. These were different. When Jonathan woke her up, twice each night during the first week, she couldn't remember what had scared her so much. But in the course of the second week, she was able to retain scarce details: people had found their way inside the warehouse and Jonathan and Charlie were covered in blood.

While Jonathan was not dismissive, he attributed Anna's visions to insecurity. It had been a long, difficult winter and her wish to see the powers that be regroup and rise from the ashes had not materialized. As far as he was concerned, Anna was only processing the realization that this new life of theirs was permanent.

On the thirteenth morning after her nightmares had started, Anna sat at the table while Jonathan, behind her, was busy preparing their food.

The thick fog of sleep deprivation clouded her senses and her thoughts. She couldn't figure out if she was about to eat breakfast or dinner. She looked down at herself because she had forgotten which clothes she was wearing. Jonathan's voice, although he stood a few feet from her, sounded muffled. Was he speaking to her at that moment or was she remembering a conversation they once had?

She feared her mind was slipping.

Jonathan set her food down on the table in front of her. He was about to walk away when she grabbed his arm to pull him closer.

"Help me," she begged of him.

Anna tried to finish her sentence, but her sobs interrupted her. Jonathan sat next to her and waited until she found the strength to speak again.

"I have to sleep," she said. "I was wondering if, hum, if maybe you could lie down behind me like you did the, hum, the night that crazy man attacked me."

Anna had never been one to rely on anyone for anything. She was as warm as could be, but also fiercely independent and not inclined to give in easily to a man's advances. Admitting to the need to be held was a crushing blow to her pride. But if she were forced to surrender, if she had to beg for some sort of physical contact, then only one man in the world would do.

And it just so happened he was right there with her.

After their breakfast, and a quick round outside the building with Charlie, Jonathan lay down behind Anna on her bed and wrapped his arms around her.

"Everything is going to be fine. I'm here now. Wink, wink," he whispered.

She once again shed a few tears, but this time as a reflex to the overwhelming sense of relief induced by Jonathan's embrace, a much more dignified sentiment than what she had carried inside of her for so many days.

"This is what, hum, what I needed," she said.

Charlie sat by the bed and looked at his humans, puzzled by the breach in the hour and the pattern of their sleep protocol.

And also quite disappointed there was no room left for him to join in.

Late in the afternoon Anna awoke, well rested, and in the best mood she had been in a while.

♦ ♦ ♦

By the end of June, Anna and Jonathan had noticed sharp differences in the weather compared to what they had seen earlier in their lives. The days were warm but dry. The nights were cooler, also free of humidity and when the sky was clear the stars appeared magnified as though they were looking at them through a powerful telescope.

The air felt pure. The disturbing smell spawned by the hundreds of thousands of simultaneous deaths in the City more than a year prior had made way for the fragrances of nature. Anna said the halt in pollution was giving the earth the leisure of becoming itself once again.

Late on the last night of June, Jonathan woke Anna and told her he was heading out to hunt. It was partly true. Even if he wasn't always successful, his goal whenever he went out was to bring back something to eat. In this instance, it wasn't meat he was after. He wanted to head back to the field where he had found the strawberries the year before and surprise Anna. He made sure to bring a bigger container this time.

When he walked behind the Renovation Depot, he felt the same softness underneath his feet he had on his first visit. He sampled a few of the strawberries and began filling the container.

He had never thought of himself as an outdoorsman. Kat was the expert at this sort of thing. He was grateful she had given him the basics, which he had worked on improving in the last year. No matter the speed at which he moved, he could now be as silent as he was invisible. His ability to sense the presence of others, even from a great distance, had also become a life-saving gift.

So while he picked the fruits, he stopped every once in a while to listen because he suspected he wasn't alone in that field. The noises, discreet at first, were now getting closer. He waited on his knees, motionless, his weapon in hand. A gorgeous adult fox soon appeared. He was so stunned at the sight of Jonathan that he froze about six feet away from him and stared straight into his eyes.

Jonathan raised his hand toward his visitor, hoping to fool him into believing there was food in it.

"It's alright buddy," he whispered. "I'm not going to hurt you."

The fox crouched. Jonathan expected he would flee in a hurry, but instead he crawled toward his empty hand and smelled it.

The sensation of the fox's thick whiskers scratching the palm of his hand was one he was certain he would never forget.

As soon as the fox realized there would be no prize to claim he walked away a few feet and turned to take one last look at Jonathan. He then left at an assured pace.

After he parked his bike behind the warehouse, Jonathan went and stood by the river, not too far from the graves by the oak. The sounds from the water at that precise spot were a source of intense peace to him. He had done this so many times by then he could have hummed along as nature sang. With his eyes closed, he soaked it in for a minute.

"You can try and be quiet all you want, I know you're there," he said.

Anna laughed on the roof.

"Charlie tipped me off. He was the one who, hum, who told on you. How was the hunt?" she asked.

"Oh, Anna, the hunt today was incredible. I'll be right up there."

She was once again delighted when he presented her with his harvest.

"Let's slice some of those and, hum, and mix them with the hot cereal," she suggested.

◆ ◆ ◆

The empty field across the road from the warehouse had become a magnet for wild animals of all sizes.

Jonathan spent a lot of time there.

The high grass portion formed a square as wide and as deep as six football fields. The woods behind it were thick and extended for many miles alongside the river. He sometimes ventured in, although never too far. The silence there, and the jungle-like scenery, made it easy to forget the City was only a few miles away.

The field was such a nice piece of land that Jonathan had gone and buried the bodies of the two thugs he had dragged there. They were not worthy of the effort, but his plan was to one day clear a path so he could bring Anna there, along with Charlie, for a picnic. Perhaps she would see something she might like to recreate on a canvas.

On a hot morning at the beginning of August, Jonathan went to the roof at sunrise, faced the graves and took what he now called his *first real breath of the day*.

A gut feeling had been bothering him for a solid week now. He could sense the routine was off, as if he and Anna were no longer alone in the area. He had yet to figure out what or who was behind this intuition of his.

Charlie derailed Jonathan's thoughts when he raised his front paws on the ledge and barked in the direction of the field. The dog's sharp hearing and keen eye, from his position on the roof, had been the initial ingredients of some of the best meals served at the warehouse in recent months.

"What is it buddy?" Jonathan whispered.

Through his binoculars, he found the reason for Charlie's excitement. There they were, near the woods: a pack of the ever-elusive wild turkeys.

Each of his attempts to deliver on his promise of a turkey dinner for Anna had so far ended in failure or embarrassment. Charlie alone had saved their lives on two separate occasions by running straight at them while barking like a maniac. The second of these occurrences had brought his hunting career to a halt.

Then, after a furious thunderstorm, Jonathan had heard a pack by the river, behind the warehouse. He had reached the edge of the grass beyond the oak only to slip in thick mud all the way down to the banks before he could even raise his weapon. He had returned to Anna upstairs, muddied from head to toe with his behind, and also his pride, badly bruised.

Whatever aura shielded those birds from him sure as hell wasn't bulletproof. Their luck had run out, Jonathan thought. He hurried back inside and found Anna wide-awake, sitting in her chair.

"I was about to, hum, to join you, guys. Why did Charlie bark?"

"He saw dinner," Jonathan answered as he handed the binoculars to Anna. He leaned forward to get closer to her.

"Tonight's the night. We're eating turkey," he declared with a wink, a smile and strong confidence.

"Oh God," Anna said, rolling her eyes.

"What?" he asked.

"It's just that…"

She tried in vain to conceal a sarcastic smile.

"What?" he insisted, knowing full well where she was going with this.

"It's the, hum, the fifth time you say that."

"Fourth. The fourth time, Anna."

"Sure. Okay. Whatever. I'll get the, hum, the pot ready," she said as they both burst out laughing.

"Just for that, you get nothing but dark meat," he told her.

Jonathan left the building while Anna went to the roof to observe him in his attempt to secure one of the birds. Charlie came and rested his chin on her thigh in the hopes of receiving a few congratulatory pats for his good work. She was more than happy to oblige.

She followed Jonathan with the binoculars and saw him get close enough to the turkeys to shoot.

"Alright, Charlie. Are you ready for this? Wild turkeys take, hum, take number six. Or five depending on, hum, on who you believe."

She held her breath when Jonathan pointed his weapon at the pack. Instead of shooting, he abruptly pivoted and aimed his rifle at the woods. The turkeys scattered as an unarmed man emerged with his hands raised in the air.

In the time it took Anna to switch to the scope of her rifle, Jonathan had lowered his weapon. He appeared to be having a cordial chat with the stranger. Much to her satisfaction, he was heeding her advice and reaching out to others.

She was already looking forward to the account of his conversation when a second man, this one holding a machete, tiptoed out of the woods from behind Jonathan. Anna tried waving her arms to alert him, but he was too far and couldn't see her. The thought of screaming at him to turn around crossed her mind. She held back in fear it would only exacerbate things.

It rested upon her to do something, and fast.

The crosshairs of her scope found the armed man's head. She exhaled, just as she had been taught, and pulled the trigger. The bullet ended its run in the man's throat. Considering the distance, it was an impressive shot.

Jonathan spun around upon hearing the commotion behind him. The man with whom he was talking seized on this and charged him. They both fell to the ground and disappeared in the high grass.

Anna kept her eye glued to the scope but couldn't see them anymore.

"Jonathan please, please, please," she said out loud.

The stranger came back into view after he rose to his feet, holding Jonathan's weapon. He raised his fist in the air as a sign of victory and then pointed the rifle to the ground where Jonathan was. His left shoulder exploded before he could fire.

Anna had hit her mark again.

It was Jonathan's turn to stand, his weapon back in the hands of its rightful owner. He wasted no time ending the life of his attacker and then walked to the man who had come up from behind him. He shot him as well and took his blade.

As he made his way back to the warehouse, Anna kept an eye out on the field in case more people tried to sneak up on him. When he neared the building, she went in to prepare water and rags to clean the blood she had seen on his face.

Upstairs, Jonathan sat at the table where a silent Anna was waiting for him. He allowed himself a few seconds to catch his breath. He then took her hand and kissed it.

"You did good. You did good," he repeated, aware these were actions from which Anna would take a while to recover.

"I'm so sorry. You were only talking to, hum, to him because I, hum, I suggested it."

She feared Jonathan would want to retreat further into isolation, now. What had just happened had shaken Anna to her very core, but it wasn't near enough to make her waver in her belief they should reach out to others.

"We'll find good, hum, good people. I'm certain of it."

She paused and then added, "One day, the Government is going to, hum, to return, and…"

He knew these were going to be her next words.

Just as he knew that this time, they would set him off.

"For the love of God Anna, please stop it with this nonsense," he screamed.

He couldn't let her finish. Not so soon after he was attacked. Not after they were forced to end the lives of two men who had wanted to kill him.

He left the table, walked to the door leading to the roof and pointed outside.

"Have you seen what just happened? This is it. That's all there is. If it ever gets any better, and that is a big if, it will be decades from now."

"Hope, Jonathan. All I'm talking about is, hum, is hope. It's allowed. We're allowed to, hum, to hope," she objected as she hit the table with her fist.

Jonathan went back to her and took a knee.

"Not blindly," he told her. "This is hoping blindly," he added, pointing to his bloodied and bruised face.

"This can't be all, hum, all there is. There has got to be more," she replied, tearing up.

"Jesus," Jonathan said, shaking his head.

He went out on the roof as a way of ending their conversation. After he calmed down, he washed up, changed his clothes and had breakfast.

A thunderstorm battered the area in the afternoon. Both worked on filtering water in silence. They were not mad at each other. After all, she had just saved his life. They just needed time to absorb the last hours and reflect.

She thought about her hopes and their relevance in this environment. He regretted having raised his voice at her.

By the time they had gone to bed, Jonathan had come

to humbling conclusions. Not only had he been wrong, he had let Anna down.

Finding the right words to express his remorse wouldn't be easy, but he had to give it a try.

It was still dark when he woke Anna to tell her he was heading out again to hunt the turkeys he had seen the morning before.

"After what, hum, what happened? Are you sure?"

"One way or another, we're getting that dinner. These assholes are not going to take that from us."

Anna wanted to get dressed and mount guard, but he told her she should sleep some more. At this hour, there was less danger and he promised he'd be extra careful. With any luck the next time she would see him he'd be covered in feathers, not mud.

"Get the pot ready! We'll talk when I come back," he said with a smile, squeezing her hand.

She watched him shut the door behind him and closed her eyes.

After he crossed the field, Jonathan entered the woods. He walked along the river for more than an hour without seeing the coveted birds.

At the warehouse, Charlie startled Anna with a long and wet lick on the face. Jonathan had forgotten to let him out on the roof so he could relieve himself.

She jumped in her chair and she was on her way to open the door and let Charlie out when she noticed a folded note addressed to her on the table. She grabbed it, went up the ramp and followed Charlie outside for a better reading light.

It appeared Jonathan had spent a good part of the night searching for those right words.

Dear Anna,

We often talk about the old world, about who and what we have lost. Rightfully so; the people and the things we once called ours were the source of such great comfort and made our lives so much easier than they have become.

This longing for the past is so strong in you, Anna. I see it in your eyes as clearly as I hear it in your voice. It's especially there in the way you say the word "hope".

And it is quite fine.

The key to our immediate survival may very well lie in finding what will help us get through each day, finding what will make today worth wishing for a tomorrow, and hold on to it with resolve. That is the very definition of Hope. And I agree with you, it should be allowed.

If hoping for a return of our former way of life is what works for you then my only response should be to hope, just as hard, right here by your side. So please forgive my lack of faith and count me in from now on. I must admit, I now see the poetry in your belief that the world could become a better place if only it became what it used to be.

As for me, if you ever wonder what makes me treasure the present and look forward to the days ahead, well, here it is:

It's you, Anna.

It's you, brave and strong you.

It's you, and the joy that lights a fire in your eyes at the sight of a ripe strawberry.

It's you, and the undying smile on your lips while you talk to Charlie or the one that grows on them after you've kissed him on the head. He told me it drives him crazy when you do that.

It's you, so you, sitting behind a canvas, your mind

gone to a place I know my own will never have the genius to imagine.

And it's you, sleeping and breathing peacefully, your back pressed against my joyful heart.

It's you, Anna. And so it's us.

Love always,

Jonathan.

Anna kissed the signature on the note, folded it and held it tight against her chest.

She turned her chair around and she was about to go back inside to have breakfast, but froze when she heard the loud announcement coming from the other side of the bridge.

"This is the Army. Do not fear. Come forward to be rescued."

CHAPTER 32

Jonathan had never gone this far deep into these woods. They were so lush he could no longer find a path ahead of him. He came upon a tree, befallen by the river and leaned on it for a pause while he munched on two granola bars for breakfast. The turkeys were nowhere to be found, anyway.

He suspected Anna might have read his note by then and smiled as he imagined her reaction. She was such a sucker for random acts of kindness.

Writing these words down on paper, and sharing them with her, had electrified his body and his soul. At this very moment, the thought of being away from her and Charlie became unbearable and he couldn't fight the urge to go back.

Before he left, he took a good look at the river. These untouched surroundings deserved a few more seconds of appreciation. He was soaking it in when he heard the announcement. It was faint, but he estimated it originated from near the warehouse.

"Anna," he said out loud.

During his desperate run, the call to survivors was repeated once more then silence returned.

He made it to the edge of the woods in twenty-five minutes and saw the warehouse as he reentered the field. His heart sank; two heavy vehicles were leaving its driveway. He made it to the road in time to catch a glimpse of the bright orange tailgate on the second truck as it drove over the bridge.

These were the army transports he had emptied the year before and that had mysteriously disappeared some time later.

Jonathan entered the building. His body quivered as he called out the code.

"Anna?"

"I'm up here, Jonathan," she answered in a broken voice.

He flew up the stairs and found Anna sitting on the floor by the door leading to the roof, her back rested against the wall. A man, apparently dead, was face down a few feet from her, wearing nothing but undergarments.

Anna was holding Charlie in her arms, pressing him hard against her chest. His beige coat, normally so bright and immaculate thanks to her incessant care, was soaked in blood.

"I'm sorry. I'm so sorry…" she cried.

Jonathan fell to his knees, looked at the dog before lowering his gaze and shaking his head. Anna then let go of her grip on Charlie who walked away from her, and to Jonathan, with surprising ease.

"He seems … fine," Jonathan wondered out loud almost cheerfully. He turned to Anna and he was about to ask her what had happened. In a moment of utter destruction, he figured it out for himself. The blood wasn't Charlie's. It was hers.

"No, no, no," he screamed as he ran to her.

She had been stabbed, twice in the stomach and once in the chest. Jonathan took her in his arms and tried to apply pressure on her wounds, but Anna grabbed the collar of his t-shirt to pull him closer.

"I can fix this. I can fix this," he kept repeating.

"Listen to me," she told him with great urgency.

"Thank you for my, hum, my note. Thank you for Charlie. Thank you for, thank you for the…"

She paused, let go of her grip on Jonathan and slid her fingers across his cheek.

" … for the strawber…"

There wasn't enough life left in her to finish that last word. She had used her final breath to express gratitude to the man who had saved her.

Jonathan looked into Anna's eyes, unable at first to comprehend what had just happened.

He eventually did.

A scream he didn't know a human being had the power to produce escaped his throat once, twice and then a third time. In the haze and the confusion, he stood, went to the roof and screamed some more, his right fist pounding at his chest.

Never had he experienced such painful, such deep and such dark sorrow. His breathing grew so heavy he hyperventilated and collapsed to the ground, unconscious. When he regained his senses, he was holding Anna in his arms again. He had no idea how long he had been out and no memory as to how he had made it back to her.

Charlie had lay down next to her body, his chin rested on her thigh.

People had stormed the warehouse. Jonathan and Charlie were both covered in blood. The visions that had terrified Anna and kept her awake for so many nights had materialized.

The stranger on the floor moved. Jonathan walked to him and rolled him on his back to reveal a pool of blood. The deep tear in his abdomen was a clue as to the most probable chain of events. Jonathan played out the scenario in his head.

After hearing the announcement, Anna had most likely signaled her presence to what she believed were army personnel. They had entered the warehouse and begun stealing the food. She had fought back by throwing one of her discs at that man. His hands weren't stained with blood and he wasn't holding a knife, so Jonathan concluded someone else had stabbed her.

They had left Anna to die. Since their accomplice had become a liability after being gravely wounded, they had also counted him for dead and stripped him of what Jonathan was willing to bet was one of the army fatigues ripped from the real soldiers manning the trucks these men had found.

In the end, and as inspiring as it was, it may very well have been her unwavering belief that order would one day be restored that had caused her demise.

It was also possible she had fought back as a response to guilt. She had flagged them. She had steered them to the warehouse only to realize she had been conned. Perhaps Anna had lost her life in an attempt to dim Jonathan's reaction to her allowing this to happen in the first place, especially after their argument from the day before.

The deception and the terror and the pain he imagined she had felt were such a heavy burden for him to bear he had to lean on the table for support. Anna's love for Charlie knew no limits. He guessed she had set aside the knowledge she didn't have long to live to take him in her arms and keep him calm until the group pulled out.

Jonathan was aggressed by different kinds of pain of his own. His stomach ached, his head was pounding and his knees were weak. Those, however, weren't the sole disturbances inside of him. He sensed each of the traits that defined who he was shutting down. It was as though an invisible but powerful force was flipping the switches — killing the lights — one after the other. Empathy, generosity, mercy and humanity: all vanished in sequence.

He saw the hammer on his worktable and grabbed it.

"Where are they going?" he asked the stranger.

He refused to answer.

Jonathan rested both his knees on the man's forearm to hold his wrist down and keep his hand flat on the concrete floor. He raised the hammer and swung downwards with such force, the tips of two of the man's fingers ruptured. The tremendous loss of blood from the gaping wound left by the disc Anna had thrown in his abdomen had rendered him too weak to fight back, yet he found it in him to scream his agony.

"Do I have your attention?" Jonathan asked, his jaw locked shut by rage.

"Take a second and tell me where they are going."

He still didn't seem inclined to speak up. Jonathan aimed at a different finger and hit him again.

"Focus," he yelled.

The man signaled "no" with his head, but the sight of the hammer being raised high in the air a third time convinced him to reveal what he knew.

"Yellow school. A yellow school on Fourth Street, down by the river," he said in a whisper.

Jonathan had his answer. He grabbed the man by the hair at the back of his head, dragged him outside and flipped him off the roof.

"I'll deal with you later."

◆ ◆ ◆

Jonathan stood behind thick bushes at the top of a hill. Behind him was the river. In front of him was the school. This vantage point gave him a clear view of the nine men going in and out of the building.

Two teams of three members dressed as soldiers left with the trucks each morning, fooled people into thinking they were being rescued, stole their food and then came back to base with the day's spoil.

On a handful of occasions they had shown up with terrified hostages, women for the most part, but a few men also. A crew of three stayed behind to keep an eye on the building and an unknown number of prisoners. None of the guards ever ventured outside at ground level when their friends were away, though they did spend some time on the roof.

Fourth Street was no more than two miles away from the warehouse.

Jonathan had found the group's hideout the same day they had murdered Anna.

Following a three-day hiatus, he had begun returning

every morning to his post by the river behind the primary school to observe and take mental notes.

He couldn't just storm the building this time: these guys were well armed, appeared disciplined and he knew nothing of the inside layout or where the hostages were being held.

Their one flaw, as far as he could tell, was their morning schedule. It hadn't wavered once and Jonathan had come to know it by heart.

He too had a schedule; every day, before sunrise, he crossed the bridge and walked alongside the river weapon in hands. His backpack was heavy with two additional loaded rifles, clips of ammo, water, food rations, a change of clothes and Anna's iPad fully charged. Once he reached his stakeout spot, he spent hours stalking the men, waiting for a moment of weakness on their part so he could strike. He headed back to the warehouse at dusk, sat by Anna's grave until late in the night and then went inside to fall asleep on her bed.

The three days after her death had been the darkest of his life. Her body, covered by a blanket, had remained where she had taken her last breath for two full days. Charlie refused to leave her side. Jonathan couldn't fathom she was gone.

In the middle of the second night, through a thick fog of despair, he had managed to push himself to do the right thing for her.

The hole he dug was, of course, next to her brother's burial site.

He had carried Anna downstairs at dawn, but hadn't immediately placed her inside her grave. He wasn't ready to let her go just yet. Instead, he had positioned her body on its side, by the hole, so he could lie down behind her and wrap his arms around her.

"I'm here now. Everything is going to be fine. Wink, wink," he had told her one last time, his face pressed against the back of her head.

He had planned the grave to accommodate Anna, but also some of her things. After Jonathan found it in him to put her in the ground, he had brought her easel along with her paint tubes, brushes and unused canvases and laid the lot next to her.

He had then begun burying her, expressing his pain out loud at each shovel-full of dirt he had dropped on top of her.

Charlie had sat by the hole and watched the scene in silence, as if he knew the moment was solemn and required for him to be good.

I just buried Anna, Jonathan had repeated to himself many times over as he stared at the site, fully aware he would never make peace with his loss. He had dragged the shovel behind him all the way back to the warehouse just as he had done after he had buried Mr. Dean. He had climbed the stairs, sat on Anna's bed and looked around the room. Every square inch of it bore her mark. The sofa, the large leather chair, the table, the stove, the ramp, the roof; she was everywhere.

And there was Charlie, too.

From that moment on, Charlie would be a constant reminder of Anna. She loved him so much. Jonathan had even grown a little envious of how he had returned that affection to her. His hunting and scavenging trips had forced him to leave them behind so often, it was normal the two would develop such a tight bond.

The entertainment he also got out of their interactions far outweighed the jealousy he felt at times.

The sight of her empty wheelchair had delivered the ultimate punch to his gut.

Her reaction when he had given it to her was one of his favorite memories. She had circled the room with Charlie on her lap and the most genuine of smiles on her face. It had been such a beautiful day, the first of a week during which Jonathan had gained her full trust by reuniting her with her brother and getting his hands on the medical supplies she so needed. Their relationship had then begun its rise to what it had become in the end: a new brand of devotion. The kind love itself could only aspire to be. The kind worth protecting at all cost and for which one wouldn't think twice before killing thugs or throwing themselves off a roof in the middle of a snowstorm.

Jonathan had sat on the floor by the footrests of her chair, his face buried in his hands, sobbing violently and repeating "Oh my God" over and over again.

Charlie was still covered in Anna's blood three days after her death. Jonathan had taken him to the roof in the afternoon, filled the portable shower and washed him up. Charlie, who had never cared for bath time, was docile and looked down while his coat had regained its shine.

Anna had taken to concealing her iPad under her mattress in case strangers ever entered the building. Jonathan had retrieved it, but hadn't powered it on fearing it would amount to an invasion of her privacy. He knew she had used it to document their time together and he wanted to see her alive and breathing again, but he needed her approval first.

In the early evening, he had gone back outside and knelt at the foot of her grave. Charlie had circled it and tried to dig in, but Jonathan had stopped him and held him in his arms.

Anna's faithful companion had begun trembling before collapsing on the dirt, crying.

"It's alright buddy, I hear you. I feel it too," Jonathan had said to console him.

He had a long talk with Anna during which he apologized for not being there to save her, something she had done for him the day before her own death. He had also told her that, with what he was preparing to do, there was a distinct possibility they could see each other again soon.

After half a dinner, he had sat in the big chair and finally looked through her iPad. There were so many pictures, so many videos, some of which he didn't even remember or know she had recorded. He scrolled down to an image from Christmas Day, when Jonathan had given her the tablet. Her head was pressed against his. Her smile covered most of the screen. Charlie, of course, was right there with them.

As darkness had settled, he had become conscious again of how strange it was to be alone in his building. Since he was always the one going out, he had forgotten how intimidating the place could be for a sole occupant. Perhaps Anna had felt the same way when she was there on her own. If she did, she had never mentioned it.

In fact, he had realized for the first time that Anna had never once complained about anything. She had never asked for anything either, not food or water or clothes. So much had been taken from her and yet she had demanded so little. His relentless efforts to find more things to give her might have missed the mark, he had thought. Perhaps all she really wanted were his and Charlie's company.

A few canvases and an occasional bowl of strawberries were nice too.

He had wiped his tears, powered the iPad off and gone to stand in front of her chair with his arms crossed.

Every single human being has a breaking point. This world was always going to push Jonathan beyond his eventually.

It was inevitable.

The more he had thought of Anna — the more he had stared at that empty, bloodstained wheelchair — the madder he had grown at those who had taken her from him in such a brutal fashion. He had fallen asleep on her bed and risen a few hours before dawn.

It was a different day to which he had awakened as a different version of himself.

Anna wouldn't have liked him this way.

CHAPTER 33

Aside from its proximity to the river, this humble part of the City had very little to offer. The dwellings, the tiny red brick houses, the few schools and stores had all been built in a hurry during the manufacturing boom of the sixties and the seventies. The area, though far from decrepit, looked frozen in a distant past.

Jonathan had scavenged there the year before, but the rewards hadn't been worth the efforts so he had quickly moved on.

His stakeout spot by the river was about one hundred and fifty yards away from the back door of the small elementary school Anna's attackers had chosen as their base. While his expertise in securing buildings was limited, he could see why the group had picked this one. It had one level, wide windows and access to the roof. It gave them ample room and was easy to guard since it stood in retreat from other structures.

The men were up at seven in the morning and took turns coming out to the backyard in pairs to relieve themselves. They used an entry code to regain access inside: one knock, a pause and four more knocks. Someone then opened the door.

Time had done nothing to lessen Jonathan's pain or repress his anger. On the contrary: he grew more enraged and increasingly unstable each evening he walked back to the warehouse without having been able to attack.

He sat by Anna's grave for hours, even after dark, looking down at the dirt. On two separate occasions, inoffensive passers-by had tried to approach him during this intense part of his day. They were greeted with a weapon pointed at their face, threatened with their lives and ended up fleeing while chased by a wrathful lunatic screaming incoherent sentences at the top of his lungs.

He sometimes awoke in the middle of the night only to see Charlie sitting in front of Anna's chair, still where she had left it on the day she had died and still stained with her blood. The dog could stare at it for hours, as though he expected Anna would reappear in it any moment.

In the mornings, Jonathan would often speak to Anna out loud while he prepared breakfast. Hearing her words and the sound of her voice made him feel good. His pain magically subsided for as long he spoke to her. He would then bring her food to the table only to realize, his heart broken anew, that she wasn't there. And that she never would be again.

On this crisp mid-September morning, Jonathan had made it to his usual surveillance cache for the thirty-sixth consecutive day not knowing the opportunity to attack he had long been waiting for was finally going to present itself.

Opportunity, much like comfort he was about to find out, comes in many disguises.

Less than an hour after the two trucks had left, the school's back door opened and a black boy, wearing only a white t-shirt and underpants, burst out and ran toward the river. Jonathan took a moment to absorb this image and its significance. He had seen the men bring in adult hostages during his stakeouts, but never any children.

The boy, all but seven or eight years old, pushed on his legs with an obvious fear of being captured again. He was near the halfway mark between the building and the river when a large bearded fellow in his early forties also came out and yelled at the kid to get back inside. Another man, on the roof this one, revealed his position after he rushed to check on the disturbance.

This had to be it. This had to be the glitch in the group's routine Jonathan had been hoping to exploit.

Because the child wasn't charging toward him, he would have to change location, and be quick about it, if he wanted to rescue him. The large man ran after the boy, and away from the school, at a pace expected for his size. Jonathan seized on this and eliminated the guard on the roof with a single bullet to the side of the head. He then let himself slide down the hill, hurried along the river and climbed back up where he suspected he would be close enough to grab the boy's attention.

"Hey, kid, over here," he whispered.

The child heard Jonathan and looked his way, but maintained the course. A few yards later, however, he ran down to the river and veered toward the voice that had just called him. He was frightened, cold and dirty. Jonathan pressed his index finger on his lips to order him to remain quiet. He removed his jacket, wrapped the boy in it and directed him to stand beside a large tree and keep facing the river.

"No matter what happens, don't turn around. Understood?"

The boy, in obvious shock, stared ahead with his mouth opened.

"Did you hear me?"

The kid regained his focus when Jonathan put a hand on his shoulder. He nodded in the affirmative.

The large man soon arrived at the top of the hill and stopped to catch his breath upon seeing the boy by the tree.

"There you are, you little shit. Thought you could just run away from me like that?" he said as he walked in closer. He also noticed something wasn't quite right.

"Hey, where did you get that jacket?"

He froze when a stranger emerged from behind the tree and pointed a silenced rifle a foot from his forehead. In the fraction of a second before he pulled the trigger, Jonathan saw all of the regrets and all of the shame that had ever plagued the planet fill the man's eyes. It was nowhere near enough to save his life.

After the man collapsed to the ground, Jonathan took the child in his arms and hurried back to his post. The boy disappeared in the hoodie and the extra pair of pants Jonathan always carried in his backpack, but at least he was warm.

"Are your parents in there, kid?"

"They're dead. The bad men killed them," he said as he bowed his head down.

Jonathan stopped moving and talking. It was possible

this child had seen his family die in front of him before being taken by their murderers. What had happened to him since that day, he didn't even want to try and imagine. He needed to shake it off for now and concentrate on his next actions.

"The trucks left this morning with six bad men. Before you came out of the building just now, how many bad men were inside, including the one we left by the river?"

"Three," the boy answered.

"How about the hostages, the "good people?" How many are there?"

The boy hesitated and then shrugged.

"Five? Six?" Jonathan asked.

"More."

"What, like eight? Ten?"

"Ten, I think."

"Alright," Jonathan said while he stood up and secured his backpack. "Are the good people all held in the same room?"

"Yes."

"I'm going in. Stay here until I come back and I tell you it's safe, okay?"

Jonathan's pressing tone was scaring the boy who retreated in silence. He lost patience and put his hand on the kid's shoulder for the second time.

"Hey, did you hear me?"

"Yes," the startled boy whispered.

He looked weak. Jonathan wasn't sure if he was petrified or famished or both.

He rolled his eyes and removed his backpack again. The boy bit into the granola bar he handed to him as if he hadn't eaten in days.

Jonathan made it to the rear entrance of the building, caught his breath and knocked using the group's code. The door swung opened.

"Were you able to find that little bast…"

The man turned mute when the suppressor at the tip of Jonathan's rifle made contact with his throat.

"Drop your weapon very slowly," Jonathan said.

The man obeyed, but with a smirk. To Jonathan, this was a sign he believed his two accomplices would show up at any moment and save him. It had all happened so fast he didn't know he was the only one left.

"Take me to the hostages."

As they walked down a hallway, the man whistled to the tune of The Godfather theme song as loudly as he could. Perhaps this was a signal the group had worked out, one to report a breach or an imminent threat. Jonathan ordered him to stop walking and to turn around. He did as he was told, but kept whistling.

Jonathan was now the one smirking.

"Did you really think I would burst in here before taking care of your two little friends first? When the trucks come back, I'll take care of the others too. No one's coming to save your ass, buddy."

The expression on the man's face downgraded from quite confident to quite unsure on the spot.

When Jonathan entered the tiny windowless room in which the hostages were held, he could hardly grasp the horror. There were eight women, three men and three young girls living in the most abject of conditions. Their cell reeked of urine and feces. Most showed multiple bruises and all of them, also wearing nothing but their underwear, were shivering. When the hostages saw the guard walking in, they huddled as a group in a corner of the room like wounded animals. Jonathan followed, his weapon pointed at their tormentor. A loud gasp filled the room.

With the help of some of the hostages, he marched his prisoner to an office with windows, tied him to a chair and forced him to reveal where the clothes, the food and the weapons were kept.

Now that they were dressed and fed, he pulled the three men aside and asked the women if any of them wanted to volunteer and assist in putting an end to all of this. Two of them came forward.

Together, they elaborated a plan for when the trucks would come back.

The element of surprise played in their favor. They could catch the two teams off guard by getting them immediately upon their return and before they entered the building. This would also help ensure the safety of innocent people they may have with them.

Jonathan taught the group how to use the rifles and guns. At the conclusion of this crash course, he gave them a strict order, one that had to be followed no matter what.

"These weapons are meant to capture them, nothing else. No one shoots anybody. That's not negotiable. We're taking them alive."

The others — the remaining women and the girls — gathered in a classroom where they were asked to be quiet regardless of what they heard. The three men headed outside, hid and waited for Jonathan to join them.

Jonathan took the two women to the roof and explained their part in the plan. They were to keep watch and alert him the very moment they saw the transports appear on the road. He wanted them to run down and point their rifles at the six men the instant they heard him say the words, "hands up."

Again, he repeated his firm order not to shoot anyone.

He went back to the main floor, but didn't exit the building. Instead, he entered the room where the prisoner was tied and shut the door. From where he now stood, about ten feet behind the man, Jonathan fired a shot at the wall mere inches from his left ear to startle him and prove to him he had bullets. He then went to stand beside him and rested the suppressor on the man's right leg, above his knee.

Theatrics or long speeches weren't his thing, but he needed to make an impression. He wanted to know where these people came from and how they had gotten together. Above all, he wanted to learn as much as he could about what had transpired at the warehouse on the day Anna had died.

He couldn't possibly live the rest of his life without a clearer image of her last moments.

"I'm about to ask you some very simple questions. If I so much as feel that you're not telling me the truth, I'll pull the trigger. Are we clear on this?" he asked, as he pressed harder on his rifle.

The man's earlier cockiness had by then vanished and made way to uncontrollable trembling. Sweat was dripping from his chin. He nodded to Jonathan and after a few attempts he was able to utter the word "yes."

"The two army trucks you guys are using, where did you find them?" Jonathan asked.

"West, on Highway 90, about fifty miles from…"

The bullet ripped the man's kneecap clean from his

leg. He tried to scream, but only air came out of his throat. On any other day of his life, Jonathan would have been taken aback by this freak occurrence. Not on this one.

"I told you this would happen if you lied to me," a calm Jonathan said. "Lets try that again. The trucks. Where did you find them?"

"Ten miles south, by the main road. They were in the ditch," he spewed out in a hurry.

"See, that was easy. If you had done that before, I wouldn't have wasted a bullet. Oh, and your kneecap would still be attached to your leg where it belongs instead of, you know… over there… on the floor… by the wall."

Jonathan switched sides and rested his suppressor above the man's other knee.

"I have more questions to which I already know the answers. So if you want to keep your one and only good knee, I suggest you tell the truth from now on."

Through his interrogation, he was able to paint a broad picture of the group's history.

This one was among four men who had stumbled upon the army trucks. They had pulled the first one back on its wheels with their car then used it to retrieve its twin.

After stripping the dead soldiers of their fatigues, they had driven to the next city, a smaller town, where convincing residents that the Army had arrived had proven to be easier than they had anticipated.

They had recruited more men with equally flexible morals to complete their crew. Winter had been rough, so after they ran out of people to con and consumed all they had stolen, they did a one eighty to come and try their luck in the City.

Their MO was simple enough; they parked the trucks on a street, got out and made some noise to attract attention. Desperate survivors, relieved to see that the "Army" was still active, didn't hesitate to approach them. Then came an uplifting story about a camp with supplies, doctors, gardens and electricity.

It wasn't rare for groups of up to ten people to board the transports with their belongings, the little food they had and high hopes of a better and safer life just a short drive away.

The trucks would travel a few blocks and stop again. Everyone was ordered to get off. Most were executed. The teams then hid the bodies inside buildings before returning to base with their bounty.

They had found a bullhorn the day before they had raided the warehouse and murdered Anna.

They had used it for the first time while driving at low speed by the bridge when they heard a woman calling out to them from the other side of the river. The food they had taken from the top floor was one of their best scores since they had begun their scam.

"What do you know about the woman who was there?" Jonathan asked.

"Only what I was told. Apparently after they got in, things went sideways pretty fast," the man said. "She started screaming and there was a dog barking. They weren't going to kill her, but Big J got real mad at the dog and pointed his gun at its head. She threw a knife or something at him."

"Which one of your friends stabbed her?"

"I don't know, they didn't tell me. I have no clue how these things work. I don't go with them on those runs."

He began sobbing. "I used to be a counselor, for crying out loud. I never killed anyone, I swear."

Jonathan frowned and looked at him, incredulous. This man seemed to believe that not being present for the murders somehow made him less of a killer than those who were.

His anger grew.

"I'm sorry I hurt your knee, earlier. I'll be back in a few minutes and we'll fix it, alright?" Jonathan said in a comforting tone. He then walked to the door and opened it.

Before he left the room he turned around, aimed his rifle at the back of the prisoner's head and pulled the trigger.

CHAPTER 34

Jonathan had come out of the school and was now hiding with the three men behind bushes a few yards away from where the drivers usually backed up the trucks for easier unloading of their stolen goods.

While they waited, the three hostages stared at their benefactor. The resolve in his actions was matched only by the anger shooting out of his eyes. Even after their own ordeal, they couldn't help but notice it. They hadn't yet decided whether they should be reassured or scared by it.

"Who are you?" one of them asked.

"I'm just a guy," Jonathan answered, looking straight ahead. "I'm just a very pissed guy."

"They stole from you?" another guessed.

Jonathan's entire body stiffened.

"More than you could possibly imagine."

It must have been noon when the women on the roof ran from their position at the front of the building and signaled the trucks were on their way. Jonathan saw his recruits become tense. He reminded them of what these people had done and that after this they were all going to be free.

The army trucks backed up in their respective spots, the two teams stepped out and walked to the rear of the vehicles exactly as expected.

Jonathan, flanked by his crew, snuck in on them from behind. When they got within fifteen feet, he screamed: "Hands up, nobody moves." The others by his side followed suit and also barked commands at the top of their lungs. Even Jonathan was startled by it. This sudden and thundering outburst stunned the six criminals into surrendering without a fight.

When the two women arrived from their post, Jonathan asked them to look inside the trucks for hostages. They returned with a teenage girl they had found, gagged and bound, on the floor of one of the cabins.

Jonathan ordered the six men to march to the back of the building and form a line, leaving a space of four feet between each of them. He then instructed them to strip to their underwear. There were no practical reasons for this other than to humiliate them as much as they had those he had freed earlier.

With five weapons pointed at the group Jonathan put down his own, removed his backpack and retrieved Anna's iPad from it. His finger tapped the screen a few times until a video began playing. It was Anna's favorite. She had done a montage of a series of clips of her, Jonathan and Charlie together. The long opening scene, captured by Jonathan at her request, was of her sitting in her wheelchair and Charlie, still a puppy at the time, sound asleep in her arms.

Jonathan walked to the first man in the line up, ordered

him to watch the footage and waited for his reaction. He then moved on to the next man and restarted the playback. This went on until he got to the fourth member of the group.

When that one recognized the woman in the wheelchair, he bit his lower lip, averted his eyes and closed them.

It was he who had murdered Anna.

Jonathan took offense at the man's refusal to look at his victim. He held the tablet up with one hand and slapped him in the face with the other to force him to keep watching. The loud sound from the impact of the palm of his hand with the man's cheek startled the hostages behind him.

"Look at her," he yelled in an explosion of anger.

The man regained his composure and stared at the screen, shivering. In a calmer tone, Jonathan addressed him while he slid his right hand in his pocket.

"Her name was Anna. She was better than you. I thought you should know that. Heck, she was better than me. In fact, she was so much better than any of us she would've wanted me to forgive you. That's how good she was. She would've insisted I forgave you and let you live. She believed, she hoped. She believed in the goodness of people. And she hoped I would too. The last thing I want is to disappoint her."

The prisoners looked at one another and wondered. Was he about to let them off the hook? Was he really going to let them live? Anna's murderer, for one, seemed convinced he was going to be spared. His relief was so intense it had lit a bright spark in his eyes.

When Jonathan saw it, he knew he had accomplished what he wanted.

This — that exact moment — would be his revenge; give these guys hope and then take it away just as fast. Wasn't that what they had done to Anna?

Jonathan moved in closer and took his hand out of his pocket.

"Then again, as I said, she was so much better than me."

He dropped the iPad. Before it had even hit the grass, he had plunged a knife in the man's stomach and grabbed him by the hair at the back of his head to hold him up. He pulled the knife out, stabbed him once more in the stomach and one last time in the chest; the same locations and the same number of wounds Anna had sustained.

He released his grip on the man's hair to let his body collapse to the ground, picked up the iPad and, as he stepped away, spoke to the remaining members of the posse.

"Do you know what she did with her final breath? She tried to thank me. She tried to thank me for a handful of strawberries I once brought her."

Two of the men in the line up sobbed and begged for mercy. Unmoved, Jonathan turned to the armed hostages.

"If you don't want to be a part of this, no one will blame you, but we can't let them go. They'll come back. They'll do it again. I can…"

At the sound of the gunshots, Jonathan covered his head and ducked as the five half-naked men behind him dropped to the ground, dead. He stood up straight and saw that the two women had taken matters into their own hands. After what they had endured in their captivity, the hint Jonathan had given that he was about to lift his ban on shooting was all they had needed to pull the trigger.

"Next time, maybe wait until the good guy gets a little bit more out of the way," he told them with his eyes opened wide.

"Sorry," both women answered in unison.

◆ ◆ ◆

The hostages were in a hurry to leave and formed two parties. None of them planned to stay at the school, or in the area for that matter, not with what it represented. They would take the trucks and perhaps drive south. Winter was just around the corner after all.

With the supplies from inside the building split between the two groups and now loaded, they were about to board. Jonathan surveyed the crowd with the feeling something was amiss.

The three young girls had been kidnapped along with either their mother or both their parents. It was the sight of one of them hugging her mom that reminded him of the boy he had left alone by the river.

"Wait here, don't go yet," he told the group.

He ran across the schoolyard. Before he reached the hill descending to the river, he called for the kid to come up, but received no answer. He called again as he went down by the river.

The child emerged from behind a tree, holding his loose pants up above his waist. Jonathan carried him in his arms back to the trucks and set him down in front of the adults.

"Alright, who's going to take him?" he asked.

They all looked at each other, but no one stepped forward.

"Come on people, someone has to take him."

"We can't, there's enough on our plates as it is," one of the men said.

"Well, I can't keep him," Jonathan replied, losing patience.

"No, that's too much. We can't," another one complained.

Each group boarded its designated transport and they were about to leave when Jonathan raised his voice in a panic.

"Hey! Hey! You know why there's too much on your plates? Because I put it there, I saved you guys. Don't you leave him with me."

In desperation, he hit the second truck with his fist as it drove away and he screamed his anger at the ingrates.

"Goddamn you people. Goddamn you all."

Out of breathe and devastated, Jonathan turned to the kid. The boy was old enough to know rejection when he saw it. He could now feel the pain of its sting.

He looked to the ground, on the verge of tears, still holding his pants up with both hands.

◆ ◆ ◆

"Sit here. And don't touch anything."

Mad as hell at the people he had freed for leaving him with a responsibility he did not want, Jonathan had carried the boy to the warehouse in his arms, all the while swearing and cursing at the entire world.

Charlie, on the other hand, was quite excited. He had never seen such a small human, so he hurried to the couch and smelled the kid who responded loud laughter as he rubbed the dog's face.

Jonathan went to the roof, by the ledge, and looked down at Anna's grave.

"It's done," he whispered. "But this…"

He paused. The task to which he was about to refer was too big, too difficult for a man this broken. He had sunk so deep in despair he didn't think he could ever climb his way back to the surface and resume being who he was before her death.

He pointed his finger toward where the boy was, toward the room he and Anna had shared for more than a year.

"…I can't do this," he said before covering his mouth with his hands.

He went back inside and ordered Charlie to his bed.

"Tonight I'll go out and get you some clothes. Then we'll find someone who will take you. You can't stay here."

"Why not?" the boy asked.

"Because I said so kid," Jonathan answered sharply.

"My name is…"

"Stop it right there. Don't tell me your name," he said with force as he took a step forward. "Don't you ever tell me your name, I don't care what it is."

The kid looked at Charlie who had barked as a response to Jonathan's unusual tone of voice.

For the moment this child was nothing more than an obligation. With a name, he would become a person and Jonathan had had just about enough of people already.

The men who had attacked Anna at the warehouse hadn't found the hidden meals and weapons on the first floor, so there was plenty of food left. They both dined on army rations, after which Jonathan filled the portable shower and taught the boy how to use it. Their day had been long and exhausting, so they went to bed before it was even dark outside.

Charlie ignored Jonathan that night, mounting guard instead by the couch where the boy was instructed he would sleep until someone else would take him in.

The dog was mesmerized.

The mood had been so grim at the warehouse since Anna's death; a change in the atmosphere was a welcome relief, even for him.

The boy fell asleep with a hand on Charlie's head.

CHAPTER 35

"There's food and water on the table. I should be back before the sun is up," Jonathan said to the boy after he woke him.

He then went outside and took a knee at the foot of Anna's grave where he seized on the darkness and the solitude to reflect on the last twenty-four hours.

In seeking to avenge her death, he had freed hostages and prevented many more killings. He had once again done what was right, though this hadn't played a part in his planning. He knew how much she would have hated the manner in which he had achieved his goal, even with the unintended good that had come out of it. She had learned to keep on going despite the necessity of violence, but she had never accepted it.

"You were so beautiful, Anna. Inside and out," he whispered to her before he stood and walked away.

He combed through houses in residential areas near the City, focusing on the ones with swing sets or scattered toys in their backyards. The first twenty homes gave him nothing, but as he got deeper into one of the neighborhoods he found clothes he thought matched the boy's size. Pretty soon, he had put together a wardrobe that would fit him either now or in a not-so-distant future.

On his way back, he stopped on his bridge and listened to the river flowing beneath him for a while.

It was past the middle of September. The nights were cool and crisp again. His goal to eliminate those behind Anna's death had dragged on much longer than he had anticipated. And now, he had to find people willing to take this child off his hands.

His favorite time of the year was nearing; the possibility he wouldn't be able to draw healing energy from it before winter troubled him.

These were selfish thoughts, he was aware of it.

On the top floor at the warehouse, he looked around the deserted room and called out to the kid.

"What are you doing?" he asked when a small head peeked from behind the couch's backrest.

"Nothing," the boy answered, embarrassed as he came out of his hiding spot with Charlie.

The sun was about to rise. Jonathan wanted to get back across the river again so he could try and approach people migrating through the area on foot and see if he could convince them to relieve him of his guest. Travelers, although much lower in numbers than the previous year, still walked in front of the warehouse and crossed the bridge to enter the outskirt of the City.

Jonathan and the boy stood by the building he had stormed the year before, the perfect location to observe movements from all sides.

Nobody showed up during the first two days. On the third, five adults appeared on the horizon.

"Alright, get ready," he told the boy. "Don't say anything, let me do the talking."

When the group got close enough for him to realize it was composed of five men, Jonathan announced it was a false alarm and the two hid. He wanted this to be over and done, but not at the detriment of the kid's safety.

It was another week before more people came in their direction. Jonathan had grown more worried with each passing day. These two couples looked promising.

Once they got within reasonable distance, Jonathan revealed his presence. He raised his hands, his weapon strapped to his back. He knew he was taking quite a risk, but this was the only way to show peaceful intentions nowadays. The couples, in their mid-thirties or so, approached him.

"I need to ask if you can take a kid with you," he said.

One of the two women walked to the boy standing behind Jonathan, his arms also high in the air.

"Oh my goodness, have you seen this beautiful child. Look at him. Isn't he just gorgeous?" she proclaimed in a loud voice.

Her terrible acting and her over the top praises were as bright a red flag as they could have been. Jonathan knew right then and there that something was about to go down. He lowered his hands and put them both in his pockets. Since there was nothing he could do to stop it, he risked it all and played along.

While at it, he went out of his way to trigger the group's actions.

"Yeah. He's a heartbreaker. And he also comes with a

backpack full of clothes and has enough food for a week."

Upon hearing these words, the man closest to the boy pulled a gun and pointed it at his little head.

"We'll take the food. You can keep the stupid kid."

Jonathan's knowledge of firearms had grown exponentially in the last year. This gun didn't look right to him. He tilted his head, surveyed the weapon's barrel and frowned.

"Are you kidding me? An unloaded gun?" he told the man. "In this day and age, you couldn't take the time to scrape up a few bullets before coming at us. I'm almost insulted."

With his con exposed, the man lowered the pistol. Jonathan took his hands out of his pockets, a disc pinched tight between his fingers in each of them. The foursome backed off.

"Why would you want to do this?" Jonathan asked.

"For the love of God, why would you even want to do this?" he repeated, losing his calm.

"Isn't there enough crap to deal with in this messed up world? Are we in that much of a hurry to die that we just can't wait and must kill one another before the virus does? This isn't a game. This kid is flesh and blood and you just put a weapon to his head. I swear to God on any other day, this right here, is the moment you died."

Jonathan took a moment to regroup and catch his breath. He lowered his head and shook it in discouragement.

"Look at the ground," he ordered them.

They didn't seem to understand his command.

"I said look at the ground," he screamed.

Now they understood and all lowered their gaze.

"This is where your dead bodies are. Blood and guts spilled all around you. Everything you ever were, everything you ever wanted to be, gone forever. And why? Because you were too damn lazy to fend for yourselves. Because you pointed an empty gun at a kid's head. And there's no one left to mourn you. Was it worth it?"

Jonathan gave the group a few seconds to absorb his words.

"I have drained the blood out of too many assholes like you. I can't be bothered anymore. Just go, okay? Just go."

They looked at Jonathan, uncertain how to react. All that violence they had no doubt witnessed in the last year and a half, not to mention the one they had probably inflicted, and there they were, listening to a man in full army gear give a sermon about, what? Peace? The sanctity of life?

"Get the hell away from here and don't you ever come back," he finally yelled at them.

The four fled at such a pace, Jonathan was convinced they wouldn't dare retrace their steps and try their luck again. He called it a day in an angry tone and he and the kid went back to the warehouse.

"Go, I'll be up there in a minute."

On the second floor, Charlie greeted the boy and ran to the door leading to the roof. The kid opened it and followed him outside. He heard a faint voice coming from near the river and he walked to the ledge to check on who was there.

Jonathan was on his knees at the foot of Anna's grave, his hands buried deep in the dirt as though he wanted to get closer to her while he spoke and sobbed.

"Please show me something, anything. I'm begging you," the boy heard him say.

Ever since her death, Jonathan had been caught in a loop of extreme anger, pain and grief. His suffering was so profound he had now come to envy the fate of all of those resting by the oak.

He needed an escape from it all, even if only for a few hours.

Later that night, he laid out the plan for the next morning. He would go hunting while the kid would remain at the warehouse and watch over Charlie.

At sunrise he woke the boy up to let him know he was leaving, but he promised he wouldn't venture too far.

For the first time since he had buried Anna, Jonathan exited the building and ignored her grave. On any other day he would have gone to her, but this morning was for him and for him alone. It had to be.

This last week of September was cold. The rising sun lit the fog of his breath as he walked through the field across the road. He reached the wooded area, but only went in a few steps deep so he could keep an eye on his home.

A large tree had fallen there many years before. Its limbs had provided some of the wood that had helped maintain the warehouse habitable during the winter. On the day he had sawed the last of those branches, Jonathan had tried to sit on the oversized naked log, but its slanted angle had made it uncomfortable. He had carved a leveled seat in it with his tools.

With his feet dangling, took his *first real breath of the day* and cleared his mind.

The warehouse's roof was visible from where he sat.

Kat, Mr. Dean, Matthew, Anna, Charlie, himself and now the kid: so many people were linked to that building and yet he felt so alone, so abandoned.

Achieving justice for Anna hadn't been as liberating as he had hoped it would be. The image of her, dying in his arms as she tried to express gratitude, was haunting him. He could still feel her fingers sliding down his cheek as she had struggled and failed to finish her last sentence. Each time he thought of that moment, he'd bring his own fingers to his face and retraced the path hers had followed.

Nearly six weeks had passed since he had lost her. Peace was nowhere in sight. He doubted he would ever find it again. It wasn't self-pity. On the day he had saved her and taken her to the warehouse, Jonathan had sensed Anna's arrival was going to turn his life upside down.

It hadn't.

Her presence had instead put his life back in order and straightened its path. In time, he had come to lean on her, and rely on her strength, to remain on that path. Without her, he no longer knew where he was supposed to go.

He bowed and covered his eyes with his hand. A man with flawless control over his emotions when going toe-to-toe with ruthless murderers was incapable of holding back his tears at the thought of a woman.

He just missed her so much.

His heart was the midst of exploding again when he heard movements in the nearby high grass. He tightened the grip on his rifle in anticipation of who or what would appear.

Jonathan recognized him immediately. It seemed his old friend the fox had been on a quest for a change of scenery since they had met in the strawberry field. The unexpected visitor brought a much-needed smile to his face and when he got within twenty feet of him, Jonathan whistled to get his attention.

The fox stopped and gazed in his direction. Jonathan was still taken by his looks and his confidence; instead of running away, the fox crouched in the grass, his two paws pointed at him.

There was more noise. This time, Jonathan saw what was coming much sooner. The long ears peeked above the vegetation. The graceful deer paused beside the fox, looked down at his tiny companion and followed his line of sight until he noticed Jonathan. The deer wasn't fleeing either. He walked in closer, so close in fact that Jonathan could have touched his face had he stretched his arm. The two stared at each other for a while.

"Hey," Jonathan finally said.

He was reminded of the night Anna had told him of her own standoff with a deer. For the half hour she had spent in the animal's company, she had said, her mind had taken her to a place free of the hardships of this world. Jonathan's, still in darkness, wasn't ready to go to such a place just yet, but he now understood what she had meant and he too was grateful for his moment of luck.

"Thank you," he whispered as he broke down and lowered his head.

The deer took a step forward and hit the ground with his foot, almost in anger, his eyes locked on the depressed man. Jonathan, startled, looked up again. The fox and the deer walked away and disappeared by the river.

◆ ◆ ◆

"Three adults and four children. This could be the day, kid. You know the drill."

The first week of October had come and passed. Barely anyone had walked by since the encounter with the two couples that had tried to steal the boy's food. The few people they had seen after that had inspired such little confidence, Jonathan hadn't bothered approaching them.

He was worried the migration might be over and he'd be forced to tend to the boy all winter. The last thing he needed was to postpone the inevitable until spring.

The kid's stay at the warehouse had been far from warm until then. In truth, the only comfort he received there came from Charlie. Jonathan was cold, distant. His part as far as he was concerned was to give the child food and shelter until someone better suited to care for him came along.

The days across the bridge were long. They hid in the lobby of the building Jonathan had once stormed. He looked out the windows while the boy sat on a lounge chair, his hands in his pockets. Few words were ever spoken.

They adjourned to the warehouse for dinner, just before sundown. Jonathan then retreated outside, to the graves, with a folding chair. Some nights he spoke to Kat, others to Mr. Dean. Most nights, however, he sat in silence at the foot of Anna's plot. The boy played with Charlie on the top floor or on the roof, where he sometimes took pauses to look down at Jonathan.

He knew exactly what the man was thinking. He too had people he missed. He too worried about what life was going to be like without them.

Above all, he dreaded the prospect of being sent away with strangers again.

Whenever Jonathan addressed him, and it didn't happen often, he always did as he was told. He said very little and was obedient for his age, reserving his outbursts for when Jonathan would wake him up. Regardless of how gentle he was in his approach, the boy was violently startled the moment he was touched. Once awake, he was fine and eased back into his calmer disposition. The two had breakfast before the sun was up then made their way to their post.

When he saw the group of seven walk over the bridge and proceed in the right direction, Jonathan's hopes were high. Both he and the kid raised their hands and stepped forward on the road to show themselves to the oncoming people, still at a good distance. In an encouraging sign, all of them also raised their hands.

As they got closer, Jonathan got a better look at them. They were dirty, but it wasn't out of the ordinary. Two of the kids were about the same age as the boy, the other pair seemed a bit older. This would be perfect, he thought.

"We don't want any troubles," he said.

"Good," the one man answered in an energetic tone. "'Cause we don't have any of those to give."

Jonathan took the three adults aside and explained the situation. They told him the harshness of the previous winter had convinced them to move south, though they were quite late on their departure.

The four children, silent and quite well behaved, stood away from the boy. They stared at him, envious of his clean clothes and skin. For his part, he was more focused on the adults, on Jonathan to be precise, as he pleaded with the others to take him.

There was a pinch to his heart.

However bleak the atmosphere was at the warehouse, he had deemed it a great deal for him from the start. Charlie sure was a lot of fun. And Jonathan, despite the permanent dark cloud that hovered over him and the tears he often tried to hide, made him feel safe.

The adults adjourned their meeting and Jonathan kneeled by the boy.

"They agreed to take you. You're going to be fine. Just be good, okay?"

The kid needed to dig deep to remain brave. Jonathan got back on his feet and helped him put on his backpack filled with clothes, food rations and water. He stayed out in the open, in the middle of the street, as the group began walking toward the City.

The boy looked over his shoulder, stopped and turned around. He then took a few steps, back in Jonathan's direction.

"What is it?" he asked.

"The lady in your iPad, is she the one you talk to? The one by the big tree?"

Jonathan was unaware the kid had been through the pictures and videos Anna had recorded.

"Yes. It's her."

"She was nice," the boy said.

That statement, which Jonathan interpreted as a question, overwhelmed him.

"Yes. Yes, she was," he answered in a shaky voice.

"I mean she was nice to me."

"I don't understand," Jonathan said while he extended

his hand to invite him to come closer. The child explained himself while he moved forward.

"She told me *Family is the True North of your life. Know where it is and you'll never lose your way.*"

Hearing these words made Jonathan feel as though Anna had just spoken to him again. He was confused, dizzy even, by what was happening.

"How do you know that saying, kid?"

"I met her with my parents once. She was hiding in a shed. I think she liked my name a lot."

"What's your name?"

"My name is North," the boy answered.

Jonathan then remembered Anna at Christmas when she had wondered out loud, *"where North was now."* This was what she had meant. He went on his knees to look North in the eye.

His heart was pounding; he was about to translate his unbearable grief into words for the very first time.

"The men who killed your parents and took you, they also killed her. I was out hunting when it happened and I came back too late to save her. We barely had enough time to say goodbye."

He stopped talking and fought to keep his composure while he wrapped a hand around North's left forearm.

"When she died, a part of me died with her. I know for certain it will never live again. I'm fine with it. She was worth every bit of the pain I feel. But…"

He brought North closer to him after he grabbed both of his arms.

" … if you want to give me a chance, you could come back to the warehouse. We could try and make the most of it."

He had gone to Anna's grave every single day since her death and asked her for a sign. Now that she had sent one this obvious, he wasn't about to ignore it.

"What do you say?"

"Yeah, let's try it," North answered.

Jonathan reached inside the backpack, took the food and the water out and offered it to the group. He thanked them for their willingness to help and walked in the opposite direction with his hand on North's shoulder.

"My name is Jonathan, by the way. And I have a confession to make."

"What is it?"

"That warehouse isn't actually mine. You'll need the real owner's permission to stay," Jonathan said.

"Who's the owner?" North asked.

"Charlie. Charlie owns the place."

CHAPTER 36

North stood at the foot of the fresh grave by the red oak and stared down at it with a broken heart. The other plots to his left had served as the backdrop of his daily life since he had moved in at the warehouse. In all of that time, not once had it ever occurred to him that a day would come this new one would be needed.

He found solace, but no more than a spec of it, in allowing that his loss was now Anna's gain. At long last, the two would be as close in death as they had been while she was alive.

His plot even looked like an extension of hers.

The years to adulthood had blessed North with impressive strength split in equal measures between his body, his mind and his character. The fatigues he wore were a perfect fit as though they had been custom-made for his height and broad shoulders.

He was a man in every meaning of the word. Jonathan, with much pride in his tone, had reminded him of that recently.

North took a knee, touched the dirt and broke down as he remembered the day the two had met.

Thirteen years had gone by since Jonathan had saved his life. Fifty-two seasons during which the two had learned to first live with, and then rely on, one another. All in a world they barely knew and that had continued to offer its surprises, for better or for worse.

Jonathan never really healed from Anna's passing, nor did he ever make peace with what he had come to see as his failure to protect her. Regret, guilt and the manner of her death had stained his soul and rendered irrelevant the good he had done for her prior to that horrific morning.

He went to her grave every Sunday regardless of the weather or the season. Her plot wasn't marked with a stone or a plaque as he had done for the others. Many times he had tried to find the will to do it. He never could.

He made the trip to the strawberry field twice a year and pedaled back to the warehouse with a container full. Before joining North upstairs, he would stop to visit with Anna and place a handful of fruits on top of her resting site. The memory of her reaction when he had first surprised her with those was sweeter to him than the strawberries themselves could ever be.

North often caught Jonathan browsing through the pictures and the videos Anna had recorded on her iPad. On many occasions he had asked him why he subjected himself to these images since they appeared to cause him so much pain.

"You met her only once, in a dark shed, for less than two minutes and she left quite an impression on you," Jonathan finally answered. "Imagine spending more than a year with her. She saved my life, and made it so beautiful, in more ways than words can express."

North had dropped the subject and eventually accepted that grieving would be a part of Jonathan's personality for as long as he would live. He had, after all, been forthcoming about this; a part of him had indeed died with her.

The torment that was Anna's loss, however, existed in isolation from his other traits. Every night during the winter months he sat with North by the stove where he taught him to read, write and count. He took him hunting and showed him to him all he knew about survival. In time, he became a surrogate parent, although he didn't think of their relationship in those terms. He preferred to say he was just a friend, a title as simple as it was true.

North was a good boy, but he too had been through his fair share of traumatic events.

He eventually recounted how the men who had abducted him had killed his family. It had all unfolded before his very eyes, just like Jonathan had suspected. As for what had happened to him during his long months of captivity, he never told. He did reveal that on the day of his escape — the day Jonathan had saved him — he was well aware of the probability he would die out there on his own. Death was still a better prospect than one more minute with these monsters.

Jonathan didn't press North on this issue. He did tell him early on that if he ever wanted to discuss his ordeal, he shouldn't hesitate. It was also fine if he preferred not to talk about it. He, of all people, knew it wasn't always necessary to talk about everything.

Perhaps words weren't the balm North's wounds

required. Comfort does come in many disguises. Jonathan's strong guidance was one of them. Charlie's unconditional love was potent medicine too.

Despite the safety he felt in Jonathan's presence, the memories of his misfortunes haunted North's nights for years.

They both became skilled outdoorsmen and bow hunters. North, however, unbound by habits acquired in the old way of life, surpassed Jonathan at a young age. The featherweight could go anywhere undetected, day or night.

At fifteen, following a days-long negotiation with Jonathan, North began going to the City's downtown core on his own. No one lived there anymore. The winters, increasing in harshness from one year to the next, had pushed most of the survivors down south.

The greater part of the remaining few had found houses or farms away from the edge of the City where they hoped open spaces and isolation would give them a better chance at survival.

The decision to let North roam the streets by himself wasn't to be taken lightly. Nature was swallowing the world at an impressive pace while imposing its own set of laws in the process. In a matter of a few years after the first wave of infections, the source of danger had tilted from humans to wildlife, regardless of where people lived. Animals were reclaiming the world as theirs. Humans were becoming trespassers on their turf.

The two weren't the only ones still living near the City, though. Jonathan flew into a rage when North told him he had made contact with people on the opposite side of town. In fact, at the time he confessed to it, he had been visiting with them on a regular basis and already counted a few close friends among the group.

The beautiful Olivia was also part of the small community of about twenty.

Jonathan knew the group to which North was referring. Two of its members had saved him from a pack of coyotes and had been quite the gentlemen afterward. It didn't matter how nice they had appeared to be back then. After Anna's death, he had vowed to stay away from all people, good or bad. Trust wasn't an option anymore and seldom a day had gone by he hadn't reminded North of how fast wishful thinking could turn into a nightmare.

He eventually looked at it from North's perspective. This desire he had to explore the world, to experience more of it, had been a human instinct since the beginning of times. And while North had broken his fair share of rules in his young life, he had thus far kept his solemn promise to never reveal to anyone where he lived. Jonathan relented and trusted North's judgment. He also understood his feelings for Olivia. He did remind him, however, that he still preferred to be left alone. The boy's and Charlie's were all the company he would ever need. The group had nonetheless relayed frequent invitations to Jonathan to come and break bread with them. He turned them down each time.

Jonathan and Charlie did walk with North toward that side of the City once, although they had parted ways long before reaching the community.

Jonathan had preserved Anna's old map, the one on which she had marked her studio as her final destination when she had left the Center. He found her street and inspected the entrance of each of the buildings until he came upon a faded red tag that read *A. Cobb* next to a buzzer.

The door to her atelier was open. All that remained were a few decrepit pieces of furniture and a mattress. A thick layer of dust had also covered her scent so Charlie didn't get to guess where he was. Honesty had forced Jonathan to admit he couldn't feel her presence as he had hoped, but it was good to be in a space he knew she had once occupied and where he knew she had been so happy. He had flipped her mattress and spent the night there with Charlie.

With Jonathan's permission, North took Olivia to the warehouse so the two could meet.

He was welcoming and the sitting was warm, but North had understood then that it was a bit much for him. What Jonathan had come to fear the most had less to do with bullies, bullets or now bite marks, and more with letting others find their ways to his heart. The graves by the oak were a reminder of the high price to pay for love and devotion. Anna's death had brought him on the verge of bankruptcy.

So they paced themselves, the frequency and duration of Olivia's visits increasing with each passing season. She was a kind, thoughtful and quite cleaver young woman. She read Jonathan's moods and demeanors and patiently worked on tightening their bond in tiny increments one visit at a time. By the time he realized she owned a piece of his heart, it was already too late.

This contact with the outside world also came with the benefit of crucial information on the rate of infections. Olivia told Jonathan about the latest death from the virus within her group, which had happened five years after the initial wave. A man in his seventies had also been infected about a year later, but the virus hadn't killed him. The infection had been limited to his right arm. Because the muscles in his shoulder and his neck were also contracted, amputation hadn't been an option. The atrocious pain had driven the poor man to madness and he had ended his ordeal by jumping off a high-rise building two days later.

No one else had been infected since.

The virus, which by all accounts had only ever affected humans, had dissipated. At least, it was the opinion of the elders in the community.

When North turned nineteen, those on the other side of the City began discussing a plan to move south. With Olivia's help, he had persuaded them to postpone their migration. He too was anxious to see more of the world, but he knew Jonathan would never agree to leave. He needed more time to prepare him to his departure by stocking up enough resources at the warehouse and know his two friends would be safe after he'd left.

More than two years later, last April, Jonathan had hardly been surprised when North and Olivia had informed him that the community had come to the firm decision to leave early in the summer. He had expected the group would eventually hear the call of the south. North's recent urgency in piling up wood and doing repairs at the warehouse had been the tip off that the young couple had decided to join them.

The night of the announcement had been quite emotional, but mostly for North.

The guilt over leaving behind the man who had saved

his life had been hammering at his conscience for some time. Olivia had been moved to tears as she had watched Jonathan walk to North, take him in arms and tell him how proud of him he was.

"I found my home here a long time ago. It's time for you to find yours. You're a man now. You're a man in every sense of the word. I trust you, kiddo" he had said not realizing he had just sounded like Mr. Dean.

And now…

Now North was standing at the foot of this new grave by the oak. The timing was lousy, but the day had come. There was no postponing it. Leaving this early in June would give the group plenty of time to find a suitable place in the south before the cold weather would set in the northern part of the country.

He wiped away more tears and gazed at the impressive stone that now sat at the head of the enlarged burial site.

"You were a good friend," he said out loud.

"He sure was," Jonathan concurred as he walked up to North from behind and put a hand on his shoulder.

"I'm so sorry. You'll be all alone now," North said.

"Don't worry about me," Jonathan replied. "Charlie was very old and in so much pain at the end. It's a miracle he lived this many doggy years with no real care available. But you are right," he added looking down at the dirt. "He was a good friend."

Charlie's health, already precarious, had taken a sharp decline just before North had gone to the community to help them pack up for the trip ahead. Jonathan had told him to give their dog an extra long kiss goodbye before leaving. When he'd returned three days later Charlie was under the ground, which made him suspect that it was Jonathan who had ended their faithful chum's suffering soon after he'd left.

All he knew was that Charlie had been buried on his bed, the remnants of his beloved teddy bear and one of Anna's t-shirts tucked in between his paws.

"They must be having such a blast right now," Jonathan said while shaking his head at the thought of Anna and Charlie, reunited after all these years apart.

"Are you going to tell me how you got that big rock up here?" North asked.

"Nope. But I do need your help with something."

Jonathan walked inside the warehouse and reappeared holding a plaque he had taken more than a day to craft. Once it was affixed to the rock, both men retreated and admired the finished result.

"It's very beautiful," North declared after reading it. He then looked up to the sky to see the sun's position.

"Listen," he continued. "Something is about to happen. I don't want you to worry. And please, I'm begging you, don't get mad. This is what I want."

Before Jonathan could ask what North had meant by that, the sounds of footsteps and rattling on the road alerted him that people, and a lot of them, were crossing the bridge and approaching the warehouse. He reached for his weapon, but North stopped him.

"It's alright, it's okay. They're coming to pay their respects. They're coming to say goodbye."

The entire community advanced toward the two men. Jonathan took three steps back. The arrival of all these people at once felt at first like an aggression, but as they moved in closer, he recognized some of them. Three of the women and one of the men he had freed on the day he had rescued North were among the group. Also present were the two men from downtown, the ones who had saved him from the pack of coyotes.

Two young women, about North's age, approached Jonathan and hugged him both at the same time. He had no idea who they were and why they were so eager, so he raised his arms, but didn't quite reciprocate.

"This is Eloise and Sarah. You saved them too on the day we met," North explained.

Some asked North to take them to the top floor so they could see Anna's painting for themselves. He looked to Jonathan who hesitated, but nodded to give his approval. Others should have the opportunity to enjoy Anna's immense talents, he decided in a flash. Those who remained outside gathered by the graves and held each other. Jonathan, in retreat by the warehouse's entrance, heard their whispers as they pointed at the stones and read the plaques as though they were visiting some sort of exhibit or a museum.

When North came back from upstairs, he noticed Jonathan's puzzled expression and then turned his attention to those by the oak.

"I told them the stories so many times, they refused to go without seeing it all with their own eyes."

"What stories?"

"Your story, Jonathan. Anna's story. Ours."

Unbeknown to him, Jonathan had become somewhat of a legend. The community had known all along not only who he was and the good he had done, but also where he lived. This entire time, they had respected his wish to be left alone. It had even become law. In their view, he had earned whatever peace he desired or could find.

The time to leave had come. A line formed to shake Jonathan's hesitant hand. Those whose lives he had saved thanked him for it. Some, to his dismay, broke down as they tried to express their gratitude. The group then retreated by the road to give North, Olivia and Jonathan some privacy.

"You have enough wood in there for three winters, maybe four. Don't let it drop too low before you replace it," North said while pointing at the warehouse. He then paused and looked intensely at Jonathan as if to etch a clear image of him in his mind.

"I knew it would be hard to leave, but I never imagined it would hurt this much. Are you sure you don't want to come with us?"

"This is my home. This is where I belong, North," Jonathan said before turning his head toward the graves.

"My place is here, with them," he added.

He grabbed North and took him in his arms for a long embrace. After he did the same with Olivia, he put a hand on her stomach.

"Once the three of you find your own home, teach that kid to read, write and count. Tell your child that somewhere up north, there is a crazy old man who loves him or her very much, even if we haven't met."

Jonathan waited for the young couple to rejoin the community by the road. He then rushed upstairs where he came upon a basket filled with fresh bread and cured meats his visitors had left for him.

He went to the roof to keep an eye on the group as they walked across the bridge. Before they headed west to reach the highway, and before disappeared for good behind trees, North stopped and turned for one last glance at the warehouse.

He saw Jonathan staring back at him.

North waved and then pointed his index finger to the sky like Anna had done for him on the day their paths had briefly met. He moved on when he received the same as a response.

Though Jonathan was excited for North's adventures to come, he was also worried and sad.

Watching him leave the City from the roof reminded him of the day he had caught a glimpse of a woman making her way to it in a beat up wheelchair from the opposite direction.

In a fraction of a second, he had chosen to break each of his own rules and run to her.

Whenever Anna was on his mind, he inevitably circled back to that instant.

That blessed instant the two had worked so hard to stretch to a little more than a year.

Among what had helped him preserve his sanity in the last thirteen years were the responsibility he felt toward North, Charlie's presence and his memories of Anna and the others he had buried by the Red Oak.

They all inspired him to live in the present day while hoping for a tomorrow, although he was doing so with a heart he had long accepted would never be whole again.

He was fine with it.

They were worth a million tears just as they were a million smiles.

Jonathan walked to the edge of the roof, on the side facing the river, and looked down at the fresh grave.

From where he stood, he couldn't read the inscription on the plaque the two now shared, of course.

He didn't need to.

It was engraved on his very soul:

> *"Family is the True North of your life.*
> *Know where it is and you'll never lose your way."*
> *Here lie Anna Cobb and Charlie the Fur Ball.*
> *I know where they are. I will never be lost.*
> *J.F.*

Steve Marchand is a French Canadian author who currently lives in Québec. He also wrote **Citizen of Happy Town – An Orphan Remembers** in which he recounts the events of his early life as an orphan.

For more on this, please visit www.steve-marchand.com

Printed in Great Britain
by Amazon